BATTLE MOUNTAIN

D1527676

BATTLE MOUNTAIN

BLOODY JOE MANNION BOOK EIGHT

PETER BRANDVOLD

WOLFPACK
PUBLISHING
— EST 2013 —

Battle Mountain
Paperback Edition
Copyright © 2023 Peter Brandvold

Wolfpack Publishing
9850 S. Maryland Parkway, Suite A-5 #323
Las Vegas, Nevada 89183

wolfpackpublishing.com

Paperback ISBN 978-1-63977-836-2
Large Print Hardcover ISBN 978-1-63977-835-5
eBook ISBN 978-1-63977-837-9

BATTLE MOUNTAIN

PROLOGUE

THE GIRL RAN THROUGH THE WIND AND THE RAIN, THE rain slashing at her, the wind sucking the air from her lungs. She was barefoot, and her feet caught in the soggy sand of the New Mexico desert while cedars and creosote shrubs tore at her soaked nightgown that clung to her bare, brown legs.

She ran as fast as she could, hearing the soggy clomp of galloping hooves behind her, and the frustrated voices of men trying to pick up her trail. Several times, she tossed a glance behind her, and in the flashing lightning, she could make out the shadows of five galloping riders in Stetson hats and yellow rain slickers. They were closing on her fast. She couldn't avoid the scream of raw terror that exploded from her lips when she saw one rider closing on her more quickly than the others and paying out the loop of a lariat, swinging it above his head, preparing to toss it at her.

"No!" the girl cried, recoiling inside herself at the horror of being hanged. They would hang her, too. After they did what they'd done before. She knew that. It was a cold stone in her belly. "I beg you...plea—"

She gave another scream as the ground suddenly dropped out from under her feet, and she found herself falling straight down through the night-black air and the white sheets of wind-buffeted rain. During another flicker of lightning, she saw the arroyo with its murky black water shepherding mud chunks and branches downstream. She sucked a sharp breath just before she dropped into the chill, quickly moving water and was swept downstream like the flotsam that had so quickly become her life.

As the current carried her with violent swiftness, she could hear the crack of gunfire above and behind her. She pulled her head down in desperation beneath the surface of the floodwater and prayed this would not be the last of her.

Or if it was, let it be fast. Faster than this...

CHAPTER 1

"BLOODY JOE, WOULD YOU DO ME A BIG FAVOR?" ASKED Mannion's prisoner, Buzzard Lee.

"No."

"Oh, come on! Loosen these damn ties on my wrists. I haven't felt my fingers for the three days we've been on the trail out from Del Norte!"

Mannion reached up to cut the ropes tying his prisoner's wrists to his saddle horn but left the ropes tying his wrists together in place.

"I don't think so, Buzzard."

"You're a hard man, Bloody Joe."

"So I been told a time or two." Brusquely, Mannion reached up to pull his prisoner down off the man's saddle.

"All right, then, Joe. You got it comin'!"

Suddenly, Lee swung toward Mannion, bringing both tied wrists around like a club. Mannion had seen it coming. This wasn't Bloody Joe Mannion's first rodeo. He'd been a town tamer for a good many years and the town marshal of Del Norte for another seven.

Joe ducked. Lee's wrists made a *whooshing* sound as they cut through the air where Mannion's head had been an eye wink before. The prisoner's momentum turned him around to face his horse again. Mannion chuckled and punched him once in each kidney and then twice in the back of his head.

Lee dropped to his knees, breathing hard and groaning—a big, shaggy-headed man in his mid-forties. Mannion himself was on the north side of fifty, pushing sixty, but he was still strong and fit, standing well over six feet and broad through the shoulders, lean in the hips.

"You never cease to amuse me, Buzzard. You know, I might just stay and watch the good people of Battle Mountain hang you for shooting their deputy sheriff. Just for the satisfaction of watching you dance the midair two-step, choking."

The outlaw told Mannion to do something physically impossible to himself.

Mannion laughed and then dragged the man over to a tree and tied him to it, wrapping the rope around the tree and the man's chest several times. Buzzard groaned. "That's too tight, Joe! I cain't hardly draw a breath!"

"Good!"

As it was late in the day and the shadows were growing long, Mannion stripped the tack off Buzzard's steeldust and his own bay, Red, and set up camp. Nearly an hour later he had a fire burning and had hung his dented, fire-blackened coffeepot over the flames from an iron tripod. He fixed some beans and bacon and gave some to his undeserving prisoner along with a cup of piping hot mud.

It was dusk by the time the men finished their meal.

Mannion hauled the dishes down to a little stream to clean them and then settled back against his saddle to watch the sun slide down the far side of the Black Range in the west. Buzzard asked for another cup of coffee.

Mannion grunted his disdain for the man and then refilled the man's cup. As he did, he noticed Buzzard glancing owlishly, furtively toward a near western ridge.

"What you see over there, Buz—"

Suddenly, the cup blew out of Mannion's hand, and hot coffee splashed across his wrist.

"Shit!" Joe bellowed as he reached for his Yellowboy repeater and rolled behind a rock as the rifle that had shot the cup out of his hand barked loudly, echoing.

Another bullet blew up dust just off the heels of his boots as he drew them behind the rock with the rest of him.

"Oh, hell—that must be Duke Alvarez!" Buzzard seethed. "That greaser can't shoot for crap!"

Several more bullets came hurling toward Mannion and smashed into the rock he hunkered behind. The horses picketed south of the camp whickered and whinnied, pulled against their picket pins.

Buzzard shouted, "If you fellas can't shoot any straighter than that, just forget it! Kill Bloody Joe when he's asleep tonight!" The outlaw laughed.

Mannion glanced over the top of his rock. He could see three hatted heads silhouetted against a stained-glass sky. He triggered several rounds then rolled out from behind his rock and ran crouching toward several larger rocks and stunt cottonwoods to his left. He'd figured Buzzard's gang might try to spring the outlaw but somehow he'd still let himself be surprised by it.

That infuriated him as much as the actual bushwhack.

Dodging more lead, he ran toward the ridge from atop of which the lead was raining down around him and hunkered low against it, where the men on top of it couldn't see him. Then he looked around until he saw a notch in the ridge and clambered through it. He reached the other side in time to see the three members of Buzzard's bunch galloping into the sunset, the rataplan of galloping hooves quickly dwindling until there was only the sound of piping birds calling a close to the day.

Cursing, Mannion walked back through the notch in the ridge and back into the camp.

Buzzard laughed. "You're wolf bait, Joe. Wolf bait, you hear?"

Mannion walked up to the man, jacked a fresh round in the Winchester's chamber and aimed the rifle at the man's broad, sunburned forehead. "Which one of us is wolf bait, Buzzard?"

Buzzard's washed-out brown eyes grew fearful. "Don't kill me, Joe." He gave a halfhearted grin. "Wouldn't want to cheat the hangman, now, would you?"

"Nah." Joe depressed the Yellowboy's hammer, poured himself a fresh cup of coffee, and kicked dirt on the fire, dousing it. "You're right about that, Buzzard."

He sat down against his saddle, sipped his coffee, and prepared to stay awake for the rest of the night in case those three polecats returned to clean his clock. It was a quiet night, so he or the horses or both would likely hear Buzzard's men approach if they came. He'd make it to Battle Mountain town by midday the next day. He'd be glad to get there and then head back home to his family —his wife, the lovely Jane, his daughter, Vangie, and Vangie's husband, Doctor Ben Ellison.

He was a harsh man, was Bloody Joe Mannion. An uncompromising lawman. But he dearly loved those close to him.

It was a long night. But Joe was used to them. He had plenty of coffee to help keep him awake and keep his senses sharp. Meanwhile, Buzzard Lee snored with his head tipped back against the tree, a perpetual sneer on his mouth, knowing his men were stalking Mannion with the intention of freeing their outlaw leader.

The stars wheeled overhead, flickering.

Gradually, there was a paling in the east. The desert shrubs and cacti began to gain definition. The birds began piping, and finally the rising sun made the shadows long and thin. Mannion kicked Buzzard awake then saddled both horses, led his prisoner to his steeldust and ordered him into the saddle, giving him a brusque shove.

"How'd you sleep, Joe?" the man asked with that lingering sneer curling his mouth.

"Like the prince I am, Buzzard. Like the prince I am."

Mannion climbed into the leather and began continuing southwest toward Battle Mountain, leading Buzzard's steeldust by its bridle reins. As he rode, he kept a close eye on the terrain around him—mostly desert scrub but here and there a rocky arroyo or stone outcropping from behind which Buzzard's men might effect an ambush. When they approached one such outcropping ahead on the left side of the old freight trail Mannion was following, Buzzard said, "You think they're behind them rocks, Joe? Might be layin' a bead on you right now."

He snickered.

"Might be," Mannion said. "But I don't think so."

"Why's that?"

"I don't feel that cold finger against the back of my neck."

"What cold finger?"

"The finger of the witch that warns me when I'm ridin' into a bushwhack."

"Pshaw," Buzzard said. "Joe, you're gettin' old an' squishy in your thinker box."

"Well, I'm gettin' old," Mannion admitted, noting the

ache in his behind. A few years ago—well, maybe ten, twelve years ago—a ride of this length hadn't phased him.

An hour later, the sun high overhead, he stopped both horses.

"What is it, Joe?" Buzzard asked, keeping his voice low and pitched with jeering menace. "You feel that ol' witch's finger proddin' ya, do you?"

"Shut up."

Mannion gazed straight ahead toward where the trail dipped into an arroyo sheathed in post oaks and willows. Indeed, the witch was poking the back of his neck with that January-cold finger of hers. He spied brief movement behind the foliage lining the arroyo and abruptly reined Red and Buzzard's steeldust behind some rocks on the right side of the trail.

"Careful, boys, he's on to ya!" Buzzard yelled, grinning down at Mannion.

Joe dismounted, cut Buzzard free of his saddle, pulled him down from the steeldust's back, and smashed the butt of one of his two big, silver-chased Russian .44s against the back the man's head. Buzzard gave a grunt and dropped to the ground like a hundred-pound sack of parched corn. Joe bound the man's ankles and left him lying belly down on the ground, out like a blown lamp, then tied both horses to willows. He shucked his Yellowboy from his saddle boot, jacked a live round into the action, then off-cocked the hammer.

He edged a look around the rocks and saw where an arroyo ahead and on his right jogged off to join the arroyo in which he believed Buzzard's men were hunkered, ready to perforate his hide. He gave a grim nod, deciding his course of action, then took a drink from his canteen, returned the canteen to his saddle

horn, and strode off, jogging, crouching, toward the inter-
secting arroyo.

He pushed through the willows and dropped into the
ravine, which was about ten feet deep, twenty feet wide,
and paved with rocks and sand. He began moving south
slowly, holding the Yellowboy up high across his chest,
closing one hand around the brass breech so a glint of
sunlight wouldn't give him away.

Ahead, the ravine curved sharply to the left.

He moved more slowly, quietly, pricking his ears,
listening closely.

He stopped abruptly. He'd heard the soft crunch of
gravel under a stealthy tread.

He stepped behind a bulge in the ravine wall to his
left, and crouched, squeezing the rifle in his gloved
hands, waiting.

CHAPTER 2

A TALL, MUSTACHED MAN IN A RED SHIRT AND BLACK Stetson stepped out from around the bulge in the ravine wall behind which Mannion crouched, waiting. The man, whom Mannion recognized as Spider Finch, moved slowly, quietly, holding a Winchester carbine straight up and down in his black-gloved hands.

When he was even with Mannion, Joe gave a slight whistle. Finch wheeled toward him, eyes widening in surprise. He was just bringing his carbine around when Mannion smashed the butt of his own Winchester against the man's face, his nose exploding like a ripe tomato.

Finch grunted, stumbled backward, and dropped, instantly out.

Joe stepped quickly out from behind the bulge in the ravine wall and dropped to one knee, thumbing the Yellowboy's hammer back to full cock and aiming the rifle straight out from his right shoulder. He knew the other two gang members would be along shortly, and he was right. Both men came around a bend in the ravine fifty feet away, spread out roughly twenty feet apart.

Both men saw Mannion and stopped abruptly, startled.

They both raised their rifles at the same time, yelling. Mannion's Yellowboy roared once, throwing the man on the left straight back off his feet, firing his own rifle straight up in the air. The Yellowboy roared again, and that bullet took the man on the right in the gut. The man folded, cursing loudly. Joe saw no reason to spare him. He was the cold-blooded killer Duke Alvarez, a half-Mex from southern Texas who mostly shot men in the back or from close range with a pistol, as his eyes were bad.

The Yellowboy roared again as Alvarez raised his face toward Mannion. Joe's bullet took him between his dung-brown, nearsighted eyes, finishing him. Mannion spied movement in the corner of his right eye. He whipped around to see Spider Finch sliding his six-shooter from the holster tied low on his right thigh, eyes pinched angrily above his ruined nose, lips stretched back from tobacco-stained teeth.

"Bad idea, Spider," Mannion said, and shot him.

Joe ejected the spent cartridge. It clattered onto the rocks behind him. He jacked a fresh round into the action and then depressed the hammer, resting the Winchester on his right shoulder and glanced at the three dead men lying twisted in death around him.

"Another day, another dollar."

He had no intention of burying the men who would have killed him if they'd been good enough. The wolves and wildcats had to eat, too. He retraced his route back to the rocks where he'd left the horses and his prisoner, who was conscious now and lying on his back like a big, ugly, bearded turtle, glaring up as Joe stood over him.

"You get 'em all, Joe?"

"What do you think?" Mannion shoved the Yellowboy

into its brown leather scabbard strapped on the right side of his saddle.

"I hope someone kills you slow and bloody, Mannion," Buzzard bit out. "Just like you deserve!"

"If wishes had wings, pigs would fly." Joe reached down and hauled his prisoner to his feet.

"You know there's more where them three came from. There's six more in my gang. True, they're spread out a might, coolin' their heels, but they'll come fer me. My boys—we take care of each other!"

"Don't worry—I'll be watching for your loyal jugheads."

Mannion had no idea how Buzzard's scattered gang had known Mannion had taken Buzzard down in a whorehouse in Del Norte late one Saturday night, when Buzzard was asleep beside a sleeping Mexican whore in a musty back room of the All-Nighter Saloon on San Juan Avenue. Outlaws were witchy that way. He knew there were several more in Buzzard's gang, and you could bet the seed bull he'd likely run into them, too.

A lawman had to have eyes in the back of his head.

And a sixth sense in the form of a cold witch's finger to know when he was riding into a whipsaw.

He untied Buzzard's feet and prodded him onto his horse, tied his wrists to his saddle horn, mounted Red, and set out once more for Battle Mountain town, which, if they ran into no more problems, they should reach in a couple of hours. He was in need of a drink and a hot meal. He'd spend the night in a bed. He'd like to head back to Del Norte in the morning, but first, he wanted to inquire around for the killer Harry Marcum, who'd killed a deputy U.S. marshal in Gunnison a few weeks ago. Mannion had a deputy sheriff's commission, and the county sheriff in Salida had assigned him the task of running down the notorious killer. Marcum had been seen in the area and since Battle Mountain was a notorious backwater and known hideout for men on the run, he had a feeling Marcum might be holed up there. He'd spend a day or two looking around for him and then head home whether he found him or not. Del Norte needed him more than the sheriff did, as his town was still growing, what with the coming of the iron horse and all, and he had only three deputies.

He was weary of the journey. Nothing bored him more than prisoner transports, though the marshal of Battle Mountain had a claim on Buzzard since Buzzard had shot his deputy in a back alley in Battle Mountain, in a messy shootout witnessed by several half-drunk townsmen.

The Battle Mountain town marshal, Sylvan Story, had sent out telegrams to neighboring towns, and Joe had picked one up as well as Buzzard himself. So, here he was...transporting another damn prisoner, sparring with his prisoner's gang, and yearning for a shot of rotgut whiskey, his favorite kind of hooch, and a big hot platter of steak and slow-cooked pinto beans followed up by a big wedge of peach pie topped with a liberal dollop of freshly whipped cream washed down with hot, black coffee. He knew he could get such a meal at the Continental Hotel in Battle Mountain manned—or womaned, rather—by the best cook in town, Ma Lonnigan, though that wasn't saying much. Ma was known for her rattlesnake stew, as well, but Mannion had eaten enough rattlesnake, usually roasted on a stick, in the frontier army that he'd had his fill.

"You tied my hands too damn tight again, Joe," Buzzard complained as they rode toward a steep, red ridge at the base of which the town of Battle Mountain sat, though the town was still too far away for Mannion to see it yet. The large, red, vaguely anvil-shaped formation, Battle Mountain, named for an Indian battle once played out on it long ago, had given the town its name.

"Shut up," Joe told his prisoner.

"Why, my fingers are swollen to the size of sausages!"

"Buzzard, don't make me shoot you."

"Just be cheatin' the hangman, Joe." Buzzard chuckled.

They were about to cross another arroyo when Mannion checked Red down abruptly. "Whoa, whoa, whoa, boy!"

Mannion had spied something lying on the north bank of the arroyo. A human figure. Now he saw it was a girl—dark-haired and clad in only a nightgown. She looked like a muddy rag lying there flat against the bank, shivering, hugging herself. Her lips were moving, and she was muttering but, as far as the lawman could tell, was saying nothing coherent.

Mannion swung down from Red's back, ground reined the bay, and hurried over to kneel beside the girl. "Good Lord, honey, what're you doing way out here?"

He touched her shoulder and she jerked with a start, gazing up at him with haunted, brown eyes. "No," she said. "No...no...leave me..."

Her lips were caked with mud. A small stream ran down the sandy bed of the arroyo at her bare feet.

"I can't leave you here," Mannion said, utterly baffled at finding a scantily clad young girl, seventeen or eighteen years old—definitely Mexican—way out here in the middle of nowhere, a good two miles as the crow flies from Battle Mountain. "How'd you get here?"

"What you got there, Joe?" Buzzard asked, where he sat the steeldust behind Red.

Mannion ignored the man.

"Did you hear me, honey? How did you get here? Where are you from?"

She'd lifted her head from the arroyo's muddy bank and gazed up at him, her dark-brown eyes cast with both fear and befuddlement. She seemed to stare right through Joe, her eyes opaque, as though she were trying to peer into her own dark past but couldn't see much of anything. She wrinkled the skin above the bridge of her nose and parted her muddy lips as though to speak but no words emerged.

"Did you hear me, honey?"

Her muddy lips parted again. She looked around as though seeing where she was for the first time and, returning her gaze to Mannion, said, "I...don't...know." Tears glistened in her eyes, and her voice grew shrill with terror. "I don't know!"

"Easy, easy," Mannion said, caressing her slender, bare shoulder. "It's all right. You're safe with me. What's your name?"

The girl stared up at him, tears dribbling down her muddy cheeks. Her voice heavily accented, she said, "I don't know." Her voice was pinched with a building terror.

"You find you a female down there, Joe?" Buzzard said, amused.

Mannion turned to him. "Buzzard, shut up, or I *will* shoot you out of your saddle."

"I was just askin'!"

Joe turned back to the girl who had squeezed her eyes shut and was sobbing and saying, "I don't know...I don't know..."

"That's all right," Mannion said, caressing the girl's shoulder again. "We'll get you to Battle Mountain. Huh?

How would that be? You must have come from there. Don't you think?"

"I don't know...I don't know..."

"Well, we'll check it out. Maybe once we get you there, it'll come back to you."

The poor girl had lost her mind. Or at least her memory. Mannion could imagine how terrifying such a situation would be. Not knowing who you are or where you are from.

How in holy blazes had she gotten here?

Like he'd told the girl, maybe he'd find the answer to that question in Battle Mountain. Surely someone there would know who she was even if she wasn't from town but from a farm or ranch in the area. A girl as pretty as she was behind all that mud would be memorable.

"I'm scared," she said.

"No need. I'm Joe Mannion." He swept his thumb across the five-pointed, nickel-plated badge pinned to his dark-red corduroy shirt. "Town marshal of Del Norte. Don't mind that ugly polecat back there, on the steel-dust. He's got a mouth on him, but he's bound up good."

"Who am I?" the girl said. "I should know."

"It'll come back to you."

She looked around again. "I don't know if I want to go to Battle Mountain."

"You don't? Why?"

She shook her head. "I don't know." Again, tears glazed her eyes. Her lips trembled.

"Well, I can't leave you here. Come an' climb up on my horse with me. Don't worry—I'll protect you. We'll get you to town and get you cleaned up. Someone will know who you are. I'm sure of it."

She looked at the badge pinned to his shirt, then gave a single nod.

"All right, then." Mannion snaked his arms under her and lifted her as he rose. He carried her over to where Red stood, gazing at his rider and the girl dubiously, and set her up on the saddle.

"Good Lord, child," Buzzard said. "You take a mud bath?"

Mannion glared at him with his wolfish gray eyes. "Not another word, Buzzard. Or I'll be cheating the hangman."

"All right, all right. I can be a gentleman as good as anybody."

"See that you are."

Mannion swept up the reins of both horses, climbed up behind the girl, and booted Red on into the arroyo and then up the other side. The old freight trail, now used by a stagecoach line, swung to the left, and Mannion and his two charges followed it along the arroyo that— after nearly a mile—became a deep canyon. Joe wondered if the girl had tumbled into the canyon. Maybe that's how she'd lost her memory. Floodwater from a recent rain must have swept her westward down the canyon until it became a shallow arroyo and deposited her on the bank.

Poor girl.

What in holy blazes was she doing out here in the rain practically clad in only her birthday suit?

He'd likely find out in Battle Mountain.

Maybe she'd run from an orphanage. Those could be bad places. On the other hand, she appeared too old for an orphanage.

Oh, well. He'd find out soon. What a mystery.

The trail climbed gradually through scattered cedars and pines and then Battle Mountain town appeared at the base of the red stone mountain that loomed above and behind it to the south, stunted pines and cedar growing out of cracks scoring its steep face. The town wasn't much anymore, as the gold and silver had pretty much played out of the mountain it had been named after. However, a gaudy Victorian mansion with a red tile roof and several turrets and stone towers stood on a rocky shelf on the town's west side, to Mannion's right, between the town and the mesa. It was easily the most impressive building in town, if not within a couple of hundred square miles of it.

The improbable place, a diamond in the rough to be sure, was shrouded in legend. Apparently, the house had been built by a wealthy Englishman who had expected Battle Mountain to become the next Leadville until the gold and silver in the mountain flanking the house played out after a promising start. The man—Kennecott, Mannion thought his name had been—owned a large mine on the other side of Battle Mountain, and when the mine went belly up several years ago, he'd hanged himself from a wrought-iron rail of a balcony wrapped around one of the castle-like house's two stone turrets. The one in which his office resided.

The last time Mannion had ridden through town, the man's wife and daughter had still been occupying the mysterious, disparate, castle-like digs overlooking the dusty, dying settlement. Mannion knew little about them. In fact, he didn't think anyone in Battle Mountain knew all that much about them, both apparently being recluses, though he'd heard a female teacher had been brought in from the east to educate the girl at home. Joe had also heard the mother and daughter usually had a maid or butler do their shopping in town; the woman and the girl were rarely seen.

At least, that had been the case the last time he'd visited, which was well over a year ago now.

Why the dead mogul's wife continued to reside in the house was anyone's guess. Maybe she simply had nowhere else to go, or maybe she was too stubborn to admit defeat and leave. Maybe she was an eccentric who liked living a solitary life in the shadow of Battle Mountain.

As Mannion and the girl and the sullen Buzzard Lee clomped slowly down the broad main street of the town, Joe saw that at least half of the mud brick or wood frame businesses were boarded up. Several men were standing out front of the town's two saloons, one on each side of the street. Two of the men watched Mannion and his unlikely charges in grim, silent fascination, one of the two elbowing a third, directing his attention at the newcomers.

Mannion swung Red over to them, where they stood out in front of the Blue Dog Saloon, the saloon's sign running along the rundown place's second floor, above the porch awning; the badly faded words would likely be gone in another year or two.

"Good day," he said.

The three bearded, obvious prospectors or miners, possibly woodcutters, eyed him suspiciously, each holding a foaming beer mug in his bony, calloused, sun-browned fist.

"G'day," said one of them, a scrawny, gray-bearded gent in a floppy-brimmed canvas hat trimmed with three bear teeth sewn into its crown. He had a tattoo of a naked lady on his weathered neck.

"Found this young lady outside town," Mannion said, glancing at the girl before him. "She seems to have lost her memory. Do any of you know who she is, by any chance?"

The three men glanced at each other in dubious

silence and then the gray-bearded gent said, "No...no, can't say that I do. Found her outside town, you say?"

"That's right."

"Got no idea," said the tallest of the three, standing with his back to the Blue Dog Saloon's batwing doors, one of which sported two bullet holes.

Then he turned and disappeared into the saloon's cool shadows.

"Yessir, we got no idea," said the scrawny, red-bearded gent.

Then they, too, retreated into the saloon.

Mannion turned his gaze to the saloon on the other side of the street. Five men had been standing on the boardwalk outside of it, between the four horses tethered to the hitchrack and the saloon—the Holy Moses—flanking it. The batwings were still clattering back into place.

Buzzard Lee chuckled. "You sure know how to make friends, Joe. Yep, you sure do!"

He laughed.

The girl bowed her head and sobbed.

CHAPTER 3

THE TOWN MARSHAL'S OFFICE WAS ON A WEED- AND sage-infested side street.

The mud-brick, tin-roofed hovel was shaded by a large cottonwood. Three crows were perched on the roof, side by side, taking the afternoon sun. As Mannion and his motley procession approached, a medium-sized yellow cur got up off the rickety stoop fronting the place, trotted down the rotting wooden steps, and crossed the street at an angle, heading for a vacant, rundown stable and pig pen nearly buried in sage. The dog disappeared into the brush beyond, casting wary looks over his shoulder at the newcomers who had disturbed his sleep.

"Sorry, Earl," Mannion called to the dog, whom he had gotten to know—as much as you could get to know the shy cur Marshal Sylvan Story had adopted when the dog's outlaw owner had been shot in a gunfight on the main street of the town several years ago. Mannion had passed through Battle Mountain several times over the years, swapping prisoners with Story, who was just now taking a drink from a gourd olla hanging from the stoop's sagging ceiling.

Story was a large, middle-aged man who looked older with his gray bib beard and belly that bulged so severely that he couldn't close two buttons above his waist encircled by the cartridge belt of his low-slung .44. He had a broad, rosy-cheeked face with the keen, amused blue eyes of a much younger man. Story didn't take his job very seriously. In fact, he approached it with a good dose of humility and irony, knowing that taking a lawman's job seriously in the outlaw town Battle Mountain had become in the years after the Kennecott Mine closed would get him fitted rather quickly for a wooden overcoat and a not-so-prime piece of real estate on the local Boot Hill.

"Don't mind Earl," Story said now, dropping the gourd dipper back into the gourd olla and ambling in his bandy-legged fashion to the top of the porch steps to greet his visitors. Doing so, he brushed a sleeve of his wool work shirt across his mouth, all but concealed by the thick, wiry beard. "That jasper who owned him was a drunk who treated him poorly. Even shot at him a few times just fer fun. I'm good to old Earl, so he trusts only me."

"You've given him a good home, Sylvan," Mannion said, reining up in front of the bowed hitchrack fronting the jailhouse.

"I need to give somebody a good home. I'd give a woman a good home, but which one would have me?" Story grinned, blue eyes glinting. They clouded up like two windows on a rainy day when he saw the girl riding in front of Mannion and then Buzzard Lee tied to his steeldust's saddle. His interest seemed to be more in the girl than the man who'd shot his deputy, however.

He frowned, lips moving inside the tangle of beard, but he didn't say anything.

"You know this girl, Sylvan?" Mannion asked. "Found her outside town, in an arroyo. I think she must've got caught out in the rain."

"Pshaw—you don't say," Story said, frowning sympathetically. "Dressed like that? Why she's got more mud on her than nightgown!"

"That's how I found her. She seems to have lost her memory."

"Oh, no, no, no," Story said, the sympathetic frown in place. Well, surely she's from somewhere around here. Unless someone just dumped her. Some of these farmers and ranchers around here...not to mention the prospectors...ain't such nice people, if'n you get my drift, Joe." He looked at the girl again. "Are you sure that ain't what happened, honey?"

"I don't know," the girl said in her small, terrified voice. "I don't know *who* I am or where I *come from*. It is a strange, sad feeling. I am very afraid, señor!"

Again, she sobbed.

"You best take her over to Ma Lonnigan's Continental, Joe. Ma'll get her cleaned up, get a meal in her. Give her a good, soft bed until we can rundown who she is and where her family is. In the meantime"—Story looked at Buzzard sitting the steeldust looking a might sheepish— "I'll get some fellas workin' on a gallows for this polecat. The judge should be here in a few days. Have us a nice necktie party in Buzzard's honor!"

Story winked at Mannion. Then he glanced at the girl again, and his own expression grew sheepish. "Uh...sorry, honey. My crude talk in front of a girl—one who's lost her memory no less..."

The girl, preoccupied with her frightening dilemma, said nothing.

"Sylvan," Mannion said. "Have you seen Harry

Marcum in the area? He killed a deputy U.S. marshal in Gunnison, and I've been given the enviable task of running him down if I can."

"Well, I'll be hanged," Story said, fingering his beard. "I heard he was seen over to the Holy Moses a time or two in the past few days. I was gonna inquire, but...but, well, you know, I got a plateful, I do."

His cheeks reddened with chagrin, and he gave a lopsided smile.

"Best leave him to me," Mannion said, meaning it. Sylvan Story had been a good lawman in his time. That time had passed. He was no longer good enough to take down a snake-like Harry Marcum, a notorious regulator out of Denver known to sell his gun skills to wealthy cattlemen. "I'll see to him later."

He sighed at his own plateful.

"Stay here, honey." Mannion swung down from Red's back, pulled his Bowie knife from the sheath strapped on his left side, behind the Russian .44 holstered for the cross-draw on his left hip, and cut Buzzard down from his saddle. He gave the surly prisoner a shove toward the jailhouse. "He's all yours, Sylvan."

"Been chompin' at the bit for him," Story said, unsheathing his old .44, stepping back, and waving the pistol toward the open jailhouse door behind him. "Inside, you murderin' devil."

"Careful with that hogleg, you old jackass," Buzzard growled, clomping slowly, heavily up the rotting porch steps. He stopped by Story and looked down at the man who was nearly a whole head shorter. "It's liable to go off by mistake, an' I want me a last meal, at least."

Story glared up at him, one eye narrowed, and pressed the maw of his six-gun against the taller man's belly.

"You'll get bread and water and if you give me any grief, you'll only get water."

Story gave the big, beefy Buzzard a hard shove through the jailhouse door.

Mannion reined Red and the steeldust away from the jailhouse. He'd stable both horses together after he'd taken care of the girl. He started to gig Red back up toward the main street, First Street, then stopped suddenly. He'd just seen a man poke his head out from a gap between a boarded-up grocery store and a still open gun shop, then pull it back into the gap, out of sight.

The girl must not have seen the man, for she did not react but only sat the saddle in front of Mannion, hanging her head in fear.

Joe himself had gotten only a glimpse of the man's black-hatted head. Hadn't seen much of his face, just saw that it was long and pale and that a black mustache mantled his mouth.

Apprehension touched him.

Marcum?

The notorious regulator might have seen Mannion ride into town. Might wonder if Mannion was on the scout for him. Might want to clear Joe from his trail.

Mannion unsnapped the keeper thong from over the hammer of his cross-draw .44 and then booted Red on ahead. As he passed the gap from which the hatted head had appeared, he looked carefully into it, ready to pull the .44 if needed. No need. The gap was sage and trash-peppered, with a small pile of rotting lumber. No pale-faced killer on the lurk.

Still, apprehension touched Mannion as he turned Red onto the main drag, heading east toward Ma Lonni-gan's Continental Hotel, the only flophouse in town for the past three or four years. The three-story, shabby, wood frame building sat on the street's left side, abutted on each side by boarded-up saloons. It had once been painted white, but the wind and sand of this high New Mexico desert had scoured the paint nearly completely from its boards, which were gray-weathered and rotting just like the rest of Battle Mountain. Mannion could smell the dry rot on the wind, as well as the stench from the overfilled privy flanking the place, as he approached the humble building.

The Continental, identified by a faded sign stretching into the street, would have seemed abandoned but for the little, wizened, manly-looking lady in blue jeans and wool shirt beating several colorful rugs hanging from a rope line between two pines with a willow switch, on the building's far side, in a gap between the hotel and the boarded-up Denver Saloon and Dining Hall.

"Take that, demon dust! Take that!" the wizened woman said with each blow of the switch, causing dust to billow.

Mannion reigned up before her. She was about to take another swipe at a rug when, catching sight of Mannion out the corner of her eye, she stopped suddenly and stepped back with a start, gasping. She placed a hand on her chest, and said, "Dear Lord, you scared a good seven years off my life, you devil! Don't you have the good manners to announce yourself, sir?"

"Sorry, Ma," Mannion said. "Joe Mannion."

The old lady, who couldn't have weighed more than a hundred pounds dripping wet and fully clothed, glanced from Mannion to the girl before him and back again, and said, "I see that." Her gaze returned to the girl. "What're you doin' in these parts again, Joe? I bet you're huntin' Harry Marcum. Who you totin' with you...half-dressed and dirtier'n an orphan coyote pup, no less?"

"You've seen Marcum, Ma?"

"Oh, hell, yes. He struts around town like the cock of the walk."

"Pshaw!"

"Sure enough."

Hope rose in Mannion that he might be able to run down his prey, after all. He'd prefer not to return to Del Norte empty-handed. That was never a good feeling. Especially if you were Bloody Joe Mannion.

But, at the moment, he had bigger fish to fry. Namely, the girl.

"You know this child, Ma?" he asked, glancing down at the girl before him.

Frowning curiously, Ma moved forward. She wore boy-sized, silver-tipped stockman's boots. Her face was as dark as an Indian's, and deeply lined, her emerald-green eyes drawn up at the corners. Her coal-black hair, not showing a trace of gray, was pulled back severely from her face and hung in a tight braid down her back. Little puffs of dust lifted around her boots as she came out of the alley, tripping slightly over a sage shrub, to stare up at the girl sitting at the bay before Mannion.

"Why, no. No, I don't," she said. "You don't know who she is?"

"She doesn't know who she is," Mannion said. "Found her in an arroyo a mile or so from town. I think she fell into the canyon and was washed downstream when it was flooded. You have a hard rain here recently?"

"Night before last. Good Lord, what were you doin' out in the rain, dear child? Dressed as you are?"

"I don't know," the girl said, shaking her head. "You don't know me, señora?"

"I'm sorry, child. I don't. I know one thing, though. We gotta get you inside and clean you up. Joe, what're you doin' sittin' there like a lump on a damn log? Get this poor girl inside. Take her upstairs to the first room on the right side of the hall. There's a big zinc tub in the closet. Pull it out for me. I'll be up shortly with water for a bath."

"Is there a sawbones in Battle Mountain, Ma."

"Ain't been a sawbones here for years. Not since he got shot by the gent whose dislocated shoulder he wrenched back into place!"

"Ouch," Mannion said.

Ma wheeled and headed for the hotel's front door in her hunchbacked, quick-stepping way.

Mannion swung down from Red's back. "You heard the lady."

The girl gazed worriedly down at him. "I'm scared, Marshal Mannion. I don't know why, but I'm scared."

"No reason to be. I'll be close by," Joe said, pulling her gently down from the saddle.

He carried her through the front door and into the hotel's small lobby, the smell of dry rot competing with the succulent smell of the slow-cooking beans and peach pie Joe had imagined on his way into town. Ma didn't do much of a hotel business, but her steak and beans were famous county-wide so that the small dining room off the lobby to Mannion's right was often filled to capacity every noon and night. If you didn't want steak, you could have the rattlesnake stew, which was also considered Ma's specialty. She kept traps set in the ravine behind her place. There must have been a den back there, because, as Mannion had heard it told, she'd never been without enough snake to fill a pot bright and early every New

Mexico morning. The rattlesnake stew was a preference mostly of old desert rat prospectors, whom you'd have thought, like when Joe was in the army, would have gotten their fill out in the desert.

The stairs rose just beyond the lobby desk flanked by a cabinet clock and a dozen wooden pigeonholes. Mannion climbed them. They swayed so badly beneath his boots he was a little afraid they'd collapse beneath him, sending him and the girl in battered heaps to the lobby floor. But he and the girl made it up the stairs and into the first room on the hall's right side, no worse for the worry. The room was tiny. Mannion eased the girl onto the bed and drew the covers up around her shoulders.

He hated the blank, shocked look he saw in her eyes. Again, she seemed to stare right through him toward her own haunted past, obscured by the fog of forgetfulness.

He pulled the zinc bathtub out of the closet and set it on the braided rug at the end of the bed.

"You'll be all right here, honey. Ma'll be up soon with hot water for a bath."

Her eyes turned less opaque as she stared at him, the fog of her shock lifting a little. "Where are you going?"

"I have to tend the horses, but I'll be back soon."

"Please don't go."

"Ma'll be back soon. You'll be fine. You're just disoriented, is all. Soon, we'll find out who you are and where you came from, get you back to your family."

"I don't even know if I have a family."

"I'm bettin' you do." Mannion doffed his hat and leaned down to plant an affection peck on her forehead. Straightening, he set his hat on his head and turned to the door. "I'll be back to check on you soon."

Joe left the room and closed the door behind him.

He crossed the lobby and went outside. The horses stood ground, reined where he'd left them. He gathered up their reins and was about to mount Red when hoof thuds sounded along the street to the west. He pulled his foot out of the stirrup and turned to see two men on horseback riding toward him side by side, spaced about ten feet apart.

They stopped their fine stallions roughly twenty feet away—two tall, lean riders dressed in trail gear, including hand-tooled chaps and leather vests, crisp Stetsons on their heads, six-shooters bristling on their hips. Their attire was crisp and well-cared for. These were not your average 'thirty-a-month-and-found' cowpunchers. They worked for a good, proud spread.

One wore round-rimmed, steel-framed spectacles and a thick, dragoon-style mustache. He curveted his fine tobiano stallion, and said, "You Mannion?"

"That's right."

The other man, a little shorter than the bespectacled one and clean-shaven except for long side whiskers, sandy-haired and wearing a crisp cream Stetson said, "You really oughta mind your own business, Mannion!"

Both men reined their horses around, put the steel to them and galloped back in the direction from which they'd come, saddlebags flapping like wings. Mannion stood in the street, watching them dwindle in size until they rode on out of town and disappeared in a cloud of their own billowing dust.

Men standing out front of the two saloons watched them, too. The watchers turned toward Mannion and then slowly retreated into their respective watering holes.

"Now," Joe said, deeply befuddled, "what in holy blazes was that all about?"

A shadow moved in the street to his right.

He'd just started to turn his head in that direction when he glimpsed a black-hatted head and a rifle barrel bearing down on him from the peaked roof of an old harness shop on that side of the street. Joe dove forward and hit the dirt just as a bullet tore up dirt behind him.

CHAPTER 4

THE RIFLE'S WHIPCRACK ROCKETED AROUND THE street.

As Mannion heard the metallic rasp of a cocking lever jacking another round into the rifle's chamber, Joe heaved himself to his feet and ran. Another bullet plowed into the dirt and ground horse manure just off his right heel an eyeblink before he launched himself over a water trough and hit the ground behind it, a jarring flow he felt all through him.

The roar of the second blast reached his ears as, cursing, he unholstered both .44s, laid them over the top of the water trough, and returned fire at the hatted head and the rifle bearing down on him once more. He fired four quick rounds and watched in satisfaction as the hat went flying off the head of his dry-gulcher. That seemed to give the man pause. He drew his head and rifle back behind the peak of the harness shop.

"You son of a bitch!" Mannion bellowed.

He heaved himself to his feet, suppressing the pain in every joint in his body incurred from his two unceremonious meetings with the street, which reminded him he wasn't as young as he used to be. Not by a long shot. He took aim at the roof of the harness shop, but when he did not see his assailant again, he ran across the street and through a break between the harness shop and a still-open dry goods store. He leaped a small trash pile and the smelly body of a dead dog and gained the rear of the harness shop in time to see his dry-gulcher galloping off to the southeast, just then leaping a dry arroyo and pushing through cedars.

Then he was gone, the thuds of his fast-moving mount fading fast.

The man wore a black hat and a black vest, and he was riding a brown-and-white pinto pony. That's all Mannion had seen. He thought he'd also been firing a Henry repeating rifle because when Mannion had glimpsed the rifle, he'd seen no forestock. That was how witnesses to the murder of the deputy U.S. marshal had identified the killer, Harry Marcum. A tall, rangy devil with a black mustache, a black hat, black vest, and wielding a Henry repeating rifle.

"Marcum, you cowardly devil," Joe growled.

Staring in the direction the man had ridden, through scattered shacks, stock pens, brush and pines on the north edge of town, heading into the open desert, Mannion reloaded his .44s and dropped them into their holsters. He swung around and limped on creaky knees back into the street fronting the Continental. Ma Lonnigan stood out front of the place, shading her eyes with one hand, regarding Mannion curiously.

"I bet you found Harry Marcum, eh, Joe?"

"You could put it that way." Mannion angled toward where Red and Buzzard's steeldust, frightened by the gunfire, had sidled down the street a ways.

"Watch your back. He's a slippery, tricky devil. He loves killin', Marcum does."

"Now you tell me." Mannion grabbed Red's reins. "How's the girl?"

"Soaking in a hot bath. I'll feed her later and put her to bed. You could use a meal yourself, Joe. After your long ride." Ma gave a froggy laugh. "And the bullets you just dodged."

"You're a laugh a minute, Ma." Mannion swung up into the leather. "I'll be back for that meal after I tend the horses."

"You do that. An' you an' me'll have a heart-to-heart."

Mannion looked at her. "About what?"

Ma gave a wry smile. "Don't worry—I ain't gonna propose. I already wore out four men, turned 'em under." She cackled.

"I don't doubt it a bit."

Mannion booted Red on down the street in the direction of one still open livery barn he'd seen when he'd first ridden into town. As he walked Red and the steeldust, he felt eyes on him, saw shadowy figures staring out at him through the dusty windows of the two saloons and the other few businesses still open in the near ghost town of Battle Mountain. He surveyed the rooftops, half expecting another attempted bushwhack by Harry Marcum, though he doubted the man would try it again this soon.

He was likely holed up in the desert, waiting for Mannion to let his guard down again.

Joe turned Red toward H.G. Finlay's Livery & Feed— a sprawling wood frame structure as age- and weather-silvered as the rest of the buildings in Battle Mountain. An old, potbellied man in bib-front overalls sat in a hide-bottom chair on the right side of the broad, open doorway, smoking a meerschaum pipe. He grinned coyote-like as Joe reined Red up before him.

"H.G. Finlay, I assume?"

"Ain't wise to assume anything. But as long as you are, I assume you're Bloody Joe Mannion."

"Your assumption is correct."

"I assume he missed," said H.G. Finlay, that coyote grin in place.

"Your assumption is correct. Came within a cat's whisker."

Finlay smiled.

Mannion swung down from Red's back. "Did he house that brown-and-white pinto here?"

Finlay puffed his pipe and nodded. "Only remaining livery in town. Just came to get him not a half hour ago."

"I'll be damned."

"I dared ask him where he was headed, because he, like so many owlhoots on the run, seemed to like it here in Battle Mountain well enough to stay for a while— walks around like he's the mayor, don't ya know—and he just said I'd know soon enough." More smoke issued from the corner of the man's thin-lipped mouth. "I heard the gunfire."

"How'd he know I was in town?"

Finlay shrugged a thick shoulder. "He was over to the Holy Moses, playin' cards, when you rode in. I assume he saw you ride in like the others did. Most around here know who you are, Bloody Joe. I got a feelin' he was gonna get a big kick out of turnin' you toe down."

"For kicks an' giggles, eh?"

"And the reputation. He could've just kept playin' cards. He was snickerin' when he rode out of here."

"What's he look like? I know he wears a black Stetson and a black vest and rides the pinto. Didn't get a look at his face. Seen it on a wanted dodger, but those are unreliable."

"Ugly as sin!" Finlay laughed. "Face like wax. And wears one of them fancy handlebar mustaches with waxed, upswept ends." He raised a hand to the side of his mouth and prissily flicked his thumb and index finger together. "Uh...but, uh...don't tell him I said so."

He chuckled devilishly.

"If I run into the bastard again, I doubt there'll be much conversation other than the six-gun kind."

Mannion tossed the liveryman the reins of both horses then shucked his Yellowboy from its boot, set it on his right shoulder, and draped his saddlebags over his other shoulder. "Feed, water, and curry these two, will you? In exchange, you can keep the steeldust. Buzzard Lee won't be needin' him again anytime soon."

Finlay heaved himself up out of the chair, making the chair creak and shudder precariously. "Sure, sure. Fine-lookin' mount."

"Buzzard didn't deserve him."

Mannion turned and started to walk back the way he'd come.

Finlay said, "Marshal?"

Mannion turned back to him, one brow arched.

Finlay narrowed one eye warningly, more smoke from the pipe slithering out of the corner of his mouth. "You watch your back. There's more owlhoots than civilized folks in Battle Mountain these days. And that badge of yours would make a mighty fine target."

Mannion pinched his hat brim to the man and continued walking along the street's north side, noting more faces staring out at him from dirty windows. The grocer was butchering a big buck hanging upside down from the porch roof in front of his grocery store, tossing chunks of meat into a wheelbarrow, the scraps to a shaggy shepherd dog sitting behind the wheelbarrow, watching the big, bald, apron-clad man eagerly.

As Mannion approached, the man stopped cutting and turned to stare at him with dark interest.

Mannion said, "Fine-lookin' dog you got there," and kept walking.

The man just stared at him, turning his head to track Mannion's passage.

Mannion approached the Holy Moses Saloon. Four men were standing out there. When they saw him coming, they glanced around at each other and then moseyed back into the saloon through the batwings. Mannion stopped in front of the batwings, still clattering back into place. He pondered the situation, then shrugged a shoulder. Curiosity killed the cat, but he couldn't help wondering if he'd recognize any of the owlhoots here in Battle Mountain.

He shifted the saddlebags on his left shoulder and then pushed through the batwings and stepped to one side so light from the doors wouldn't outline him and make him an easy target.

Almost instantly, the low roar of conversation faded to the silence of a Lutheran church on a Saturday night in Dodge City. There were twenty or so men in the place and two scantily clad doxies. A half dozen men stood at the bar, a couple of big, bearded miners and obvious gunmen, two rather nattily clad with trimmed mustaches and two pistols on their broadcloth-clad hips.

Mannion looked around at the other men sitting at tables, several playing cards. All eyes were on him. Smoke hung in a thick cloud over the room, which smelled of tobacco, sour beer, whiskey, pomade, and cheap perfume.

A plump, dark-haired doxie hovering over one of the

gamblers lowered her head to whisper in the man's ear. He frowned annoyingly and waved her away with a pale, beringed hand, keeping his gaze on Mannion. Joe recognized him as a wanted stage robber named Omar Sledge. There was a fifteen-hundred-dollar reward on Sledge's head, if Mannion remembered correctly. He wore a three-piece suit and a gray felt sombrero. Sledge's long, blond hair flowed over his shoulders to hang down his back, brushed to a silky texture. A bulge in his Prince Albert coat bespoke a shoulder rig.

Mannion recognized a few of the other faces in the room.

A bounty hunter with balls enough to try could make quite a killing in the Holy Moses. Mannion was tempted to make his own play, but he was smart enough to know it would be sure suicide. There were just too many obvious gunslingers here.

He smiled at the room, pinched his hat brim, then turned and moseyed up to the bar running along the wall on his right, with an elaborate and nicely polished backbar mirror. He set his rifle and saddlebags on the bar. The barman—a short, fat man with pomaded hair combed straight back from a pronounced widow's peak— watched him warily, one fist on his hip, the other on the bar.

Mannion kept one cautious eye skinned on the backbar mirror as he said to the barman, "Set me up with a beer and a shot, will you, amigo? Been a long, dusty ride. You can pour the whiskey from a low-shelf bottle. My preference."

He grinned.

Behind him the room remained silent save for a few whispers and grunts and the creaking of chairs as men shifted their weight. As the barman filled a schooner from a tap, scraped off the foam with a stick, and filled a shot glass, Mannion saw that the two card games in the room behind him began to resume haltingly, the conversation among the players conspiratorially hushed.

Eyes flicked toward him.

Mannion felt like a rabbit at a rattlesnake convention, but he couldn't help himself. He felt like a kid unable to resist teasing a rabid fox with a stick. He was liable to get a bullet in the back, but he resolved to enjoy his drinks.

He threw back the shot of rotgut, smacked his lips, and sighed as he set the glass back down on the bar. Enjoying his beer, he surveyed the room in the mirror.

The hushed silence filled the room like a large, dark cloud.

It was like the near total quiet preceding a violent storm.

In the mirror, Mannion saw one man in particular eyeing him frequently and fidgeting around in his chair, grunting and sighing. He was a half-Mex outlaw named Herman Torrez. He was sitting with Jack Dawson, whom he was whispering with. They were a pair of known cattle thieves. Mannion had cost them both several years in the Colorado Territorial Pen. They sat at a table about ten feet away from Mannion and to his right as he faced the bar.

He knew if trouble came, it would come from that quarter.

As he casually sipped his beer, he furtively reached down and unsnapped the keeper thongs from over the hammers of both his holstered Russians.

Sure enough, he'd no sooner finished his beer and set the empty schooner down on the bar when Torrez leaned over to snarl into Dawson's ear, flaring his nostrils before rising so quickly, his chair went flying out behind him.

Slapping leather, he glared at Mannion and bellowed, "Bloody Joe, die you son of a—"

Mannion swung around, fists filled with both cocked Russians.

Torrez didn't get the last word out before Mannion's six-guns spoke the language of instant death, filling the room with their simultaneous, twin roars.

CHAPTER 5

MANNION STARED THROUGH HIS WAFTING POWDER smoke, over the smoking barrels of both Russians extended straight out before him, at Herman Torrez lying belly up over his overturned chair, the twin holes in his chest oozing blood slowly as his heart fell still.

His open blue eyes, opaque in death, reflected the light slanting in through a window to the right of the batwings.

Joe turned to Jack Dawson, still sitting in his chair, but his hands closed around the grips of his two-holstered Schofield .44s. His chin was dipped, and his eyes were hard with malign intent. A fly buzzed around his thick, gray-brown mustache that drooped down over both corners of his knife-slash mouth.

One eye twitched.

His chest rose and fell heavily.

Mannion said, "Want some of this, too, Jack?"

Dawson looked at Mannion's still-smoking Russians and shook his head slightly, the malign intent in his eyes turning to apprehension.

"Well, then get your cotton-pickin' hands off your pistols, you stupid son of a bitch!'"

Dawson removed his hands from his six-guns and raised them shoulder high, palm out.

Laughter broke the room's funereal silence.

"You sure know how to win friends and influence others, Bloody Joe—I'll give you that!" called Omar Sledge.

A few of the other men in the room laughed. One of the doxies covered her mouth and tittered.

Behind the bar, the fat apron said, "If you came in here attracting trouble for yourself, Mannion, you sure accomplished the task."

Keeping one Russian trained on the room, Mannion holstered the other one. He dug coins out of his pocket, tossed them onto the bar. "Just a habit I have," Joe said, knowing it was a bad habit. "I just can't help myself."

He holstered the second Russian, picked up his rifle, draped his saddlebags over his left shoulder, and aiming the Yellowboy straight out from his right hip at the room, moseyed toward the batwings. "Thanks for the drinks," he told the barman.

"Oh, anytime, Joe. Anytime."

More laughter from several quarters.

All eyes followed Joe to the batwings, which he backed out of, keeping the Winchester trained on the room. Once outside, he shouldered the rifle and continued eastward along the main street, heading toward the Continental.

"You damn fool," he muttered. "On the other hand, I've been wantin' to turn Herman Torrez' toe down for years. Mission accomplished."

He grinned.

As he walked, he noted that shadows were growing

long and the western light had turned that deep orange, salmon color. It was late afternoon, pushing on toward suppertime. Birds were chirping and flashing gold and silver as they winged over the main drag. Two young dogs were fighting over a bone at the mouth of a side street, on the other side of the main street from the casually strolling Del Norte lawman, who knew his bad habits were going to catch up to him one day.

One day soon.

He'd just kicked a hornet's nest.

He couldn't help chuckling drolly at himself.

There were already a few diners in the dining room of the Continental, two Chinamen who must have been driving the big dray filled with pine logs sitting outside the hotel. They were conversing in Chinese. Ma Lonnigan was just then setting big, smoking platters of steaks and beans down in front of them, and both big, round-faced, mustached sons of Han brightened with rosy, eager glows, bowing their heads at the little, mannish woman.

"Bon appetite!" Ma said in her smoker's rasp. She usually carried a corncob pipe in the breast pocket of her wool shirt and was often seen sitting in a chair on her front porch, legs crossed, puffing away like a gandy dancer.

She turned to see Mannion walk into the room.

"There you are, you big lug. Been courtin' more trouble, have you?"

"Been to church," Joe said, setting his rifle on a table by the front wall and draping his saddlebags over one of the table's four chairs. "Said a little prayer for all you sinners."

He tossed his hat down on the table and scrubbed a big hand through his longish, salt-and-pepper hair.

"You're liable to get struck by lightnin'," Ma said, "prayin' for me."

Joe sagged into a chair with his back to the wall. "How's the girl?"

"Clean as a whistle and sound asleep last I checked. Hungry?"

"So hungry my belly's making time with my spine."

"Steak or stew?"

Mannion chuckled. "Steak'll do me."

"You don't know what you're missin', Joe. I trapped me the largest bull yet. He alone nearly fills the pot!"

Ma laughed and headed for the kitchen. She came out a few minutes later with a steaming coffee mug and a large, smoking platter over the sides of which an inch-thick T-bone hung. Mannion's mouth watered.

"Ahh," Joe said. "I need to visit here more often."

"That's what I wanted to talk to you about." Ma dropped into a chair across from Mannion.

"Oh?" Joe said around his first mouthful of meat and beans.

Ma crossed her arms on the table and leaned over them conspiratorially. "Battle Mountain is no place for a lawman. Oh, Sylvan, sure. He wanted Buzzard on account o' Buzzard shot his deputy an' Sylvan can look only *so* bad an' still keep his job. He's smart enough to keep from prodding the snakes in their lair. But it's no place for you, Joe. I knew from how long you were gone you probably already stepped in it."

"You know me too well." Mannion was sawing into another large chunk of the succulent, medium-rare beef.

"Joe," Ma said. "This is a notional place. Lawmen come here and they either leave right away or they disappear. A couple of Pinkertons came here about a year ago. They overstayed their welcome an' they disappeared."

Mannion stuck a forkful of beans in his mouth. "How do you know they didn't ride out of their own accord?"

"Because they never checked out of my humble digs, and their horses were still in the livery barn long after they disappeared."

"Ah."

"A notional place. A dangerous place. Sylvan leaves well enough alone. He just mans his office to collect a paycheck and to break up a fight between drunks from time to time. Same with his deputy till he caught a bad case of lead poisoning from Buzzard Lee."

"I have to see to the girl, Ma."

"I'll see to her. I'll find out who she is and where she came from and get her back to her people."

"Well, I'm right curious myself, so I think I'll stick around. I told her I'd stay close. She's scared."

Ma reached across the table and closed her hand around Mannion's left wrist, giving him a direct, pointed look. "Joe, you listen to me. You ride out of here straight-away in the morning, or you won't ever ride out of here except maybe belly down over your own horse and dropped in the nearest ravine."

Mannion swallowed a mouthful of steak and beans and frowned across the table at the woman. "I saw the breed of owlhoot here, Ma. I stopped at the Holy Moses for a boilermaker. They're the usual cut. I can handle them. Hell, I tamed towns from—"

"I know where you tamed towns, but there'll be no tamin' Battle Mountain." Ma squeezed his wrist harder. "You mind me now, Joe. You take the first room in the second story hall, left side, across from the girl's. Then, first thing in the morning, you go."

With that, she rose from her chair and went over to

take the orders of several more customers who'd arrived while she'd been reading to Mannion from the book.

Joe frowned at her as he continued eating, puzzled. Suspicious. He had a feeling she hadn't told him everything she'd meant.

Really meant. Just a feeling he had. He'd been a lawman long enough to trust those feelings.

He finished his meal, left some coins on the table, doffed his hat, grabbed his saddlebags and Yellowboy, and headed for his room. He'd turn in early. It had been a long day and he needed a good night's sleep.

He was interested to see what tomorrow would bring.

————

IN THE SPRAWLING STONE CASTLE OVERLOOKING THE town of Battle Mountain, Ruth Kennecott lifted her pen from the ledger she'd been adding up figures in, her heart quickening a little at the realization of the cost she would incur when she reopened her mine—the Kennecott Mine on the backside of Battle Mountain— and turned her head to frown curiously toward the open French doors of her office. Which had once been her husband, Hayward's, office until he'd hanged himself from the balcony rail, though she'd tried time and time again to scour the horrid memory from her consciousness.

The shame was always there, however, like a heart condition or a cancerous growth on her spine. The only way she thought she might exorcise it from her consciousness was to reopen the mine on the advice of a team of Canadian geologists who insisted there was, indeed, more gold and silver to be plundered from the formation albeit with more, and more costly, modern mining techniques, and to make the Kennecott—as well as the Kennecott name—a success at last.

A mine and a name to be proud of.

"Lottie?" Ruth called.

"Yes, Mrs. Kennecott—I'm here," her maid, Lottie Jefferson, called.

Footsteps sounded and then the heavy Black woman in her black, lace-edged uniform dress with a clean white apron appeared in the office's open doorway, holding a feather duster in one hand, a soiled white cloth in the other. She'd been dusting and polishing the wooden furniture of the parlor. Ruth had been hearing her huffing and puffing with the effort, occasionally humming one of the old songs she'd brought with her from the Alabama plantation she'd been raised on before the Emancipation Proclamation had taken effect.

"More tea, ma'am?" Lottie asked, glancing at the silver tea set on its silver tray resting on the large, gold-riveted, leather-covered desk before Ruth, near Hayward's cherry humidor, which she had not scoured from the room for some reason, unlike so much of him she'd tried to rid the house of. Athena had given it to him after her trip to Philadelphia, to visit her grandparents the winter before Hayward had died. Ruth supposed that was why she hadn't tossed it as she'd discarded most of his other belongings aside from his books. Athena had taken after her father in that she read nearly every waking moment when she wasn't playing the piano or collecting wildflowers from the bank of the spring-fed creek that wound along the base of Battle Mountain.

"Don't you hear that?" Ruth said, frowning curiously. Distantly, through an open window overlooking the garden at the rear of the house, she could hear her daughter talking and laughing. She also thought she could hear the deep, throaty voice of a man. "Athena is talking with someone. You told the grocer not to send that teenage boy of his with our groceries, didn't you, Lottie? I distinctly told you I did not want that vermin anywhere—"

"Oh, yes, yes, Mrs. Kennecott. I told him you wanted that vermin spawn of his nowhere near the house! That's Mister Sledge. I'm sorry, I thought I told you he was here. I told him to wait in the parlor, but he's out in the garden, talkin' with Miss Athena, I reckon. I told him you'd be right with him."

"Oh!" Ruth returned her pen to its holder. She'd been so absorbed in her figures and in the prospect of reopening the mine that she'd forgotten that Lottie had told her Sledge, her troubleshooter, was here to discuss a certain matter. In her mixed excitement and consternation about the mine, and her remembered conversation with the team of highly optimistic geologists, the information had gone in one ear and out the other.

Anger rippled through her, however.

She'd distinctly told Sledge she wanted him to have no contact with Athena.

She rose quickly from her brocade armchair, long gown swishing about her long legs still slender at forty-seven, as she fumbled open a drawer of the desk. She removed her .38 caliber, pearl-gripped Merwin & Hulbert pocket pistol—also once a possession of her disgraced late husband—and dropped it into a pocket of the black leather vest she wore over a simple blue blouse. She hurried past Lottie and down the broad, carpeted staircase, toward the house's rear garden from where her daughter's imbecilic tittering played her nerves like the creaky strings of an ancient violin.

CHAPTER 6

THE FRENCH DOORS AT THE REAR OF THE LARGE dining room with its mile-long oak table at which politicians, diplomats, and railroad moguls were once supposed to dine—but had never come because the mine proved a failure—were open. The gauzy curtains danced on the breeze like the wings of angels. On this breeze came Athena's musical voice and damnable tittering punctuated by the deep, masculine voice of Omar Sledge.

Ruth stopped in the doorway and gazed out into the brick-paved garden in which roses and a dozen other plants were kept alive by Ruth's hired men—a full-blood Ute named Charlie Three Knives and the big German, Hans Kreutzer—both of whom were repairing the door to the stable in which Ruth kept her two blooded steeds and Athena's cream mare. Ruth rode with Athena twice a week around the remote backside of Battle Mountain, to revisit the remains of the mine and for Ruth to imagine what it would look like once she reopened it...that was, with the help of Grant Kincaid, owner of the Horsehead Ranch, the largest spread in the region, and several eastern investors.

Sure enough, Omar Sledge was in the garden with Athena. The tall, lean gunman with the long, silky blond hair flowing over his shoulders and down his back, from beneath the gray sombrero with a black silk band he always wore, stood before Athena, who sat in the wooden swing suspended from the bough of a ponderosa pine at the rear of the garden, near the very base of the mountain. Athena wore a day dress that was growing too tight for her maturing figure. Part of her auburn hair was drawn up on her head and fixed with blue ribbons that drew out the lilac in her eyes. She held a wooden apple crate before her, and she was smiling and speaking in low, intimate tones while Sledge held his hand in the box, also smiling and muttering in his intimate, masculine voice.

"Athena!" Ruth barked. "What on earth is going on out here?"

Athena gasped and jerked her startled, blue-eyed gaze to Ruth. "Mother! Stop! You've frightened Zeus!"

"I don't care who've I've frightened! *Mister* Sledge, what are you doing back here *alone with my daughter*, pray tell?"

Sledge turned his seedy-eyed, freckled face toward Ruth and gave a sneering grin, showing one chipped front tooth. In his petal soft, Southern accent, he said, "Oh, you don't need to pray for me to tell you anything, Mrs. Kennecott. I was waitin' for you in the parlor, fiddling with my hat, until Miss Athena here came in and invited me to the garden to see the magpie she rescued. He's a cute little fella, I'll give him that. She healed his wing up good. I do believe he'll be ready to fly away soon."

He turned his supercilious smile to the girl, who smiled brightly and with way too much naïveté, as was her way, damn the simpleminded child, anyway. She might have been the best-educated person in the entire

Kennecott clan, had breezed through a classical education, which Ruth had provided right here at home, in record time, could recite endlessly from Socrates and Homer, and was a masterful pianist, but still had the mind of a child. Most of the time, anyway.

Though sometimes Ruth had to admit suspecting if she wasn't putting on the dog a bit.

"Be that as it may," Ruth said, frigidly, "I do remember telling you I wanted you to stay away from my daughter."

"Mother!" Athena intoned, drawing the wooden crate back close to the aggravatingly well-filled corset of the day dress. "How dare you keep me in solitary confinement! I merely invited Mr. Sledge back here to see Zeus and for some innocent conversation. Nothing more and nothing less. Your restrictions on me are going to drive me absolutely insane until the only fitting place for me will be an *asylum*!"

The twenty-year-old rose from the chair and stomped, barefoot, the crate in her arms, past her mother and into the house, yelling behind her in her melodramatic fashion, "What you've done to me is best described by Mr. Shakespeare: 'Life's but a walking shadow, a poor player that struts and frets his hour upon the stage, and then is heard no more. It is a tale told by an idiot, full of sound and fury, signifying *nothing*'!"

Inside the house, a door slammed.

Omar Sledge scowled at Ruth. "What'd she just say? 'Shadow,' 'player,' 'idiot'...?"

"Never mind. I don't know half of what she says myself. All I know is I strictly forbade you from being alone with her."

"Oh, come on, Ruth."

"*Mrs. Kennecott* to you, Mister Sledge!"

"All right, all right." Sledge threw up his hands in supplication. "Mrs. Kennecott, the girl's lonely. Can't you see that? Ain't she supposed to be *married* by now?"

"She was, yes." Ruth moved out into the garden and sank slowly into a cushioned wicker chair. "We ran into a bit of a stumbling block. That's partly what has Athena fit to be tied. She doesn't understand any of it. I can't say as I do, either. Neither of us is accustomed to being rejected."

"Yeah, well, most of the town understands it. Includin' me." Smiling knowingly, Sledge sank into a cushioned wicker chair on the other side of a small wicker table on which the book Athena was currently reading—*Ivanhoe* by Sir Walter Scott—lay open and face down.

"Wipe that sneer off your face, *Mister* Sledge. I have a revolver in my pocket, and I came out here fully prepared to use it in defense of my daughter's honor as well as my own reputation." Ruth patted the bulging pocket of her vest.

"Jesus," Sledge laughed. "You, *Mrs.* Kennecott, are a piece of work."

"Yeah, well, you're a known criminal with a price on your head!"

"And you hired me. You sent for me all the way from Council Bluffs, remember? Had me a good payin' job workin' for a stockmen's syndicate."

"Yes, well, my last, uh...underling *associate*, who shall remain nameless...took a bullet he couldn't digest. In my employ."

Ruth wasn't sure why, but she was proud of that. Her husband had acquired many enemies over the years, and when he died, she'd had the bad luck of inheriting them. Hayward had had other business interests—none as

successful as what he'd dreamed the mine would become
—and with those interests had come rivals who were not
exactly choirboys. Those interests, including shares in a
shipping business, a railroad line, and several saloons in
and around St. Louis, often evoked the ire of those she
perpetually found herself in competition with.

As well as more than a few corrupt politicians and
government officials wanting a piece of the pie, not at all
uncommon in the frontier west.

Some of those rivals and genuine burrs in her bonnet
she had found more convenient to kill than, say, to air her
dirty laundry before attorneys and a judge—all of whom
could be extremely expensive. Because of the failure of
the Kennecott Mine, Ruth had found herself wealthy on
paper but poor in the vault.

That, too, had been Hayward's fault. She sometimes
wished she could resurrect the SOB, if only to slap the
holy snot out of him.

"I admit you did come with several good recommen-
dations. Be that as it may, please don't forget that you are
a criminal—how common we'll not be so indelicate as to
discuss—and you do have a price on your head."

Sledge snorted and jerked his head back. "Are you
threatenin' to blackmail me, *Mrs.* Kennecott?"

"Just stating a fact, *Mister* Sledge." She sent that home
with a brown-eyed, pointed look. "Now, what are you
doing here? I did not call for you. I just want you to
remain handy."

"Yeah, well, remaining handy, I learned something
about the topic a few minutes ago...before you decided to
discuss my checkered pass."

"What topic?"

"Athena's marriage or lack thereof."

Ruth frowned. "What *in particular* about it?"

"The Mex."

"Who?"

"The...*Mex*."

"You mean...the...the...girl?"

Sledge grinned. "One an' the same."

Ruth's frown grew more severe. So did her curiosity, tinged with just a hint of apprehension she feared would grow. "Just what about the girl?"

"She appeared in town earlier. With a lawman...a fairly famous if not *notorious* lawman known as Bloody Joe Mannion."

"I've heard the name." Yep, her apprehension was growing, all right. "I take it there's more."

"She'd been badly beaten up. Mannion found her in a ravine. She was muddy, dressed in only her nightgown. No memory."

"No, what?"

"Memory. Gone. Shot to hell. Kaput."

"How could that be?"

"I don't know. Shock, maybe. Who knows. Anyway, she didn't know what happened to her that she found herself in a ravine some distance from town. Back in the direction of her family's estancia. That's 'farm' in Spanish."

"I'm sure I know as much Spanish as you do, Mister Sledge."

"Just sayin'."

"What happened?"

Sledge shrugged innocently. "I thought maybe you'd know."

She stared at him as though he were dung a dog had left on the paving stones for a full five seconds before she said, "What are you implying?"

"I'm not *implying* anything. I was just wondering if you knew what might have happened to the girl."

"You're implying I did something."

"Did you?" Again, he threw up his hands in supplication. "I mean, I don't care whether you did or not. I just thought, acting as your *underling associate*...I should let you know what happened to her and that she rode into town with one of the nastiest SOB lawmen the territory —not to mention the entire frontier west—has ever known. And I hear Bloody Joe's bein' right protective of the sweet little Mex and seems determined to find out what happened to her that was so bad she don't even remember what it was."

Ruth stared at him. The wheels were churning in her head. The apprehension was building. If Omar Sledge suspected she might have had something to do with causing the Mexican girl to lose her memory, others in town might, too. And these suspicions might filter to the notorious former town tamer and current town marshal of Del Norte, Bloody Joe Mannion, a man she knew only by reputation.

If she'd had nothing to do with the girl losing her memory, who had?

"Grant."

"What's that?" Sledge asked.

"Nothing."

"No, you'd said something. Grant?"

"Never mind."

"Grant Kincaid?"

Ruth rose from her chair and walked to the low stone wall bordering the garden, separating the sprawling house from the sheer sandstone wall of Battle Mountain. She crossed one arm on her chest and raised the other to her mouth, worrying her bottom lip with her beringed index finger.

"Surely not. Surely, he didn't. Something like that could endanger us both...all we've worked for. All we will work for...together."

"What?" Sledge said, cupping his ear and scowling. "Speak up. I can't hear you."

"Never mind."

"If you don't mind me sayin' so, I did see a couple of men who used to ride for Kincaid ride down from your place. Don't worry, don't worry...I know you got more *underling associates* than just little old me." Sledge laughed ironically.

Ruth turned to the man favoring her with an ironic half smile on his almost effeminate lips to go with his long, silky blond hair that was distinctly feminine, as well. He shrugged. "Just sayin'."

"They patrol the mine entrance...on the other side of the mountain. Keeping claim jumpers away from the old shaft. Several have tried breaking in over the years."

"Ah, I see."

"You may leave now, Mister Sledge."

"You got it, Mrs. Kennecott." Sledge raised his long, lean frame with his spaghetti-thin legs from his chair, the hem of his long, black Prince Albert coat falling into place around him. He pinched his hat brim and smiled. "Say goodbye to Miss Athena for me, will you? Tell her I wish her an' Zeus the best."

Ruth just flared a nostril at him.

When he'd sauntered into the house, heading for the front door, Ruth turned to stare worriedly at the sandstone ridge of Battle Mountain.

"Oh, Grant," she said. "Oh, Grant."

CHAPTER 7

MANNION WASN'T SURE HOW LONG HE'D BEEN ASLEEP when something roused him.

He opened his eyes and sat up in bed, listening.

Seconds passed.

Distantly, he could hear the cabinet clock ticking away in the lobby. Ma slept several doors down from him, but he could hear her sawing logs as though she were in the next room with the tree and a long saw. Somewhere outside, a dog was barking. Also distantly, he could hear the tinny patter of a player piano in one of the town's two saloons.

None of those sounds had roused him.

It had been something closer.

Then it came again: the creak of wood under a stealthy foot. Another creak and a faint shuddering sound. Someone was coming up the stairs.

Mannion's heart quickened. He reached for one of his two Russians hanging from the bed's front post to his right. He slid the big popper from its holster, threw the covers back, and rose, holding the Russian straight up and down by his right shoulder, thumb on the hammer.

The creaks grew more frequent and louder.

There was a faint whisper. His heartbeat quickened.

Someone was coming for him. They meant to kick in his door and fill him so full of lead he'd rattle when he walked!

Not his first rodeo.

Clad in only his longhandles, he padded in his stocking feet to the door and pressed his left shoulder to the wall beside it, turning his head to listen.

The creaking had stopped.

Were his would-be assailants outside his room?

He frowned, waiting.

Then he heard a man whisper, "Which room's she in?"

Another man whispered, "Fritz was in the dining room when Mannion brought her in. First room on the right."

Mannion frowned. His heartbeat quickened evermore.

They were after the *girl?*

He twisted the knob and opened the door in time to see the silhouette of one of two men draw his right foot back to kick the girl's door in.

"Hey!" Joe bellowed.

Both men wheeled toward him. Ambient light glinted off the pistols in their fists.

The Russian roared twice quickly, sounding like a shotgun in the close quarters. Both men grunted and stumbled back, one of them firing his own six-gun into the ceiling just before he struck the floor. The two lay, one atop the other, groaning and writhing briefly, grinding the heels of their boots into the floor, then making a last exhalation before giving up their ghosts.

"Hey!" Ma Lonnigan cried from down the hall. "Not in my consarned establish you don't!"

In her own room, the girl screamed shrilly with stone-cold terror.

Mannion hurried across the hall and into the girl's room. She sat up in bed, to the right of the window through which light from a guttering oil pot angled, limning her silhouette.

"It's all right, honey! It's all right, honey! It's Joe Mannion. You're safe now—no harm done!" He took the sobbing girl in his arms and drew her close, feeling her lithe, supple body shudder against his.

"What the hell's goin' on?" This from Ma Lonnigan standing in the open doorway behind Joe and the girl, looking down at the fresh beef piled up to the left of the girl's door as Joe faced the hall.

The girl continued to sob in his arms.

"They were after me, Ma," Joe lied for the girl's benefit. "You were right. The town's damn notional. They were here to trim my wick." Continuing to hold the girl closely against him, he said, "It's all right, honey. They were after me. I had to shoot 'em. I'm sorry I frightened you so bad, but you're gonna be just fine."

Why in holy blazes were two men out to kill the girl?

———

MANNION GENTLED THE SOBBING GIRL BACK DOWN ON the bed, tucked the covers around her, and walked to the doorway where Ma Lonnigan stood, looking down at the two dead men. She wore men's longhandles under a ratty deerskin robe.

"You recognize 'em?"

She shook her head. "Never seen 'em before in my life."

"You sure?"

Ma gave Mannion a peevish look. "Yes, I'm sure!"

"You stay with the girl. I'll drag their bodies outside and then fetch Story."

Ma went into the room, drawing the door closed behind her, saying, "Say, say, dry those tears now, child! No one's gonna hurt you!"

Mannion dressed then dragged the first body down the stairs and out the front door, which had been barred from the inside, meaning the girl's two would-be killers must have entered by a back door. He'd just dragged the second body onto the porch when he heard footsteps and heavy breathing out on the street. He reached for his cross-draw .44 but staid the motion when he saw the bulky figure of Sylvan Story angling toward the hotel, wearing baggy denims, a longhandle top, and suspenders, with his cream sugarloaf sombrero glowing dully in the light of a near oil pot.

Sylvan stopped at the bottom of the porch steps, wheezing like he'd run a mile dripping wet. "You already shootin' up my town, Bloody Joe? You ain't been here a full day. You shot one fella over to the Moses, riled a whole *passel* of rattlesnakes over there, and now—what? You done shot two more?"

He spat to one side and planted his fists on his broad hips.

"Come up here and take a look at 'em. See if you recognize 'em."

Sylvan sighed and wearily climbed the porch steps. He stood looking down at the two dead men, both clad in the garb of your average range rider, complete with hand-tooled leather chaps and billowy neckerchiefs.

"You recognize 'em?" Mannion asked when the Battle Mountain lawman didn't say anything for nearly a full minute.

Sylvan shook his head. "No. No, can't say as I do."

"You sure?"

Sylvan lifted his gaze from the dead men to Mannion. "Yep. Don't know 'em—sure enough."

"They were after the girl."

"They was?"

"Yes. Why, do you suppose?" Mannion asked, thoroughly befuddled. "Why would two cowpunchers want to kill the girl upstairs?"

"I got no idea."

"You sure?" Something told Mannion the man wasn't telling the truth.

"Sure, I'm sure," Sylvan said in the same peevish tone Ma had acquired when Mannion had prodded her upstairs about the identities of the two dead men.

"They must have mounts around here somewhere. Probably around back." Mannion moved down the steps and headed for the Continental's front east corner.

"I'll fetch the undertaker," Sylvan said.

"Hold on."

Mannion walked around to the rear of the hotel. A minute later, he led two saddled horses, one buckskin and one black with one white sock, around to the front where Sylvan still stood on the porch, facing the street.

"They came in the back. Jimmied the back door. Doubt it was very hard. The door's as rickety as the rest of the place." Mannion stopped the horses at the bottom of the porch steps. "Horsehead brand on each of 'em. Where's the Horsehead, Sylvan?"

Story fingered his beard. "Horsehead, you say, huh? Hmm."

"Come on, Sylvan. You must know all the ranches in this country. Unless these two fellas aren't from around here, but I'd bet the seed bull they are." He paused. It was his turn to strike a peevish tone. "Aren't they?"

He thought he'd heard the Horsehead name tossed around a time or two on one of his previous visits to Battle Mountain town.

"Listen, Joe," Story said. "You're startin' to dig too deep into somethin' that ain't none of your business. You'd best leave now. You brought me Buzzard Lee. You done your job. You head back to Del Norte first thing in the mornin'."

"My job isn't officially done until I've run down Harry Marcum. He'll likely show himself again sooner or later."

"And when he does, you'll likely get your head blown off!"

"It's my head." Mannion paused and gave the local lawman a pointed look. "Where's the Horsehead, Sylvan? If you don't tell me, somebody will."

"Oh, hell, Joe!" Story sighed and wagged his head fatefully. "Southwest of town. There's a side trail. It's marked. Let me give you one more warning, Joe. You stay away from the Horsehead. You let me deal with this matter. I'll take care of it."

Mannion climbed the porch steps and stood threateningly close to the thick-set lawman who was a couple of inches shorter than he was, slump-shouldered and pot-gutted. "Take care of what?"

Story threw out a hand to indicate the two dead men lying side by side on the porch fronting the door. "This. These two. The Horsehead. If they're even from the Horsehead. They might've just stolen a couple of Horsehead horses. Grant Kincaid is known for his horses."

"Grant Kincaid runs the Horsehead?"

Again, Story gave a weary sigh. "Yes, yes, yes. Grant Kincaid runs the Horsehead."

"What beef would he have with the girl upstairs?"

"I got no idea!"

"Yes, you do. Tell me, dammit, Sylvan. I'm gonna find out sooner or later. If I find out you been holdin' out on me...with that girl's life in the balance...I'm gonna kick the stuffing out of you from both your fat ends!"

"Ah, hell!" Story walked heavily down the porch steps. "I don't have to listen to this crap." He started angling across First Street toward the mouth of the cross street down which his jailhouse sat. He stopped, turned around, and thumbed himself in his lumpy, longhandle-clad chest. "This is my town. Not your town, Mannion. *My* town!"

He swung back around so quickly he nearly tripped over his own feet and then headed for the cross street, the light from the oil pot on the other side of the street silhouetting his thick figure.

"Then the girl's your responsibility, Sylvan. I'll be riding out with these two dead men for the Horsehead in the morning. There better not have been a hair harmed on her head when I get back, or I will gutshoot you and leave you in the street, howling!"

Story threw up a dismissive hand and headed down the cross street.

"Bright and early, Story!"

"Go to hell, Joe," came the local lawman's weary voice.

———

MANNION UNSADDLED THE DEAD MEN'S TWO HORSES but left their bridles on. He tied them both to one of the hitchracks fronting the Continental. He fed and watered them both—he wanted them both fresh in the morning

—then spent the rest of the night in Ma Lonnigan's smoking chair on the front porch.

A passerby might have thought he was holding a vigil for the two dead men. The fact was, he had nothing but contempt for both and was eagerly awaiting his ride out to the Horsehead to find out why in hell they'd been about to kick in the girl's door and fill her full of lead. He took up a position on the porch to watch for more assailants. If anyone came in the back again, he'd hear them inside when they headed up the creaky stairs.

He doubted more would come.

On the other hand, he had no idea why the first two had come, so what in hell did he know, anyway?

He didn't want to leave the girl alone, but he had a feeling Sylvan Story had more spine than the man himself gave himself credit for. Mannion was betting the man would let no harm come to her when Joe was out powwowing at the Horsehead.

Whether or not she knew who wanted the girl dead, Ma Lonnigan would look out for her, too. Few would tangle with Ma.

Gradually, the saloons fell silent. The oil pot guttered out.

Darkness aside from starlight was almost complete.

The only sounds for a long time were coyotes warming up like choirs from insane asylums in the mountains outside of town.

At dawn, Mannion saddled both horses. He'd just finished tying both bodies, wrapped in their bedrolls, belly down across their saddles when Sylvan Story appeared, approaching as he did the night before—heavy-footed, breathing hard. Only this morning, he held a double-barrel Greener across his chest.

He stepped past Mannion, who was tightening the

black's saddle cinch. He said nothing until he'd climbed the porch steps and had taken a seat in Ma's smoking chair.

"Let me know what you find out," he said, tonelessly.

"Something tells me you already know. Or have your suspicions."

"Suspicions is one thing."

Mannion led both horses down the street to the livery barn, where he roused H.G. Finlay, who was not one bit happy about being awakened so early in the morning. Finlay watered, fed, and saddled Red and led the bay out the broad open doors. Clad in a tattered, checked robe over longhandles, and wearing high-topped mud boots, he glanced at both spare horses obviously carrying dead men. He didn't say anything, only gave his head a single, fateful wag, then, yawning, retreated back into the bowels of the barn and, presumably, to his sleeping quarters.

Mannion mounted up and, leading both packhorses by their bridle reins, booted Red out of town to the west and back along the trail he, Buzzard Lee, and the girl had taken into Battle Mountain only the day before. He continued past where they'd picked up the trail and followed a two-track wagon trail southwest.

The sun was well up when he came upon a fork in the trail and a weathered wooden sign standing between two ponderosa pines identifying the southern fork as the route to the Horsehead Ranch. The trail climbed a steep, forested ridge and then followed a canyon with forested slopes on both sides.

Mannion had ridden a quarter mile past the ridge when he checked Red down and stared up the ridge on his left. Three men hung from three separate pines. They'd been hanging there a good two weeks, judging by the stench and the bloated, purplish condition of their bodies inside their range attire. They were so bloated that the seams of their shirts and pants were splitting. Their swollen, purple tongues stuck out of their mouths, and their eyes had been pecked out by birds.

One appeared Mexican. The other two were white men—one with long, flowing gray hair, the other with short, sandy hair and a thin, sandy mustache. The sandy-haired one was just a kid.

A wooden sign hung around his neck by a rope.

On it, painted in red, was one word: *RUSTLERS*.

"Well, all right," Mannion said to himself, wryly. "Good to know who I'm dealing with."

Grant Kincaid was obviously a hard man.

Hard enough to order a young woman killed in cold blood while she slept?

Mannion booted Red on ahead. "Reckon I'm gonna find out."

The canyon opened and Mannion found himself following the trail through pine forest. Where the forest played out, he found himself sitting Red at the edge of it, staring down into a broad, grassy, stage-stippled valley through which a narrow, meandering stream cut. To the right of the stream lay a picturesque and obviously wealthy ranch headquarters with a large, lodge-like log house sitting off to the right of the bunkhouse, barns, corrals, and other outbuildings. White-faced cattle peppered the valley around the headquarters, which included a large corral teeming with horses that even from this distance of a quarter mile, Mannion recognized as prime stock.

A hitch-and-rail fence encircled the headquarters.

A lookout tower stood near a windmill and a stock tank in the middle of the yard. There appeared to be a man in it, but Mannion couldn't be sure until he rode down into the valley and was loping Red toward the broad portal into the high crossbar of which the Horsehead brand had been burned, and a man bellowed hoarsely, "Riders comin' fast, boss. Three hosses!"

Mannion heard the loud metallic rasp of the rifle in the lookout's hands being cocked.

CHAPTER 8

THE LOOKOUT AIMED HIS WINCHESTER AT MANNION and ordered loudly, "Hold it right there, Mister!"

Mannion stopped Red just inside the headquarters and returned with: "Joe Mannion, Del Norte town marshal. I'm packing fresh beef that, judging by the brands on these two horses, belongs here."

Men were working around the yard, most gathered around or sitting on a breaking corral in which two others were working with a wild-eyed grulla at a snubbing post. All heads turned to regard Mannion and his grisly cargo with interest. Several men turned to each other to confer in low tones.

"Wave him in, Don!" came a man's resonant voice from the broad porch ringing the main lodge.

Don lowered his rifle and, with a great air of self-importance, waved Mannion toward the lodge, where Mannion now saw a man his own age standing atop the broad, high, halved log steps. Mannion booted Red toward the lodge, passing through a fringe of pines then climbing a slight rise to the impressive main house.

Mannion reined up at the two, wrought-iron

hitchracks, each with the Horsehead brand formed at the ends, to either side of the porch steps. A gravel-paved drive formed a *U* at the bottom of the steps, and Mannion imagined horses and carriages parked here during parties at Thanksgiving and Christmas and maybe the Fourth of July or whenever Kincaid invited moneyed guests here from the east for hunting excursions in the fall and maybe the winter, his tony guests carried about in fur-laden sleighs warmed with heated bricks and drawn by the finest horseflesh in the territory.

Kincaid looked the regal old frontiersman dressed in blue shirt trimmed with a bolo tie, a brown alligator hide vest, and gray whipcord trousers. He was tall and broad-shouldered, with a broad, red-weathered face and piercing blue eyes. Thick, gray hair was combed to one side. Muttonchops the same color as his hair ran down both sides of his face. They were in stark contrast to the almost Indian copper of the man's skin.

His big hands hung straight down at his sides. He'd already taken in his guest. Now, he was looking owlishly at the two horses flanking Mannion.

His eyes returned to Joe. "Mannion, did you say?"

"Joe Mannion, yes."

"Bloody Joe?"

Mannion gave an ironic smile. "Yeah."

"Hmm."

"Are these your horses?"

"If they're wearing my brand they are. Or were."

"What about the men riding belly down across the saddles?"

"I don't know. I can't see them."

Mannion swung down from Red's back. "Come on down."

"I know who they are," Kincaid said. "I recognize

them by their horses. I know my horses better than I know my men. They are Hattersby and Plum. Slash Hattersby and Roy Plum. Former hands of mine. They were let go after roundup last fall and I didn't hire them back in the spring. They were not top hands, and I only hire top hands."

Kincaid's attention was drawn toward the bunkhouse. He threw up a hand, palm out, and yelled in his deep stentorian: "James, stay there!"

Mannion turned to see beyond the fringe of pines, a young man who'd started walking toward the lodge, away from the breaking corral, stop and stare this way. He was of average height, ever so vaguely stocky, slightly potbellied, fair-skinned but tanned, and dressed in range gear, including batwing chaps. His sandy hair hung nearly to his shoulders, and a soot-stain mustache appeared to mantle his upper lip. He wore a sun-coppered, bullet-crowned, black hat with decorative white stitching along the brim. Nothing in his stature told Mannion he was the rancher's son, but the facial features were ever so vaguely similar.

His interest in what was happening up this way did, as well.

The young man started forward again, stubbornly.

Kincaid stopped him with a pugnacious, menacing: "Did you hear me, boy?"

The young man turned reluctantly and walked back toward the breaking corral, chaps flapping against his legs. The men sitting on the rails had their heads turned to watch the doings at the lodge.

Mannion turned to Kincaid. "These two tried to kill an innocent young woman last night in the Continental Hotel."

"Innocent young woman? Damn, few of them around Battle Mountain. Doxie?"

"Dunno. Don't think so."

Kincaid frowned, impatient. "Well, who is she?"

"That's what I want to know. She lost her memory."

"Nicely setup little Mexican? Woman's body, little girl's voice and manner?"

Mannion just stared at the man.

Kincaid said, "Giannina Calderon."

"Who?"

"Giannina Calderon. From the Calderon family between here and Battle Mountain. She's trash. A puta. *Whore*. She had these two so twisted they didn't know their heads from their backsides. She played 'em against each other. Bad habit of hers. She made more jingle that way. Then I heard she started answering the sparkings of a gambler from town, and these two were likely so upset they got drunk and decided to clean her clock."

"That was last night. Before that, I found her in an arroyo a couple of miles west of town. Likely carried down by a flood from a rainstorm. She's in shock. Doesn't remember a thing."

Kincaid smiled and crossed his arms on his broad chest. "The gambler probably gave her a good thrashing, or tried to. Cinco Summerfield was his name. Spent some time in Battle Mountain. I even played poker with him myself. Temperamental sort. He was caught cheating, and I and several other of the men he fleeced, ran him out of town. I saw him with Señorita Calderon a time or two, in either the Moses or the Blue Dog. Can't remember which."

"No one in Battle Mountain seems to know her."

"They know her. Might've even had a piece of her."

Again, Kincaid smiled. "Just take her back to her family. They have a hayfield along San Juan Creek at the base of Battle Mountain, halfway between here and town. They'll take her in. They have no shame. They enjoy the extra dinero she brings in. Even take her to town, drop her off for a few nights. I know the squalid family. Bought hay from them a time or two."

Mannion just stared at the man. He didn't want to believe what he was hearing. That the girl he'd found was from some distant planet would have been easier to take. He'd gotten to know her as this innocent forest sprite he'd found lost and alone in an arroyo—frightened, chaste, almost angelic.

He turned to gaze through the pines toward the breaking corral. Kincaid's son, James, sat on the corral but his head was turned this way, staring toward the lodge with obvious interest.

Why?

Did he know the dead men Mannion had brought to the Horsehead?

Had he been involved with Giannina Calderon, as well?

Were the folks of Battle Mountain too ashamed to have told Mannion who she was? Possibly the roles some might have played in her life, if what Kincaid had said about her was true?

"Let her go, Mannion. Don't you get twisted around her, too. She's a cunning little devil. The thing of it is, though"—Kincaid frowned, pursed his lips, and shook his head—"I'm not certain she's totally aware of what she's doing. She's just this wild little animal acting on instinct. Probably ran in fear of the gambler, got lost in the storm, and ended up in the arroyo."

Kincaid shrugged his thick shoulders, and added, "Her memory will come back sooner or later."

Mannion thought it over. He wasn't much good at thinking at the moment, however. He found himself nodding. "All right." He nudged his hat up to scratch the back of his head. "All right. I'll leave these two with you. They're your horses."

"We'll bury the bodies. I don't think either man had a family."

Joe was about to rein Red around when Kincaid said, "Hey, Mannion. Let it go. She has this effect on men. She'll baffle you. Turn you inside out. Go back to Del Norte. There's nothing for you here."

Mannion reined Red around and booted him into a hard gallop down the hill, across the yard, through the mine portal, and back out into open range.

He was relieved to be out of the Horsehead head-quarters, for some reason. He felt as though he'd been lost in a hall of mirrors.

———

HE'D RIDDEN ONLY A QUARTER MILE WHEN RED TOSSED his head and whickered.

"What is it, boy?" Mannion asked, though he had a feeling he knew what had riled the mount. For the past several minutes he'd had the sensation that they were being followed.

He checked Red down and curveted the horse, gazing back in the direction from which they'd come. Nothing but the pines of the forest they'd entered a few minutes ago, the deep shadows of the tall, columnar trees. Birds piped. A squirrel chittered angrily from a nearby pine bough.

Mannion gigged the horse forward again and rode for another fifteen minutes. The nagging sensation that he was not alone remained but every time he peered behind him, he saw nothing. When he'd nearly come to the trail that would take him back to Battle Mountain, he halted Red once more and peered along his back trail, hand on his cross-draw Russian, wary of another attack by Harry Marcum.

As he did, a horse and rider roughly a hundred yards away veered behind a boulder.

"Ah," Mannion said. "We're not just getting nervy in our old age, Red. We do have us a shadow, sure enough."

Mannion slid the Yellowboy from its boot, cocked it one-handed, and booted Red back the way they'd come. Slowly, he approached the rock behind which his shadow had taken cover. He gained the backside of the rock and aimed the Winchester out from his right hip.

Nothing.

No one was behind the rock.

Hoof thuds sounded, and he turned to see horse and rider just then galloping up a rise fifty yards to the south. Both man and horse were silhouetted against the sky, so Mannion couldn't make out much. The horse appeared to be a cream, and the rider wore a black Stetson. That was as much as Mannion could see just before horse and rider crested the ridge and disappeared down the opposite side.

"Damn," Joe said, fingering his chin. "Who in the hell was that?"

He doubted it was Harry Marcum. The horse was the wrong color, and the rider didn't match the stature of the rider, Marcum, who'd ridden away from Mannion the day before.

Mannion turned Red around and headed back to the main trail that would take him to town. A half-hour later, he came to a creek—likely San Juan Creek, which Kincaid had mentioned—that crossed the trail before him. He studied the placid but steadily flowing stream for a minute, pondering. Then, instead of crossing the creek by the wooden bridge spanning it, he swung Red onto the secondary trail that ran along the stream to the south and that followed the meandering cut of the creek toward the backside of Battle Mountain that was turning a deep red now in the late afternoon.

As the sun angled low, the ridge was looking more and more like nothing so much as the devil's forge. Damned formidable. Almost gave Mannion a chill. He chuckled at himself and, despite his apprehension, continued following along the stream's west bank, now and then passing a stitch of whitewater rapids and deep, dark pools in which he imagined fat trout lurking, gills slowly expanding and contracting. The glowing red forge of Battle Mountain shimmered, growing larger before him until he followed a leftward bend in the trail and checked Red down suddenly.

His heart thudded as he stared into a clearing maybe seventy yards right of the stream, at the remains of what once had been a farm, judging by the hayfield between the cabin and several small outbuildings including what Mannion believed to be a chicken coop—judging by the many dead chickens around it—and a stock pen, stable, and connecting corral. To the right of the yard lay a patch of half-grown corn. Mannion was just guessing at the function of these buildings because they, too, were half-burned hulks of charred wood. Between the hayfield and the corn, the cabin was half-burned, the roof tilting precariously toward a scorched stone chimney on the cabin's right end.

Inside the corral, which was still standing though the stable was mostly burned, lay two bloated mules. In another pen, partly hidden by a stock trough, lay what appeared to be a dead pig.

The fire had been recent. Mannion could still smell the stench of charred timber and stone, kerosene, and the putrid stench of the rotting chickens, the pig, and the mules.

He removed his neckerchief and, holding it over his mouth and nose, rode forward into the yard, noting the tracks of several horses and spent brass cartridge casings. As he approached the cabin, he saw several brown patches of what could only be dried blood. An old Springfield rifle lay on the hard-packed earth ten feet off the burned cabin's charred front stoop. The rear stock was also smeared with the dried, brown remains of blood.

Near the shotgun were two women's Mexican-style sandals and a few yards beyond those was a dark-green bandanna, also bloodstained.

Scuff marks, as those of dragged bodies, led around to the rear of the cabin and beyond. Mannion followed the furrows to a dry wash roughly a hundred yards southwest of the farmyard. He stopped Red and peered into the wash, having to hold the neckerchief more tightly over his nose and mouth, because the stench of death was even stronger here than in the yard.

The edge of the cutbank had been stomped down into the wash, making an oval mound of clay, sand, and gravel stippled with sage branches and grass. A hurried, messy job had been made of the makeshift grave, for a man's brown hand, a swatch of a woman's orange dress, and a woman's bare foot stuck out from beneath the debris.

"Good Christ!" Joe said, gritting his teeth against the grisliness of the obvious murder scene.

If the girl whom Grant Kincaid claimed was Giannina Calderon had been here during the obvious attack, no wonder her mind was gone. Had she witnessed the murder of her family? If so, how had she avoided the same fate?

Mannion shuttled his gaze from the makeshift grave in the wash to the charred farmstead. If the attack had happened during the rain, the killers had probably returned to burn the place later, after it had dried, to get rid of any possible evidence, though they'd been brash enough to leave their rifle casings. But nearly every puncher in the west carried a .44. Maybe the burning had been out of pure meanness.

"Who in God's name had committed this savagery?" Joe wanted to know.

Red lifted his head suddenly and turned it to glance with apprehensive, white-ringed eyes back in the direction he and his rider had come. He gave his tail a hard switch and whickered softly.

Mannion followed the horse's gaze back toward the trail that followed the stream, reaching forward to caress the bay's left wither. "What is it, boy? We still have our shadow?"

Mannion gazed back along the trail, squinting his eyes, closely examining his back trail. Then he saw the shadows of riders moving through some mixed pines, cedar, and willows clumped along the stream, a couple of hundred yards away. The riders were just emerging from the woods when Mannion neck-reined Red hard left.

"Hy-ahh, boy!"

The bay leaped into the wash, landing hard on its front hooves.

Mannion grunted with the violent jolt and then booted the horse on up the wash beyond the makeshift grave, following a bend to the right. Behind him, a man shouted.

A rifle cracked.

CHAPTER 9

A HALF-HOUR EARLIER, JAMES KINCAID REINED HIS gray-brown gelding behind a boulder to the right of the trail on which he'd been following the lawman who'd brought the bodies of Slash Hattersby and Roy Plum to the Horsehead headquarters, tied belly down, dead, across the horses James's father had let the two men take with them when he'd given them their final wages.

A couple of known troublemakers were Hattersby and Plum.

James's father, Grant, had let them go after the roundup of the previous year and hadn't rehired them in the spring. At least, not officially. James knew, however, that his father had hired the men and paid them under the table for less legitimate work—namely, ridding the range of a family of German squatters who had ignored Grant's warnings to pull their picket pins or pay the age-old price.

James knew that Hattersby and Plum had extracted the price. He'd seen the black smoke rising from where he knew the German family consisting of a husband, wife, and two children, a few cows and as many horses and one mule and several caged rabbits, had built a small log hut and stable. He hadn't ridden over to investigate. He knew his father well enough to know what he'd ordered his two former hands to do. Nor had he addressed his father about it. It wouldn't have done any good.

His father disgusted James, who had never been able to live up to his father's toughness nor savagery. He simply followed orders along with the rest of the hands. Still, it was hard at times, knowing who your father was, shouldering the shame of his barbarity, but to continue working for him, to continue living and working on the headquarters he himself had built—him and his first foreman, Quincy Ryan.

To join him and his stern, just as uncompromising wife in church every Sunday.

And to also shoulder the fact that you were too weak, too afraid, to try to wedge yourself out from under his and your mother's strong shadows. Worst of all, to agree to marry the girl they wanted you to marry for business reasons despite the fact you had no feelings for the girl. When you were, in fact, in love with another.

Another girl your family didn't approve of.

Such thoughts swirled through James's head as he nudged the gelding forward to edge a look around the boulder. Just then, the man he'd been following stopped his own horse roughly a hundred yards up the trail. He curveted the handsome bay stallion and just started to look back behind him. Heart thudding, James pulled his own head back behind the boulder, reined the gelding around, and nudged it into a gallop back in the direction from which he'd come.

He cursed his lack of spine.

He'd followed the lawman because he'd been trying to

work up his courage to talk to the man. To try to find out what James's father had hired Hattersby and Plum to do this time. But he hadn't the courage. He feared the lawman instinctively. He feared the danger he might mean for his father and the entire Horsehead Ranch. James had lived in fear for years that his father's sins would catch up to him.

Yes, while hating and being revolted by his father's actions, he feared him having to pay for them one day. Feared what that would mean for him, his mother, and his younger sister, Sydney.

Oh, Christ, he thought, as the mouse-brown gelding galloped back along the trail in the direction of the Horsehead headquarters. It was harder than hell to both love and hate a man of Grant Kincaid's stature.

He was halfway back to the headquarters when he checked the gelding down to a trot, then a walk, then stopped him altogether. He frowned over the horse's head, watching three riders gallop toward him, a tan dust cloud rising behind and above them. He saw that the lead rider—a tall, lean man with a thick, brown, dragoon-style mustache and high-crowned, broad-brimmed black Stetson, was Grant's foreman, Wayne Cord. The two other riders were two longtime Horsehead hands, Neil Quade and Max Coffee. Both men, in their early thirties, considerably younger than Cord, who was fifty, were Cord's top hands. They were his friends, though if you knew the man, you wouldn't think he'd have any friends. You rarely saw the three men apart. They rode to town every Saturday night to drink, whore, and play cards together.

And now, judging by the speed of their horses and the strained, determined sets to their gazes, they were three men on a mission.

Thirty yards from James, Cord raised his right hand

and drew back on his gray gelding's reins with his left one, the horse skidding to a stop before James's gray-brown. The other two checked their own horses down behind Cord then walked them up and stopped on either side of the foreman. Quade was a stocky blond with a perpetual sneer on his lips; Coffee was a big, beefy man in buckskins, with bushy red hair and a curly red beard.

Scowling disdainfully at the boss's son, whom the foreman had no respect for whatever, Cord said, "What're you doin' out here, James? You're supposed to be helpin' Durham shoe those three new broncs."

"You're goin' after the lawman, aren't you, Wayne?"

"That's none of your business. You better get home before your old man finds out you rode out without permission...before the end of the workday!" The brown-mustached, black-eyed foreman, whose thick brown hair was streaked with only a little gray, pointed an accusing, brown-gloved finger at James. The demonic ramrod used to give James nightmares when his father had first put him to work for the man. He was like his father's twin, only worse. In fact, James's sleep was still disrupted by the dread of the man.

"What did Hattersby and Plum do for Pa, Wayne? What'd they do?"

"If your old man wanted you to know, he'd have told you himself." Cord's horse was skitter-hopping and blow-ing, chewing its bit. The other two men's mounts were, as well. "Now, yield the trail. We're in a hurry!"

"Don't do it, Wayne. He's a *lawman!*"

"Oh, hell!" Cord reined his gray around James and the mouse-brown dun and whipped his rein ends against the horse's left hip. The horse whinnied, rose slightly off its front hooves, then tore up the trail in a ground-chewing gallop.

The other two cursed and cast James withering glares and followed suit, both men galloping into the foreman's billowing dust.

"Damn!" James said, ramming the end of his gloved fist against his saddle horn. He shook his head fatefully, and said, "Pa, don't you start killin' lawmen."

Though he doubted the man he'd been following would be the first lawman he'd killed. No, James wouldn't put it past his father to kill a lawman. Two Pinkertons had disappeared not long after they'd gotten crossways with Grant Kincaid. That had been puredee trouble there, though nothing had come of it. Eventually, the proverbial chickens would come home to roost. It all just depended on what kind of trouble Pa might be in this time.

What in hell had Hattersby and Plum done for him, anyway?

Only one way to find out.

Calling up a bucket of courage from a deep, dark well inside him, James booted the mouse-brown dun up the trail. Twenty minutes later, he passed through the portal with the Horsehead brand burned into the crossbar fifteen feet above the trail, and continued galloping the horse until he'd passed through the fringe of pines and climbed the hill. He checked the dun down near the porch steps, fairly leaped from the saddle, hoping against hope the kernel of courage he'd found inside himself did not crumble.

He tossed the reins over one of the hitchracks and, batting his hat against his thigh, causing dust to billow, climbed the steps, crossed the porch, opened one of the stout oak doors and stepped into the broad, deep foyer, a potted plant to each side. He turned to his right and followed a dark hall through a dayroom. Before he'd left the dayroom, he heard a familiar female voice say, "Well, well—look what the cat dragged in."

James stopped and winced when he saw his pretty, blond, nineteen-year-old sister sitting on a fainting couch before a broad front window, afternoon light from the window glistening in her brown eyes and blond hair drawn behind her in a long queue. Sydney was dressed like she usually dressed—man-like in jeans and wool shirt and suspenders, stockman's boots, one of which was drawn up, its heel hooked on the edge of the fainting couch. She had one of her eight or nine cats on her lap— a fat, liver-colored tabby. Two others slept curled tightly in the sunlight on a shelf in the window.

Sydney was the bane of James's existence. She was a year and a half younger than he, but she could outwork and outride him on the range, which was her second home. She rarely helped their mother in the house. She was an outdoor, horse, cat, and dog girl. As wild as the wolves that James heard yammering to each other across the valley as he tried to drift to sleep each night.

"What's that supposed to mean?" James asked, though he knew he shouldn't humor the girl.

"Seen you ride out without permission." The blonde, pretty in a tomboyish way, her face classically featured but strong, her mouth saucy, eyes forever jeering, taunting, challenging, insolent. "Did you catch up with that lawman?"

James scowled and looked away, sheepish. "Just curious is all."

"Just curious, eh?" Sydney tilted her head to one side and gave a foxy half-smile. "About what?"

"About how Slash an' Roy ended up dead."

"That's none of your business. You'd best stick to

blowin' out water holes, repairin' harness, and cleanin' out stock tanks."

"Do you know?"

"Know what?"

James heard his mother talking with the help just down the hall. He peered that way to make sure she wasn't near, then turned back to his sister. "You know what. Why that lawman killed 'em."

Sydney's eyes grew hard, though they still glowed like a brown stream in the sunlight. She straightened her head, stiffened her shoulders slightly, and said, "Leave it alone, big brother. Leave it...alone."

James frowned and turned to face her squarely. "You know, don't you?"

"I got no idea," she said, tonelessly as well as unconvincingly.

"Is Pa in there...with Ma?"

James knew his parents were entertaining tonight a couple of neighboring ranchers and their wives, as well as a territorial senator who intended to run for governor of Colorado in the next election and was seeking Grant's backing. He could smell the two elk haunches their cook —a big, fat Scot named Billy Biggerstaff—was roasting in the outdoor fireplace behind the house. Billy had been cooking at the Horsehead for as long as James had been alive. He'd be basting the haunches with great quantities of his own homemade chokecherry wine and swilling nearly the same amount, while singing Scottish ballads to himself.

Billy was one of the few men James liked at the Horsehead. Him and old Quincy.

"I got no idea," Sydney said in answer to James's question, as tonelessly and unconvincingly as before.

James gave an impatient chuff and continued down

the hall and through the arched doorway into the dining room that was as large as any hotel dining room or saloon. He found only his mother and two maids there. His mother, still attired in a simple skirt and ruffled blouse though she'd be dressed to the nines in an hour or so, was giving quiet instructions to the two somber maids, who stood before the middle-aged, queen-like, gray-haired, not unpretty woman though her eyes and mouth were nearly always cast sternly.

No joking around with Katherine Kincaid. No sharing a tender word, either. She had more important things on her mind—mainly running an efficient house-hold and throwing dinner parties that were the envy of any moneyed Easterner. She was Grant's perfect match.

Katherine glanced at her son, the skin above the bridge of her nose wrinkling with incredulity and annoy-ance. "Yes?"

"Sorry, Mother." James fumbled his hat off his head. "I thought maybe Pa was in here."

"He's not."

"All right."

James turned to go.

"James?"

He stopped and turned back to his mother.

"You do intend to stay upstairs tonight, don't you? This evening?"

He was allowed contact with only certain guests.

"I'll do you one better than that, Mother. I'll bunk with Quincy."

Katherine Kincaid spread her thin lips in a straight line. "Better yet."

James donned his hat, retraced his steps, and made his way to the rear of the house. A minute later, he lightly wrapped his knuckles against a stout oak door, smelling cigar smoke emanating from the gap beneath it and the floor.

"Who is it?" came the stentorian voice of Grant Kincaid.

"James, Pa."

"All right," came the weary reply.

Here we go, James thought. *Once more into the breech.*

CHAPTER 10

JAMES TWISTED THE KNOB, SHOVED OPEN THE DOOR, and stepped into the office rife with the smell of tobacco smoke, Scotch whisky, varnished wood, the contents of a brass spittoon, and old leather.

The regal old lion, Grant Kincaid, stood with one boot planted on a leather-upholstered bench fronting the big bay window that took up nearly the entire far wall of his office, beyond a cold, brick fireplace, a big leather sofa, two leather chairs divided by a coffee table on which a cut glass whisky decanter and two goblets sat, beyond a big desk constructed of longleaf heart pine abutting the wall to James's left and which was covered in papers, ledgers, books on animal husbandry and rangeland management.

A fat stogie smoldered in an ashtray Billy Biggerstaff had carved for Grant out of age-silvered driftwood, on a shelf built into the window. Grant was running an oily rag up and down the ancient Spanish sword, called a Spanish *lobera*, or "wolf slaying sword," he'd long ago discovered on his range, poking out of a bank of a deep arroyo. The sword didn't look like much to James, but Grant adored it and loved nothing more than to show it off to his guests, which was why he was babying it right now and would pass it around later when the men had settled into this very office to smoke, drink, and chin about women, money, and politics, usually in that order. James knew what they talked about. He'd been listening through the door since he'd graduated from rubber pants.

Grant was already dressed for the night in a Western-cut suit complete with a turquoise encrusted, silver-capped bolo tie. He smelled like the pomade that glistened in his hair.

Grant plucked the stogie out of the ashtray, took a couple of puffs, the smoke obscuring his head, and stared at James curiously. "What can I do for you, son?" He returned the stogie to the ashtray and resumed tenderly running the rag up and down the old sword that looked as though it might crumble with his touch.

James closed the door, remembered his hat, and quickly removed it, anxiously rubbing at the rooster tail he could feel sticking up at the crown of his skull. "Uh... uh...well, Pa, I seen that lawman that rode into the Horsehead earlier."

"I know you did," Grant allowed, suddenly halting his hand with the cloth midway along the sword. "That's nothing for you to worry about."

"Well...well, Pa...uh...I am a little worried. I mean, he came in with two of your men...dead. Slash an' Roy."

"They *were* my men. Mannion made the mistake of believing they were *still* my men. You know as well as I do that they were not. I agreed to bury them here rather than having the town bury them at considerable expense. They worked here for a time, so I don't begrudge giving them a proper planting. They'll reside with the other men who've died over the years on the

Horsehead. I might even invite the preacher out from town to say a few words over them. Just to do it all right an' proper and to show that I have no ill feelings toward either man, despite their well-known and obvious failings."

"What'd they do?"

"What's that?"

"What'd they do to get themselves shot by this Mannion fella?"

"Oh," Grant said as he resumed running the oily rag slowly up and down the sword that glinted dully in the light from the big window behind the man. "They got into a little trouble in town. Like they always did." He gave a wry snort. "To think of all the bail money I spent on those two before I finally let them go." He shook his head.

"What kind of trouble?"

Again, Grant stopped the rag and now he scowled deeply, incredulously, with an obvious building anger all too well known to James, who'd been the target of his father's wrath more than a few times in his life. Damn near every day, in fact.

"Now, aren't you just full of questions."

"You, uh...you don't think I should know?"

"No, I don't think you should know. You don't need to know. It is no business of yours. Nothing to worry about. What you do need to worry about, however, is riding into town sometime this week and paying a visit to Miss Athena up at her mother's big house. Take some wild-flowers. She likes those. Her mother's expecting you. You talk nice to the girl and perhaps it's time you, uh...uh... discuss your future together."

James drew a deep breath.

Grant dipped his chin and sent a withering glare

across the room at his son. "You're done with that little Mexican whore—you understand me?"

"Pa, I told you I was."

"My God." Grant shook his head slowly, darkly. No man's glare could have cut through another man the way Grant's glare cut so cleanly through his son—nor so bone deep. Soul deep. Leaving James jelly-spined, weak-kneed, and tongue-tied. "To think a Kincaid was sparking a Mexican whore."

James didn't know where his courage to respond in such an angry fashion came from, but came it did, and he found himself stumbling forward two steps and hardening his jaws as he said, "Pa, she's not a whore! She's not like that. The men in town...they made her do what she did because she was so lonely. Her family made her feel lonely, and she had no place to turn but that little...that little..."

"Hole in the wall saloon on the Mescin side of Battle Mountain."

"She just sang and danced to the piano. She never meant to...she never meant to...those men forced her into it!"

"Whatever the hell happened, James Kincaid," Grant's voice thundered around the room, making James's eardrums rattle and his heart race, "you have nothing more to do with her—you understand? NOTH-ING. MORE. End of story! Now, you take a spray of wildflowers and go up to Mrs. Kennecott's house with your hat in your hands, and you ask Miss Athena very politely to sit and talk. And discuss your future together."

"Pa," James said, hating how his voice was quivering and the way it always rose a couple of octaves when he addressed his father. "I don't think she...I don't think she wants me anymore than—"

"She does!" Grant said, again his voice as loud as near thunder. "She does want you, boy. She sees something in you that touched her heart. Her mother said as much. I don't know what in hell it could be"—he gave an ironic laugh—"but she does. She's sweet on you, boy. You're just too damn timid to see it and to act on it. You think you're only fit for Mescin *putas*!"

The word had no sooner escaped his mouth than Grant suddenly looked chagrined. He glanced at the door and then at the floor, realizing that he'd been speaking far too loudly about forbidden things.

Grant turned back to his son but lowered his voice. There was almost some tenderness in it as he said, "You're a Kincaid, son. A *Kincaid!* It's time you acted like it."

James swallowed and nodded. He hated that his damn knees wouldn't stop quivering. You'd think by now, at almost twenty-two years old, he'd be immune to his father's wrath. But he wasn't. He still found himself wanting to please the man. At the same time, he hated him more than any other man he'd ever met. Even more than Wayne Cord.

"All right, Pa. All right." He turned to the door.

"Son?"

James glanced over his shoulder at his father, the man's red, weathered face obscured by a thick cloud of cigar smoke.

"You staying inside this evening? As you probably know, your mother and I are entertaining."

"I'll bunk with Quincy."

"Good idea. Don't leave the headquarters."

"Never."

He left the office and drew the door closed behind him.

He stood with his back to the door. His mind swirled.

Hattersby and Plum. He'd gotten no satisfying answer from his father. He had a feeling they'd died for more than causing trouble in town. But he hadn't been able to push the matter. No man made him feel more spineless than Grant Kincaid.

He went downstairs and outside and grabbed his reins off the rack. He swung up onto the back of his mouse-brown dun. He rode down the hill and through the pines. The other men were just then leaving the breaking corral and heading for the bunkhouse for supper and a night of poker and exchanging long windies—lies to make their lives seem more interesting than they were. They spent long days in the saddle or working around the Horsehead headquarters, just as they'd done on countless other ranches before being hired by Grant Kincaid. Most would never marry, never raise families, would never leave whatever ranges they were working on for thirty a month and found.

They'd get drunk in town every Saturday night, spend their need on painted ladies, and lose a month's wages to chuck-a-luck, high-low, grand hazard, poker, and three-card monte.

At least, James had an opportunity to get married and raise a family. Of course, he'd have to do it here on the Horsehead. He and his father had never discussed that aspect of his marrying Athena Kennecott. They hadn't had to. James could leave here. He was too tied to his parents, who had never accepted him, who were so embarrassed by him that they wouldn't even allow him around their dinner guests—aside from Mrs. Kennecott and Athena, that was.

They wanted him and Athena to marry, thus marrying the two families to the financial advantage of both.

Nothing like an arranged marriage to make two business associates inseparable. The problem was that James did not love Miss Athena, and he knew she didn't love him. He knew, however, what her and her mother saw in him.

A non-threat.

He was reserved and polite, if a little simple, but he was hardworking, and he would be a good husband and father. He would make a stable life for the flighty, impractical Miss Athena, who was beautiful to be sure, but she was not...

James shook his head as he opened the back gate in the fence, ringing the Horsehead headquarters. He rode through, pulling the gate closed behind him as he did, then trotted the dun over a low ridge, across a wash and up to a small log cabin turning dark in the darkening woods. Smoke rose from the leaning tin stovepipe, rife with the smell of roasting stew and coffee.

A shaggy cowdog rose from where he'd been lying on the cabin's stoop and came running down the porch steps and over to where James approached on the dun, barking happily and wagging his tail.

"Hey, Bear!" James said, always as happy to see the shaggy collie as the collie was to see him. The dun was so accustomed to the dog's raucous greetings that it no longer shied.

James dismounted and dropped to a knee to pet the dog who gave him several licks and then turned to have his back rubbed brusquely.

"How you doin', old fella? How you doin'? The old man home?"

He knew his father's very first foreman, Quincy Ryan, was home because of the smoke. The words were his way of alerting the man of his visitor's identity.

"Get in here, boy, and give my stew a stir. I'm too

damn lazy to get outta this chair!" came the deep-voiced reply from inside the cabin.

James chuckled, gave the delighted collie another pat, then tied the dun to the hitching post, mounted the porch hardly larger than a postage stamp, and tripped the door's steel latch. The door, made of three vertical pine planks that had warped badly over the years, since Quincy Ryan had retired as foreman nearly ten years ago and built his cabin on the Horsehead range, sagged and shuddered on its leather hinges. James shoved it wide and stepped inside where the smell of rabbit stew spiced with wild onions assaulted his senses and immediately made his mouth water.

Billy Biggerstaff was a mighty good cook, but for some reason, James had always preferred Quincy's fare. It was simple and just plain good—everything from his roasts to his stews to his venison steaks to the trout he caught himself in one of the streams bisecting Horsehead range and which he fried with potatoes and wild onions. Nothing complicated but simply good.

"I'll be hanged," James said as Bear followed him into the cabin and lay down at Quincy's feet. He closed the door and walked to the range, drawing deep drafts of delicious air. "I didn't even realize I was hungry until I rode up and smelled your stew."

Quincy Ryan was a stocky, square-headed man in his late sixties with short, spiked gray hair and a bristly, salt-and-pepper beard that never seemed to disappear nor grow any longer than stubble. He wore buckskin trousers and a deerskin tunic decorated with Indian beads in the form of the sun and the moon on each breast. His second wife, a Hunkpapa Sioux he'd met in Dakota when he'd been soldiering up there, had done the decorating before she'd died while delivering their only child, who had also died. He'd never remarried. He'd retired after a bull he'd been trying to pop from a hawthorn thicket had gored him so badly he'd never died. He'd been laid up for nearly a year and then he'd retired, and Grant had given him this patch of land a quarter mile from the Horsehead headquarters on which to build a cabin.

Grant Kincaid could be a roaring bastard, as he almost always was—at least, to his only son—but he was also loyal to the men he valued. There were damn few of those, but another was his current foreman, Wayne Cord, though James thought in that case his father's loyalty was badly misguided. He sat sideways at his kitchen table, which was nearly always where James found him on his frequent visits. Quincy's cabin was a sanctuary from the torment of his home life.

A tightly rolled quirley smoldered in an ashtray made from a cut-down tomato tin, and a stone mug of black coffee, no doubt spiced with a liberal jigger from the whiskey bottle that stood on the table cluttered with tack, traps, chains, ammo, and previous meal leavings, steamed near his right elbow. He was darning a wool sock, one hand inside the sock, holding it up close to his blue-eyed face so he could see the stitches he was making with needle and thread, wincing every time he poked the needle through the sock and pricking his fingers inside it. He had the eyes of a fierce Celt warrior, and he could be fierce. James had seen it. But he could also be warm and deeply amusing, and his presence was always a breath of fresh air to the man's boss's only son, whom, despite the differences in their temperaments, Quincy seemed to understand.

James lifted the lid on the stewpot and took a deep sniff of the succulent aromas. Along with big chunks of rabbit meat were the wild onion and the potatoes, peas, and carrots from Billy Biggerstaff's garden. Quincy and Billy were old friends, and they often made chokecherry wine together and sat up late right here in Quincy's cabin, partaking of the wine and perhaps an elk steak or two and sharing memories from their shared pasts right here at the Horsehead. Billy started out as camp cook on cattle drives, so the two men had been down many a trail together and had held rampaging Utes off with pistols and old Springfield rifles. Both men had taken their share of arrows and bullets and had somehow lived to tell the stories in their old ages.

"That smells almost better'n anything I ever smelled before," James said, giving the stew a couple of stirs with a long-handled wooden spoon.

"Help yourself. I figured it was time you'd show up again. So I made plenty."

James glanced over his shoulder at the old mossyhorn, who just winced again as he poked the needle through the sock. "You knew I was comin'?"

"Downright prescient, I am."

"What does that mean?"

"It means I knew you'd been away long enough you'd had your fill of your old man again and would be showin' up on my and Bear's ol' doorstep sooner rather than later." Quincy chuckled to himself and set the needle down to take a deep drag off his wheat paper cigarette. He closed his eyes dreamily as he drew the smoke into his lungs and smiled luxuriously as he blew the smoke plume at the rafters.

Quincy made smoking look so good that James wanted to try it himself, though he knew he'd likely turn green and air his paunch, just like he'd done when he was twelve years old and had swiped some tobacco and papers from Quincy's rawhide makins sack.

Eagerly, he dragged a wooden bowl down from a shelf and used a wooden gourd ladle to dipper himself a bowlful of the steaming stew. Quincy told him there was milk in the creek—from one of the Horsehead's five Holsteins—curving behind the cabin, so he fetched himself a tall glass and returned to the cabin and a chair across from where Quincy was just then finishing darning his sock. He pulled his hand out of the sock, inspected his fingers for prick marks, then took another drag from the quirley and, blowing the smoke at the darkening front window, said, "So, tell this old hermit what's new at the Horsehead."

James was already on his fourth spoonful of stew.

He winced and said around the mouthful of food, "A lawman—not from around here—brought Slash an' Roy to the Horsehead not much over an hour ago. Both were wrapped in their bedrolls and layin' belly down across their saddles."

Quincy chuckled. "I figured those two would end up in a dry ravine a long time ago. They overstayed their welcome. Who was the lawman?"

James held a fresh spoonful of stew in front of his mouth. "I heard the name Mannion. Joe Mannion?"

Quincy slapped the table. "Holy moly—Bloody Joe Mannion?"

Chewing, James said, "I think I heard Pa call him Bloody Joe. You know him?"

"Know *of* him. I was in Kansas when he was breaking heads, bloodying noses, and triggering enough lead in Abilene to fill a mountain. What did those two privy rats do to get themselves crossways with Bloody Joe?"

"Beats me. I tried to find out, but, as always, I was all but kicked out of the old man's office. All I know is Pa sent Cord and two others out to follow Mannion."

Quincy tapped ash into his ashtray as he studied James speculatively. "To follow him? Or to catch up with him?"

"You know Pa. He hanged three rustlers three weeks ago. They begged an' pleaded with their lives. He didn't bat an eye. He had Cord hang all three an' leave along the trail."

"Ahh. More of Grant's Kincaid's rustler-bearing trees." Quincy laughed a wheezing, throaty laugh as he stared down at Bear curled up at his feet, snoring softly as he slept. "Some things never change." He looked at James. "I hope he don't try that stunt on Mannion."

"Only Pa would play cat's cradle with the head of a famous lawman?"

"Why, do you think?"

"I tried, but I couldn't get to the bottom of it."

"I hope he hasn't gone off his rocker, that colicky ol' devil."

Finished with his stew, James dropped his fork in his empty bowl. "Quincy, what do you think Slash an' Roy did for Pa that was bad enough for Pa to go after the lawman...even a famous one...who turned 'em toe down?"

Quincy bunched his lips and studied the coal of his cigarette with those piercing, Irish blue eyes. "Good question..." He looked at James suddenly, his gaze darkening. "Say, uh...say, boy...you stopped seein' that Calderon girl, haven't you?"

James's stomach tightened. "Yeah. I promised Pa I'd never see her again, though I gotta admit, it burns a hole right through my belly. She and me, Quincy...we seen eye to eye on things."

Quincy stared at him. Slowly, he nodded, his eyes growing more and more pensive, darker and darker.

James leaped to his feet so suddenly his chair toppled over backward. Bear got up with a howl and barked.

"Quincy, you don't think he...he'd want to *make sure* I never saw her again, do you?"

He didn't wait for an answer. He doffed his hat, ran to the door, which he fumbled open, nearly slamming it into his face, then ran outside and down the porch steps to his horse.

Bear ran, barking after him.

"Boy, get back here!" Quincy roared.

Too late.

James had already put the mouse-brown dun into a full gallop.

CHAPTER 11

MORE GUNFIRE CRACKLED BEHIND MANNION AS RED galloped along the meandering course of the wash. His pursuers were firing from precarious perches, however, and most of the bullets sailed far wide to either side or plumed sand and dust of the wash behind Red's scissoring hooves.

Mannion rounded a rightward curve of the wash. A pine-carpeted ridge rose to the left of the wash, maybe a hundred yards away. He reined Red up the bank and out of the wash and then put the steel to the bay once more. Red lunged off his rear hooves and broke into a ground-consuming run, head down, ears back, covering the sage-stippled flat as though his tail was on fire.

Joe crouched low over the horse's neck, the bay's black mane buffeting against his face.

Behind him, men shouted as his pursuers saw that he'd left the wash. Mannion glanced over his left shoulder in time to see the first of the men—a tall man with a black handlebar mustache and low-crowned black hat trimmed with silver conchos—riding a willowy gray up out of the wash and then booting his own horse into a hard run. The two other men rose out of the wash on a buckskin and a strawberry roan, respectively, and came on hard, flanking the man with the black hat and black mustache, who hunkered low in his saddle, lips stretched back so Joe could see the white line of his gritted teeth.

Mannion gave a wry snort and turned his head back forward.

The lead rider behind him was like a caricature of a bad guy penciled on the cover of a dime novel.

Mannion glanced behind once more as the dime novel "bad guy" raised a silver-plated revolver whose maw stabbed smoke and flames as the man commenced firing at Joe once more. Again, the bullets screeched well past Mannion. Ahead, the pine-stippled ridge loomed, growing larger as Red closed the distance between it and the wash. When he gained the bottom of the rise, knowing exactly what was required, he began climbing without hesitation, lunging forward with his front hooves and pushing off hard with his rear ones, blowing hard but not faltering, picking his own route around pines, firs, and aspens and leaping deadfalls.

"There you go, boy," Mannion said into the bay's right ear as he stared at the crest of the ridge that slid toward him. "There you go! There you go! Almost there!"

Two more lunges and after a hard swerve around a fir, Red gained the top of the mountain, lowered his head and shook it, giving a proud blow.

"Good boy!" Mannion and the bay crossed the forty-foot-wide crest of the treeless rise. Joe put the bay down the opposite side and stopped him about twenty feet down from the top. Curveting the mount, he dropped the reins, grabbed the Yellowboy from its boot, and fairly leaped out of his saddle.

His left ankle gave way beneath him, and he dropped to a knee with a curse.

"You damn fool," he castigated himself with a grimace, pushing himself back to his feet. "You are not twenty-four years old anymore!"

He ran limping back to the crest of the ridge. He limped across it and then knelt beside the last fir Red had dodged. The wind was blowing up here as the sun hung low in the west, growing copper between two ridges. Mannion racked a round into the Winchester's action and aimed down the mountain he and Red had just climbed.

Cheeked up against the rear stock, he frowned as he gazed down the octagonal barrel.

Nothing down there but the darkening trees of the forest, wind-harassed pine boughs and aspen branches, pinecones tumbling from trees.

Mannion lowered the Winchester and scowled.

Where in hell were they?

No way that cartoon of a bad man had given up.

"Hey, Mannion."

Joe jerked a sharp look to his right.

The bad guy, complete with black, malevolent eyes to go with his black hat and black mustache, was hunkered down beside a boulder roughly thirty feet away at the crest of the ridge. He was staring down the barrel of a Winchester at Mannion, and grinning.

"Shit," Joe muttered.

"Over here."

Mannion turned to his right. Another of his pursuers stood shouldered up against an aspen, aiming down his own Spencer repeater at Joe. He was big and beefy, red-haired and red-bearded. A long, tan duster buffeted around him in the wind. A wind-bending crow feather stuck up from the band of his sugarloaf sombrero.

He grinned, too.

Behind Mannion, Red whinnied.

Joe turned to see the third rider riding slowly up the ridge, aiming a rifle straight out from his right hip. He was short but thick and wearing a thick blond mustache. The anxious Red whinnied again and sidled away from the roan horse and its rider, moving up the ridge to the left of the bay.

The malevolent-eyed bad guy said, "Toss the Winchester away, Bloody Joe, or your nickname is gonna take on a whole new meaning."

He smiled even more broadly at that, thoroughly satisfied with himself.

"Ha-ha," Joe growled, and tossed away the Yellowboy.

The bad guy gestured with his rifle barrel. "Stand up."

Mannion heaved himself to his feet, wincing again at his twisted ankle. *Damn fool thing to do at a damn fool time to do it in.*

The black-eyed bad man rose then, as well, and walked toward Mannion, keeping his right cheek pressed up taut against his Winchester's stock. He was dressed almost entirely in black—black shirt, black vest, black corduroy trousers—save a burgundy ribbon tie that whipped behind his neck in the wind.

"Unbuckle that pistol belt an' drop those hoglegs," the bad man ordered through teeth gritted beneath his black, handlebar mustache.

Mannion cursed and kept his eyes on the man approaching from ahead of him as he unbuckled the shell belt and tossed it and the two Russians over toward the Winchester. They landed with two heavy thuds. He winced. Damn nice way to treat such a pretty pair of hoglegs that had ridden many a dark and lonely trail with him for a good many years. The Yellowboy, too.

In the corner of his right eye, he saw the blond man stop the roan to his right and swing down from the saddle. He could hear the big red-haired, red-bearded man approach from behind him.

Nice fix you got yourself in now, Bloody Joe. How you gonna get your mossy old ass out of this whipsaw? He was alone and weaponless. A long way away from anything or anybody. His body would likely never be found. At least, not before the wildcats and wolves had strewn his bones after picking them clean.

The blond man walked up to within ten feet of Mannion.

He glanced at the malevolent-eyed bad guy. "How you wanna play it, Cord?"

Cord stopped ten feet away from Joe. Joe glanced over his shoulder to see the red-haired, red-bearded man stop about six feet behind him. He was nearly Mannion's height—six feet four, roughly two hundred and thirty pounds. Whereas Mannion was proud to boast he had little tallow on him despite his fifty-seven years, the red-haired gent was beefy, with a bulging gut. Still, he was likely only in his late twenties, early thirties—which made him damn near thirty years younger than Mannion.

If Joe made a play on him, it wouldn't go well.

Cord said, "The boss said to rough him up a little. Make him decide that remaining around Battle Mountain was a bad idea." He turned to Joe. "This ain't your jurisdiction, Mannion. You got no business here."

Joe said, flaring an angry nostril, "Did you murder the Calderon family? Burn their farm, shoot their livestock? Drive the girl out of her head?"

"Wasn't us. I don't know who it was, but it wasn't us."

"Then why did Kincaid send you out here to rough me up?"

"Because he knows how it looks. Sooner or later, you'll find out that his son had tumbled for the girl. Against the boss's wishes. He and Mrs. Kennecott want James to marry another, better girl. That gives the boss a motive to burn out the Calderons. Hell, he knows his reputation in these parts."

Remembering the three dead men he'd seen hanging from the pine just after he'd ridden onto the Horsehead graze, Joe said, "Yeah, I've seen pretty good proof of it myself."

Cord had lowered his rifle. He pointed at Mannion with his free hand and narrowed one black eye beneath the flat, black brim of his hat. "See? Now, that's the problem."

With way too much eagerness, the stocky, blond-haired man said, "I think we're gonna have to kill him, Cord. We're gonna have to kill Bloody Joe!" He grinned at the delightful notion. Oh, to be the ones who finally turned the notorious Bloody Joe Mannion under!

The big, red-haired man said in a deep, burly voice, "Ain't we gonna have to? We're gonna have to, Cord!"

"The boss said to just rough him up," Cord said with a menacing half smile as he walked slowly up to Mannion.

Joe tensed himself. Anger burned in him. He hated the stupid, dim-witted lunacy he saw in this man's black-eyed gaze. He stopped three feet away from Joe. He held his Winchester straight up and down in front of him. He stretched his lips a little beneath his coal-black handlebar mustache then grimaced savagely as he suddenly rammed the rifle butt into Mannion's solar plexus.

Joe gave a great chuff of expelled air, bent forward, and dropped to his knees, trying desperately to suck a breath. Fury overwhelmed him. It even overwhelmed the stark misery of having your breath so suddenly battered out of your lungs. He wasn't sure where he found it—maybe on the tail end of his rage—but he managed to summon every ounce of strength that remained in him to leap up off his knees and to hurl himself forward, ramming his head and shoulders in Cord's own belly.

Cord gave a loud, startled grunt as Mannion bulled him over backwards, slamming him to the ground. He straddled the man quickly and slammed his right fist against the man's mouth once...twice...three times, turning the lips to red jelly before the man even knew what was happening to him.

Cord screamed and writhed beneath Joe.

The other two roared curses and leaped forward.

Joe turned quickly just as the red-haired man was going to slam the butt of his rifle against Joe's head. Mannion deflected the rifle with his left arm and then, twisting around still further, grabbed that arm and jerked the man to the ground beside him and then slammed the end of his right clenched fist squarely against the man's nose, turning it sideways against his face. As he did, he saw the stocky blond step toward him, cursing loudly and cocking the Schofield .44 he'd filled his hand with. Before he could steady the revolver, Joe gave a bellow like that of a miffed grizzly and slammed the toe of his right boot up soundly between the man's legs.

"*Ohhh!*" the blond man howled. He triggered his Schofield into the ground beside his right foot before he jackknifed forward and dropped to his knees, closing his hands over his battered privates. "*Ohhh! Ohhh!*" he wailed, his face turning crimson, eyes so wide that Mannion thought they'd pop out of his head.

The redhead was flopping around on the ground to

Mannion's left, holding both hands over his nose, blood oozing through the cracks between his fingers.

"Kill that son of a bitch!" he wailed.

"My pleasure," came Cord's curt response.

Mannion turned to see the black-eyed demon half sitting up, one hand outstretched on the ground, the other aiming a cocked Colt at Joe's head.

"No! No! No! No! No!" a man's voice said to Mannion's left, as he turned to face Cord and the Colt that was half a second away from turning him toe down.

Cord frowned and turned his head as a man walked up through the trees to the top of the ridge, extending his own Colt in his right hand. He was young, early twenties, a few inches under six feet tall, and he wore your typical range gear, including batwing chaps and a bullet-crowned black hat with decorative white stitching along the brim.

He was the young man, a little under six feet tall, whom Mannion had seen back at the Horsehead headquarters.

He was Grant Kincaid's son.

CHAPTER 12

"Uncock it and lower it, Cord. No one's getting killed here today." James Kincaid's voice quavered with apprehension, but as he dipped his chin low, he regarded Cord with fury in his eyes. He added tightly, "Not if I can help it."

"You can't help it, Junior," Cord said, keeping his Colt aimed at Mannion's head. Mustached upper lip stretched back from his teeth, he said with a barely contained fury of his own, "Lower that hogleg, or I'll take it away from you and shove it—"

"Ease the hammer down an' lower it, Cord," James Kincaid said, again tightly.

Cord shifted his gaze from Mannion to the kid, exasperation and rage making his black eyes glint. "Have you gone mad, you little pip-squeak? You lower *your* gun an' holster it, and I *might* just decide to forget what happened here today!"

The blond was still on his knees, saying, "Ohh!" over and over, holding both hands over his privates. The red-bearded man had sat up and drawn his knees to his chest. He was holding his neckerchief over his nose and grunting with the pain of the broken beak. His incredu-lous, misery-sharp gaze was on the kid.

"Lower it, Cord," the kid said, with stubborn defiance.

He'd seen the burned-out Calderon farm, Joe knew. He'd tracked him and Mannion's three Horsehead shadows through the burned-out farmstead and up the ridge.

Cord glanced at Mannion and then swung his cocked Colt at the kid. "Drop it, Junior, or I *will* blow your heart out your back. I doubt your Pa would mind overmuch!"

The kid flinched as the Colt in his own hand roared, stabbing smoke and flames. Cord's own gun roared a quarter second after the kid's, as he jerked backward with the punch of the bullet. He lowered the smoking gun in his right hand and looked down in shock at the ragged hole in his black shirt, over his right shoulder. Mannion leaned forward and grabbed Cord's Colt out of his hand, rose, jerked the gun out of the blond's hand, who made no effort to resist, then tossed his and the redheaded man's pistols and rifles into the brush. He backed to one side of the group, cocking Cord's Colt and aiming at all three of his assailants, though none seemed capable of doing any more damage here today.

Cord seemed to have trouble comprehending what had just happened. As he studied the hole in his shirt through which blood promptly oozed, his lower jaw sagged nearly to his chest. He looked at the kid, his black eyes as large and round as eight balls.

"You *shot* me, you...little...son...of a—!"

"Who burned out the Calderons?" James interrupted.

Recocking the Colt and keeping it aimed steadily at the enraged, disbelieving Cord, the kid stepped forward. His voice quavered again with emotion as he said, "Did

Hattersby and Plum do it?" He paused, hazel eyes darkening, jaws tightening. "Or did you do it?"

"I didn't do it! We didn't do it! I don't know who did it—likely Hattersby and Plum—but I don't know who did it!"

"Whoever did it, Pa had it done." It wasn't a question. It was a stone-cold statement. He pursed his lips to keep his lips from trembling. It didn't work.

Cord looked again at the blood oozing through the fingers of his left hand, which he held over the wound. Returning his lunatic black-eyed gaze to the younger man, he said, "You *shot* me!"

James gestured with his gun. "Go on back to the Horsehead. This is over." He glanced behind him, and with his fury still barely contained, added, "I brought your horses. All you gotta do is mount up and ride out."

Just after the guns' twin blasts, Mannion had heard a horse whicker and stomp down the slope behind the kid.

He looked at the kid, and he couldn't help smiling. He could practically smell the fear radiating off young James Kincaid, his bewilderment at his own actions. Trepidation swam around in his hazel eyes below a wing of sandy hair hanging down over his forehead from beneath his bullet-crowned, sun-coppered black hat. But raw anger and sorrow were there, as well. He thought the girl had been killed with her family.

Still, he held the gun steady...held his resolute gaze unyielding...on Cord, who Mannion assumed, judging by the man's commanding demeanor, was the Horsehead foreman.

Which made what the young man had just done all the more surprising. Now, he'd have to answer to his father, and something told Mannion that Grant Kincaid was not an easy man to answer to.

But if he'd burned out the Calderon family, he'd gone too far.

Now that he had a gun, Mannion felt like stepping in. But he decided to let the young man finish the performance he'd started. The kid looked about to pass out from a toxic mix of emotions, but behind that fear lay a determination that would not let him yield. Even to the Horsehead foreman and his father.

Mannion vaguely wondered how long this had been building.

Gesturing again with the gun and raising his voice commandingly, James said, "Quade, Coffee, help Cord on his horse."

The blond and the redhead glared at the kid but said nothing. They gained their feet miserably, exchanging dark glances. Then they pulled the cursing and grunting Cord to his feet and led him toward the trees.

As he passed James, Cord said, "You just died here today, Mister. Do you realize that?"

James gave a wan half-smile. "That's the first time you ever called me Mister, Cord. I sorta like the sound of it."

Cord cursed again, loudly, red-faced, and added, glancing toward Mannion holding his pistol, "You bring our iron back to the headquarters—understand?"

James didn't respond to that. He just stared back at the man.

Cord cursed once more, loudly, the echo chasing itself around the surrounding ridges. Then he let Quade and Coffee lead him down the slope and out of sight. Mannion and James stared at the trees until they heard the hoof thuds of the retreating riders. When the thuds dwindled to silence, James turned to regard Mannion dully. He seemed in shock. He gave a deep exhalation of profound relief the ordeal was over, and then he wearily shoved his pistol into the holster on his right hip.

He dropped to his knees as though they could no longer support him.

"She's alive," Mannion said, tossing Cord's pistol into the brush. He winced at the lingering pain in his belly from Cord's savage assault. That rifle butt had bruised a couple of ribs.

James looked up at him. "What?"

"She's alive. Giannina. I found her in a ravine near here. Somehow, she got away from the attackers. I brought her to town. She's with Ma Lonnigan at the Continental."

The young man's mouth opened and formed a nearly perfect dark circle. "Oh, god. Oh, god."

"She has no memory. At least, she didn't as of last night. I haven't seen her today."

James drew a breath of deep relief. Then he said, "The rest of the family?"

"Dead. Whoever burned them out tossed them into the ravine near the farmstead and broke the cutbank down over them, burying them. How many in the family?"

"Four. Giannina has a younger brother."

"I don't know for sure, but I'd say all three are in that makeshift grave."

"But Giannina's alive?"

"Yes."

Again, James's voice trembled with emotion. "Who did it? Who burned them out, Marshal Mannion?"

"I don't know. All I know is Hattersby and Plum were about to kick her door in last night. I believe they were going to shoot her. Assassinate her. I gunned them both and hauled them to your father. I was told they worked for him."

"Only under-the-table stuff," James said. He was sitting back against the heels of his boots, hands splayed on his thighs. He glanced toward the darkening, forested slope behind him. "Pa had them burn out the Calderons because he wasn't sure he could trust me not to see Giannina Calderon again." He raised his forearm to his eyes and sobbed. "Oh, god!"

"Is he really that criminal? That *savage?*"

James kept his arm over his eyes. "Yes."

"Christ." Mannion walked over and scooped his shell belt and two holstered Russians off the ground. He wrapped the rig around his waist and buckled it, adjusting both holsters. He took two more steps and plucked the Yellowboy out of the sage.

He ran his hands over both stocks and the breech, brushing away the dirt and sand, and said, "I have no proof. I wish I could've taken Plum and Hattersby alive, but for the girl's sake, I had to take them both down hard."

"Thank you for saving her, Marshal Mannion. She means a lot to me. I had a devil of a time telling her I couldn't see her anymore. Pa and Ma want me to marry Athena Kennecott."

"For business?"

"Yes."

Mannion gave a wry snort. "A Romeo and Juliet situation, eh?"

James frowned, puzzled. "Who?"

"Never mind." Mannion turned toward the slope down which he'd left Red, removed one glove, stuck two fingers in his mouth, and whistled. When he heard hoof thuds growing gradually louder as the bay approached, he turned back to James, who remained in the same position as before, resting back against the heels of his boots, pondering all the horrible things he'd learned over the past hour.

He still appeared in shock.

"I'm gonna ride back to town," Mannion said. "It'll be dark soon but there's a Horsehead..." He paused. "What're you gonna do."

James blinked, didn't say anything for nearly a minute, then looked at Mannion. "I'm gonna ride to town with you. I have to see her."

"You sure that's best for either one of you?"

"I can't not do it, Marshal. She needs me."

As Mannion heard Red walk up behind him, whickering softly, announcing his presence, Joe scrutinized his young companion through narrowed, gray eyes. James must have seen the question in that gaze.

"Everybody says she's a whore, but she's so much more than that. Those are just the circumstances of her life." He shook his head slowly. "She's so much more than that."

"All right," Mannion said. "You'll see her. Maybe seeing you will nudge her memory. I fear what'll happen when you return to the Horsehead, though." He walked up to the young man, extended his hand, and pulled him to his feet. He kept James's hand in his own. "I don't believe I thanked you for saving my life." He gave the gloved hand a single shake and then let it go. "I'm obliged. You've complicated your own, though."

"Maybe it was time I did. If Pa burned out the Calderons, Marshal Mannion, he has to pay for it. I can't believe I just said that. I followed you out from the Horsehead a couple of hours ago, but I was afraid to catch up to you and learn that my father had done another terrible thing, one he might pay for with prison time or a noose. Couldn't see my life clearly beyond that. I still can't. But I'm not half as afraid as I was. What I fear now, knowing he might of murdered the Calderons, is a whole shovelful of anger so damn sharp I'm afraid my ribs'll split."

Mannion patted his shoulder. "Welcome to my world, kid."

He gathered up Red's reins and swung aboard.

"Let's head to town. It's a smoking caldron, but we might find some answers there."

James walked down the ridge to his own waiting horse and mounted up. Then, he and Mannion rode down the ridge and retraced their route back to the main trail by riding through the burned-out shell of the Calderon estancia. The fetor of scorched wood and the sour stench of dead flesh that had been ripening in the hot sun made Joe's eyes water.

They'd just left the yard when James said tightly, with quiet menace and unwavering resolve, "Whoever did this is gonna pay big. I don't care who it is."

CHAPTER 13

WAYNE CORD RODE SLOUCHED LOW IN HIS SADDLE, holding his left hand over the neckerchief he'd stuffed into the bloody bullet wound in his right shoulder. His left hand held his gray's reins and the brown bottle of rotgut whiskey he'd fished out of his saddlebags to dull the pain, which it maybe sorta *almost* accomplished, but not by much. Pain was like an ice pick driven through the shoulder clear through his loins and down his legs to his toes.

His anger was even keener.

He kept seeing the look in the kid's eyes. James's eyes.

He'd never seen it before. Before, the kid's eyes had always been soft and uncertain as putty. No confidence or resolve whatever. He'd flinched when Cord would bark at him so that Cord had found himself barking at him just to watch him flinch, then chuckle to himself.

The boss's cowardly little pip-squeak of a son.

This afternoon, however, he'd seen a side to James he'd never seen before. It confounded the Horsehead foreman no end.

Anger.

Defiance.

Unwavering resolve.

Threat.

And then he'd made good on that threat and drilled a bullet into Cord's shoulder!

He threw his head back and took another deep pull from the bottle.

"How you doin', boss?" asked Neil Quade, riding off Cord's right stirrup. "You gonna make it, you think?"

"I'll make it," Cord said through gritted teeth. "Don't you worry about ol' Cord." The worst feeling in the world was humiliation, he now realized. That was the single, most powerful thing he was feeling right now. Compared to that, the bullet wound was nothing.

He felt like spreading it around a little.

He turned a sneer to Quade regarding him with concern, and said, "How's your oysters? Looked like Mannion landed that kid purty sound."

Even in the dim light of the Horsehead kiting up in the east and obscured occasionally by scudding clouds, Cord could see Quade flush beneath the brim of his battered, funnel-brimmed Stetson. He made a sour expression and turned his head forward.

Cord chuckled.

He glanced over his shoulder at Max Coffee riding behind him, holding a bloody neckerchief over his ruined nose. "How you doin', Max? How's the beak? That old man fixed your wagon purty good, too, eh?"

"How 'bout you share that bottle, you smart-ass SOB!"

Cord chuckled, took another pull from the bottle, and held it close against his chest.

He was glad the moon was behind a cloud when they rode into the Horsehead headquarters an hour after they'd left the scene of their humiliation. He turned his gray toward the corral on the other side of the stable just beyond the bunkhouse, whose windows flickered umber with inner lamplight. But then, noting the buggies and carriages and several saddled horses fronting the main lodge's broad front porch steps, seeing shadows moving in the lodge's large windows, and hearing the low roar of joyous conversation—the elites were really kicking up their heels tonight at the Horsehead, everyone dressed to the nines including his boss and stately wife who had never said more than three or four words to Cord in the seven years he'd ramrodded here—he neck-reined the gray toward the pines at the base of the rise crowned by the Kincaids' regal residence.

"Where you goin', Cord?" Coffee said, his voice comically nasal due to the big man's broken beak. Cord vaguely wondered if the bunkhouse cook, Lester McNally, who often saw duty as medico, dentist, and even occasional undertaker as the need arose, would ever get the man's nose set straight on his face again.

Cord's own nose ached just by looking at the miserable big man.

"Gonna talk to the boss." At the top of the rise, Cord stopped the gray, swung down from the saddle, and tossed his reins to Quade. "Corral my horse. Tell Lester he best fix a big pot of coffee. Gonna be a long night."

"You'd best come to the bunkhouse and let Lester go to work on you before you bleed out," Quade warned.

"If I bleed out, I'm gonna do it on Mrs. Kincaid's dining room rug." Again, Cord chuckled despite the throbbing, almost unbearable pain in his shoulder and the blood running down his shirt and vest clear to his right, black twill-clad knee.

He broke the empty bottle on a rock then practically

dragged his boot toes as he made his way to the porch steps and began climbing. Climbing, he noted how weak he'd become. With each step, he grew even weaker. Blood loss. He must have lost a couple of pints. Anger spurred him on, however. He didn't know why he felt so angry with the old man, but he did. To have raised such a son. A wolf in sheep's clothing. Why, that little, weak-eyed scoundrel had likely killed Wayne Cord!

He wanted to show Kincaid in front of his moneyed guests what that little snake had done to his own fore-man, no less. That oughta change the pitch of the conversation!

He crossed the porch, fumbled one of the big, stout oak doors open and stumbled inside. He found the corridor that led to the dining room. Passing the dayroom, he heard a gasp. He stopped and turned to see Miss Sydney tuning up her violin on the fainting couch fronting the night-dark window behind her, a cat curled to each side of the girl, snug against her well-turned thighs. She was decked out in a creamy lace and taffeta gown, and her hair was partly drawn up to the top of her head and secured with red and blue ribbons.

Cord grinned. "Never seen you so well-appointed, my lovely."

Sydney's eyes bulged in shock, and she scowled as she brought a finger to her lips. "Shhh!"

Cord threw his head back with a laugh and muttered, "The Kincaid children are just full of surprises," as he continued ambling drunkenly along the corridor to the brightly lit dining room ahead. He stumbled through the entrance, tripping over the edge of the rug, and fell forward between a man and a woman sitting at the long table covered in white silk as well as gravy boats, soup tureens, china bowls mounded with mashed potatoes and butter, and several large silver roasters heaped with thickly sliced, blood-red elk with nicely charred edges.

Even in his grave state, Cord's mouth watered at the sights but also at the smells of the succulent vittles laced with ladies' expensive perfume and men's hair tonic.

A roar of startled surprise rose as Cord gripped the edge of the table, trying not to fall, sandwiched between the man dressed in a coal-black three-piece suit with red foulard tie and the woman clad in a low-cut sleeveless gown—some mucky-muck senator and his blooded wife from back east now residing in Denver, he reckoned.

Grant Kincaid rose from his chair at the left end of the table just as Mrs. Kincaid rose from her chair at the opposite end of the table, having just dropped her fork of elk and mashed potatoes and gravy.

"Wayne!" he bellowed, salt-and-pepper brows ridging severely.

"Good god, man!" intoned Mrs. Kincaid, candlelight and light from the chandelier hanging over the table glistening in her gray hair and the several coils of real pearls hanging down over her deep cleavage revealed by her own low-cut brown silk gown. "Are you drunk?"

He pushed himself back off the table and her eyes went to the large smear of blood he'd left on the white tablecloth, between the senator and his comely if middle-aged wife. Then her eyes went to the blood still oozing out between the fingers of his bloody left hand, and she gasped and covered her mouth with her own beringed right hand.

"Cord!" Kincaid bellowed once more. "What is the meaning of this?"

"The pip-squeak shot me, Mr. Kincaid. Your Mescin whore-lovin' son—good old James!" Cord chuckled. "Never thought he had it in him, but we were out to rough up Mannion, just like you said, an' he shot me, sure enough! Demon spawn is what he is. Traitor. He finally grew a pair when he realized what you done to them Mescins the little whore belongs to. Just thought I'd let you know." He glanced at the awestruck eyes riveted on him from around the table. "Forgive the intrusion, ladies and gentlemen. Carry on! Carry on!"

Cord turned to leave the room but lost his balance and dropped to a knee. He likely would have fallen flat, but Grant Kincaid grabbed his left arm and heaved him to his feet and then shoved him brusquely down the corridor. They passed the dayroom in which Miss Sydney stared, hang-jawed, at the two men as they passed, Cord laughing and stumbling and nearly falling, and Kincaid's face set sternly, exasperatedly as he muscled his wounded, drunk foreman down the hall.

When they reached the foyer at the bottom of the broad, carpeted staircase, Kincaid shoved Cord against the wall, and said, "How dare you embarrass me like this, you fool!"

"Oh, I'm sorry about that, boss!" Cord laughed. "But you know what—he's your son. I don't know what you're gonna do about him. But if you don't, I will!" Suddenly scowling furiously again, Cord rammed his fist three times against his chest. Then, quietly but menacingly, he said, "You don't kill him, I will."

"Are you trying to tell me that my son James did this to you?"

"Oh, I ain't tryin', I'm tellin' you. We went out to rough up Mannion, like you ordered, and he intervened. Didn't think he had it in him, but he does, all right. For her. For the girl. A turncoat is what he is. A damned traitor."

"I don't believe you," Kincaid said, the disbelief obvious in his gaze.

"Believe it." Cord pushed off the wall and shoved his face up close to Kincaid's, who flinched against the whiskey on his breath. "He's *disloyal*. Loves that whore, too. If you're thinkin' that's gonna change, then you got another *think* comin'!"

"Come on, dammit!"

Kincaid grabbed him by his arm and again he nearly fell as the rancher pulled him brusquely to the doors and then across the porch, Cord again nearly falling as Kincaid pulled him down the steps. Kincaid led him just as brusquely down the hill and through the pines. He was practically dragging his foreman by the time they reached the bunkhouse from inside of which issued the raised pitch of excited conversation.

Kincaid shouldered open the door and drew Cord into the bunkhouse behind him. An instant hush fell over the place. A hush save for a man groaning on one of the lower bunks to Cord's left. The big, square-headed cook, doctor, dentist, and undertaker—Lester McNally—sat on the edge of the bunk on which big Max Coffee lay, writhing and kicking his legs. Three other men gathered around the bunk and held him down while McNally appeared to be trying to straighten the man's nose.

"Stay still, now, me bucko," McNally said in his thick Scottish brogue. "If I accidentally turn that fat beak of yours the other way, I won't be doin' you any favors, eh? Bloody hell, boys—hold 'im down!"

"We're tryin'!" intoned one of the other men. "He's a strong one, Coffee—I'll give 'im that!"

Cord sagged into a chair at the long eating table in front of the door, in the kitchen and dining end of the bunkhouse. He was spent. He'd have to sit here and continue bleeding until McNally got to him. He watched his boss walk down between the two lines of bunks. The man stopped at Coffee's bunk and looked down at the writhing man, wheezing and huffing and puffing as the medico adjusted his nose.

"This Mannion's work?" he asked Coffee.

As he continued writhing and kicking in raw agony, Coffee nodded.

Kincaid turned to the stocky blond Neil Quade sitting on the lower bunk to the left of Coffee's bunk. The man sat leaning forward slightly, holding his hands over his privates. His face was drawn with his own brand of misery.

"Mannion?" Kincaid asked him.

Quade grimaced and nodded. "He's big and he's old, but he's fast. Caught all three of us off guard."

"When did my son show?"

"Just after he broke Max's nose and Cord was about to shoot him."

Kincaid swung around in disgust and strode back to the door. He placed one hand on the handle and then turned to face the room again, sliding his gaze to Cord, who now sat sagging forward in his chair.

"You three are fired. I want you off the Horsehead by noon tomorrow." He turned to a man also sitting at the table, rolling a quirley. "Pat? You're foreman. You pick three others to find my son tomorrow and bring him back to the Horsehead. I want to see him in my office before day's end. Good night."

He went out.

Head hanging, Cord gave a mirthless laugh.

CHAPTER 14

MANNION AND JAMES KINCAID, WHO WERE TROTTING
their horses along the main trail back to Battle Mountain, were in fact only about a mile away from that
former boomtown turned outlaw camp, when Mannion
frowned suddenly, stopped Red, and curveted him,
staring back in the direction from which he and James
had come.

"You heard it?" the younger man said, drawing back
on the reins of his mouse-brown dun.

"Yeah." Mannion slid his Yellowboy from the sheath,
angling up from beneath his right knee. He cocked it
one-handed, eased the hammer down to half-cock, and
rested the barrel across his saddlebow. "Riders. Quite a
few coming fast!"

The rataplan of maybe a half dozen horses grew
steadily until Mannion could see the jostling shadows of
the approaching horses and riders as they topped a rise
maybe a hundred yards back along the trail.

"Take cover!"

Mannion and James reined their horses off the trail's
left side and behind a tangle of cedars. As the thuds of

the galloping riders grew louder, Joe leaned forward to cover Red's snout with his hand, to keep the horse from whinnying. James did the same. Both men glanced at each other, darkly.

Were the riders James's father's men, sent out for Mannion and the rancher's son after his raggedy-heeled foreman and the other two no-accounts had returned to the Horsehead headquarters looking all the worse for having had the stuffing kicked out of both ends?

They were about to find out.

The thunder grew until the squawk of tack, the rattling of bridle chains, and the flapping of saddlebags joined the cacophony. Red shied a little as the riders galloped into sight on Mannion's right, racing to his left. He peered through the cedars to count six men dressed in your average trail gear. They'd galloped on passed the cedars too quickly for Mannion to have gotten a look at any but the lead rider, who had coal-black hair hanging down from a low-crowned cream Stetson flying out behind him in the wind of his passage. He wore a vest over a red shirt. That was all Joe knew for sure.

When the riders were well past the cedars and their din was dwindling quickly as they approached Battle Mountain town, Joe looked at James again. "You recognize any of 'em?"

James shook his head. "Not a one. They passed mighty fast, but they weren't Pa's men."

"Hmm." Mannion scratched his neck, scowling. "Who in hell, then?"

"Your guess is as good as mine, Marshal."

Mannion's scowl deepened. "No, it might be a tad better."

Could that group be the rest of Buzzard Lee's gang?

"Let's get to town, boy," Mannion said, reining Red

around the cedars and putting him back onto the trail. "Let's go, fella!"

Joe spurred the bay into an instant, hard gallop. He and James had taken it easy earlier, in no real hurry and not wanting to tax the horses in the darkness, so Red had plenty of bottom left. James's mount did, too. The younger man's dun easily kept pace with Red as it galloped just off Mannion's left stirrup, in the left rut of the two-track trail.

When they reached the raggedy outskirts of Battle Mountain, they checked the mounts back down to trots. Both men scoured the hitchracks fronting the town's only two remaining saloons, the Blue Dog on the right side and the Holy Moses a little farther down on the left. Mannion drew rein out front of the Holy Moses. Six sweat-lathered horses stood at one of the hitchracks fronting the Moses, blowing hard, their saddle cinches hanging loose. Several of the horses were greedily drawing water from stock tanks between the hitchracks and the boardwalk fronting the saloon. From inside the saloon came the tinny patter of a piano and a large hum of loud conversation—the kind of conversation men engage in after a long, hard dusty ride.

"You got an idea who they might be, Marshal?" James asked.

"Yeah. Yeah, I do. Let's get over to the Continental. That's where I left Sylvan Story."

"What's he doin' there?"

"Guarding your girl. I didn't know if any other would-be assassins would be coming for her."

"That was good thinking, Marshal Mannion. Thank you."

"Oh, I'm known for my reasonable thinking," Mannion quipped as they put both their own lathered mounts up the street toward Ma Lonnigan's Continental Hotel.

Not a minute later, they checked their horses down at a hitchrack fronting the decidedly humble, adobe brick building. Two men sat to either side of the front door, rifles resting across their laps. Both men stood, cocking their rifles.

"Hold it right there," one of them said with a menacing, mock-casual drag to his voice. "Who might you be an' what's your business?"

Joe studied them quickly. One was tall, bearded, and dressed in buckskins. The other was of medium height, with long dark-brown hair and the severely chiseled facial features of a full-blood Indian. He wore a calico shirt under a dark-blue gold-buttoned Union jacket with a sergeant's chevrons on both sleeves, and denim trousers. He wore two shell belts around his lean waist, and two holstered .44s were tied low on his thighs.

"Joe Mannion, town marshal of Del Norte. Who're you two and where's Story?"

"The marshal went for supper then to check on his prisoner." The bearded white man, who also wore two pistols, one low on his left thigh, the other for the cross-draw on his right hip, added, "I'm Willis Reed. This here's Eddie Shoots-the-Coyote. Friends of the marshals. We were stationed at Fort Bowie together, Eddie an' me. Eddie was a scout. *Chishi Dine*. I was a lieutenant."

Chishi Dine was the Indian name for Chiricahua Apache.

"You were a young lieutenant," Mannion remarked. He still couldn't be thirty.

"Only twenty-two when they upped my rank," Reed said. "Mustered out two years ago. "Story sometimes deputizes us when he needs extra help."

"You're here to protect the girl?"

"That's right."

"You seen her?" James swung down from his saddle, draped his saddlebags over his shoulder, and tied his horse at the hitchrail.

"Neither hide nor hair," Reed said. "Stayin' in her room. Quiet as a church mouse."

The Indian had said nothing, as was the Indian way. Mannion guessed he was at least part Apache. Maybe some Navajo, as well. He stood there like he could have been made of wood and was standing sentinel at a cigar store.

James turned to Mannion. "I'll see if she's awake. If not, I'll wait and talk to her in the morning. I'll see Ma about a room."

Mannion nodded. "I'm gonna have a palaver with Story." He turned to Reed and Eddie Shoots-the-Coyote. "You two can go. James and I'll take over."

Reed turned to Eddie. "I could use a drink. How 'bout you?"

Eddie just smiled.

As the pair came down the porch steps and headed down the street in the direction of the two saloons, James mounted the porch. He glanced back at Mannion, a dubious look in his eyes. "Her family's dead. I reckon I get to be the one to tell her."

"See if you can nudge her memory back. Give her some time. Then tell her. She's been through enough."

"You like her, don't you, Marshal?"

"What's not to like about her?"

"I don't know why, but the town's ashamed of her."

"The town's ashamed of what they did to her."

James drew a deep breath, nodded, then went into the Continental.

Mannion stood staring at the closed door, wondering at the complication James made of his life when he saved Joe's. Mannion felt guilty. On the other hand, James's life became almighty complicated when he fell in love with Giannina Calderon.

Mannion reined Red across the street and down the cross street to the jailhouse standing adjacent to the abandoned, overgrown hogpen and stable. Just down from the jailhouse, on the same side of the street as the hogpen and stable, the beginnings of the gallows stood— four uprights and the beginnings of what would, in a day or two, be the platform and its deadly trapdoor.

The tall upright from which the noose would hang was there, as well, sunk deep into the street and standing nearly twice as high as the platform supports. Mannion could smell the tang of the new wood. He wondered when the judge would arrive to pronounce sentence, for that's all the trial would be. Witnesses had Buzzard Lee dead to rights, and Mannion had seen enough backwater court trials to know how they went and that few lasted more than fifteen, twenty minutes. The judge would pound his gavel then head out to his carriage, likely driven by a secretary and guarded by a mounted deputy marshal, and light out for the next town, the next kangaroo court, the next gallows, the next necktie party which the town was likely already planning for, a four-piece band likely warming up for.

Wan lamplight guttered in the window to the left of the jailhouse door as Mannion mounted the stoop. He rapped twice on the door and tried to open it. Locked.

"Sylvan, it's Mannion."

Joe heard a chair squawk. Boots thumped on complaining floorboards. He heard the locking bar being removed from the brackets. The door was drawn open two feet and Mannion saw the thick-set Sylvan Story standing before him, partly silhouetted by the light on his desk. He held his pistol in his right hand. When he saw Mannion peering in at him, he holstered it.

"What's the matter—you didn't believe me?"

"Can't be too careful. Ol' Buzzard's been tellin' me his gang's on the way and detailin' all they'll likely do to me when they bust Buzzard out of my cellblock. He says most were in the frontier army and learned from the Apaches." Story wagged his head as he turned and ambled back to his desk.

Mannion moved into the office, closed the door, and dropped the wooden locking bar into its brackets. He doffed his hat, tossed it onto a table, and scrubbed his head brusquely with his fingertips, making a spiky mess of his longish salt-and-pepper hair. "Well, they might be here."

Story had just taken a sip from a steaming tin cup—coffee likely spiked from the small, flat bottle on his rolltop desk. He lowered the cup and wrinkled the skin above the bridge of his nose. "What makes you say so?"

"A mile out of town, six galloping riders rode past me and James Kincaid."

"You an' *who*?" Story asked, frowning incredulously.

"You heard right. He came to see the girl—Giannina Calderon." Mannion enunciated both names clearly, slowly, sending them point-blank to Story, who'd pretended he hadn't known who she was or where she'd come from.

The Battle Mountain town marshal sagged back in his chair and cursed.

"You must've known I'd find out sooner or later."

Story had his head back, staring at the ceiling, arms draped loosely over the arms of his swivel desk chair. His hat was on his desk by the whiskey bottle; a few strands of gray-brown hair did an inadequate job of hiding the bald top of his skull.

"Who are you more ashamed of?" Mannion said, standing before the man, his thumbs hooked behind his cartridge belt. "You or the girl?"

"Me, of course. The rest of the town." Story drew a deep breath, let it out, and shook his head. "She didn't deserve it. To be treated that way. Such a pretty, little thing—dancing an' singing in the *Cantina Rosa Amarilla*. On the Mex side of town, near Rattlesnake Wash."

"Never been there."

"Only the town knows about it. The dregs of the town...includin' the town marshal." Story flared a nostril in revulsion at himself. He dropped his chin to look at Mannion. "Reed and Eddie still at Ma's place?"

"They were. I released them. James and I'll take over for the night."

"Glad they were still there when you rode in. They're not always dependable. Like to drink an' whore too much. They usually go to the highest bidder, so I reckon I didn't have much competition this afternoon. They run with Omar Sledge, but Sledge, I reckon, was up to Mrs. Kennecott's. He troubleshoots for her."

"Does Mrs. Kennecott know he has a bounty on his head?"

"Ha!" Story laughed. "So do Reed an' Eddie. Hell, three-quarters of the town is wanted, Joe."

"Oh, to be a bounty hunter," Mannion said, picking up Story's bottle and taking a couple of liberal swallows. It raked several layers of skin off his vocal cords and seared his innards, just the way he liked it. "I could go to work and in a day have enough to retire."

"To Boot Hill!" Story laughed again. When he

sobered, he frowned at Mannion, curiously. "How in the hell did you partner up with James Kincaid?"

"You know he was...er, still is...in love with Giannina, don't you?"

"Oh, sure, sure." Story laced his hands on his big belly as he continued leaning back in his chair. "But his old man keeps him under tight rein. Especially after he found out he was steppin' out with the Mex. He only lets him come to town in Kincaid's own company an' only when he visits Mrs. Kennecott's daughter up to their gloomy old stone castle on the ridge. They're due to be married, you know."

"Oh, I know. I heard the story. An' one hell of a sad one, for sure. James is a nice kid. He saved my life today."

Story scowled, incredulous. "He did?"

"Shot his father's own foreman."

"*Wayne Cord?*"

"Popped him right through the shoulder."

The local lawman wagged his head darkly. "Oh, that ain't gonna go over good at the Horsehead at all. Not at all! Why, he's gonna be due a reckoning, an' I'll live in dread of what it's gonna be. Wouldn't put it past ol' Grant to draw an' quarter him!"

"There'll be no drawing an' quartering. I've seen enough of that for one lifetime." Mannion scooped his hat off the table and set it on his head. "The younker saved my life. I'll be damn sure looking out for his. Least I can do."

Mannion walked to the door. "I'm gonna tend his horse an' Red an' get some shut-eye. I have a feelin' tomorrow's gonna be a long day."

"Joe, have you ever had a short day?"

Mannion chuckled, and said, "Mind your prisoner, Sylvan." He glanced at the heavy door leading into the cellblock. "I gotta feelin' that horde James an' I saw galloping toward Battle Mountain was Buzzard's gang, all right. They might get liquored up an' decide to complicate your evening."

Story pulled his mouth corners down and leaned forward to pat the double-barrel Richardshotgun resting across the corner of his desk. "They complicate mine, I'll complicate theirs."

"I'll keep an ear skinned for a blast from that contraption an' wander over to help."

Mannion removed the locking bar from their steel brackets and touched the door latch.

"Joe?" Story said.

Mannion turned to him, one brow arched.

"Thanks for not judging me too harshly. About the girl. I been lonely since Mabel died. An' that's nigh on twelve years now."

"Just help the kid out if he needs it."

"I will."

"Good ni—" Mannion cut himself off abruptly. He was about to trip the latch and open the door, but suddenly that witch's bloodless finger poked the back of his neck. Hard.

"What is it?" Story said.

Mannion stared at the door. "Not sure. Just this strange feelin' I get when I'm about to be..."

He let the sentence trail off. He tripped the latch, pulled the door open, and stepped to one side. He hadn't set both feet beneath him before a bullet came screeching through the opening to slam against the heavy door to the cellblock with a loud *thud!* The bark of the rifle that had fired the bullet reached Mannion's ears a half an eyewink later. Two bullets sailed through the open door, one thumping into the door to the left of the first bullet, one thumping into the door to the right of it and three inches high.

Mannion pressed his back against the wall and slid his cross-draw Colt from the holster on his left hip. He pointed the Russian barrel up beside his right shoulder and cocked it, waiting for more bullets.

None came.

Instead, an oddly high-pitched voice called, "Mannion?"

Keeping his back pressed against the wall, Joe said, "What?"

"You hit?"

"Missed again, Harry!"

"Damn!" came the reply, followed by, "I'll be back, Joe. You won't know when or where, but I'll try again." An amused cackle.

Mannion turned and stepped into the doorway, crouched, Russian extended. He saw nothing but the shadows of the abandoned buildings and stockpen on the other side of the street. The only sounds were those of a rider fleeing fast.

"Marcum?" Story stood before his chair, holding his shotgun up high across his chest.

Mannion gazed out into the darkness, heart still thudding. "Uh-huh."

CHAPTER 15

EARLIER, AS MANNION HAD RIDDEN AWAY FROM THE Continental, heading for the jailhouse, James Kincaid had entered the hotel. Ma Lonnigan sat at the desk in the lobby, several ledger books open before her, a loosely rolled quirley dangling from a corner of her knife-slash mouth in a face as wrinkled as crumpled, dark-brown paper.

She glanced at James and then returned her attention to her books, saying in her smoker's growl, "What can I do for—"

She cut herself off and jerked another look at the newcomer.

Her eyes widened, and her mouth started to open until she almost lost the cigarette. She plucked it out of her mouth and blinked against the smoke. "Oh."

James moved slowly into the foyer, doffing his hat, worrying it in his fingers.

"You're here to see...her."

"Giannina, yes."

Ma drew her mouth corners down and nodded

guiltily, likely for her part in not identifying Giannina to Mannion. Instinctively, she'd probably thought she'd been protecting the rest of the town who'd done such an injustice to the girl. Mannion was a powerful lawman, and he was just passing through. Or so she'd thought.

He'd stayed for Giannina.

Ma drew on the quirley and blew a smoke plume toward the stairs. "Up the stairs. First room on the right."

"I'd like to stay, too."

Ma nodded once. "Take the room just beyond it." She flicked ashes from the cigarette, stuck it between her lips again, and returned her attention to the ledgers.

James adjusted the saddlebags on his shoulder and started up the creaky stairs. He stopped before the first door on his right and canted his head to listen through the panel. Silence.

Giannina was likely asleep. After what she'd been through, she needed all she could get. He needed some, too. He'd take only one step away from the door, the floorboards creaking beneath his boots, when a soft query issued from behind Giannina's door:

"Who's there?" A tremor of fear in her Spanish-accented voice.

James's heartbeat quickened. He turned back to her door, slowly twisted the knob, pushed the door open a foot, and poked his head into the room.

"Giannina," he said quietly, "it's me—James."

"Who?"

"James. Don't you remember?"

Silence. He could hear her breathing.

Then she said, "Your voice...it's familiar."

"Can I come in?"

He heard the rustling of the covers as she pushed

herself up in bed. She was no more than a human-shaped shadow.

"Maybe in the morning," he said, and began to pull his head back out of the room.

"No, wait." Another pause. "Come in. Light a lamp."

James let his saddlebags slide down his arm to the floor in the hall. He stepped into the room and gently latched the door behind him. In the candlelight from the hall, he'd seen a lamp on a cloth-draped table to his left. Now, the mantle glistened in the light from the half-moon angling through the room's single window. He moved to the table and opened the table's single drawer. He pulled out the box of matches there, removed the mantle, turned up the lamp's wick, scratched a match to life on the underside of the table, and touched it to the wick.

The flickering glow spread across the room, glinting in the dark-brown eyes of the girl sitting up in bed, her long hair hanging down across her nightgown-clad shoulders. Her bare, brown arms looked so slender, her heart-shaped face with plump lips like that of a doll's.

James returned the mantle to the lamp.

He turned to Giannina, looked down at her.

She stared at him with a growing intensity. The lamplight guttered in her eyes.

Her breathing grew more and more rapid. A tear collected in the corner of her right eye and slid down her cheek. Both eyes opened wider. Her mouth opened, forming a perfect, dark O. She closed both hands over her mouth, and her shoulders jerked as she sobbed.

"Oh, honey!" James hurried to the bed and sat down on the edge of it.

He took the girl in his arms and held her tight as she sobbed uncontrollably against his shoulder.

———

WHEN MANNION WOKE THE NEXT MORNING, BUTTERY sunlight shone in the window to the right of his bed in the Continental. He groaned angrily. He'd wanted to get a jump on the day. He still wanted to find out who'd wanted Giannina dead, wanted to run down Harry Marcum, and help Sylvan Story hold off Buzzard Lee's bunch, if the six men whom he and James had seen on the trail to Battle Mountain had indeed been a part of his bunch. He was betting they were.

He tossed the covers back, rose, and walked stiffly to the chair by the door on which he'd deposited his clothes. He'd spent most of the previous day in the saddle, and he'd tangled with three toughnuts from the Horsehead. His body was unabashedly informing him that he was getting too old for this crap. Even his feet hurt. He couldn't seem to get them to lie flat on the floor but shuffled around like a man pushing ninety, not sixty.

He cursed as he took a whore's bath at the washbasin, with tepid water from a pitcher. He'd take a long, hot bath once he got back to his and Jane's home in Del Norte. At least some of the trail dust scrubbed from his person and he dressed, having to sit down to pull his socks on.

"You old bastard, Mannion," he grumbled at himself.

He donned his hat, grabbed his rifle, and stepped out into the hall. He arched a brow with interest when he saw James's saddlebags on the floor outside Giannina's door, where he'd seen them last night when he'd tramped over from the jailhouse.

"Hmm."

He went downstairs and resisted the succulent aromas wafting from the kitchen and dining room.

Pancakes, bacon, coffee, and maple syrup. Damn! He'd slept in too late. His punishment would be an empty stomach until lunch.

He went out and noted how different the main street of Battle Mountain town was from Del Norte. At this hour, San Juan Avenue would be choked with traffic and roiling with dust and the pistol-like pops of black-snakes being popped over mule teams' backs. Battle Mountain's main street was all but deserted. A couple of drunk cowboys who'd spent the night in the Holy Moses were having a devil of a time mounting their horses. A single ranch wagon was parked out front of the mercantile. A single dog was trotting proudly down the middle of the street with a dead rabbit hanging from its jaws, a trophy won after a night's hunt in the countryside.

That was it.

The outlaws from both saloons were likely asleep in the livery barn or the town's hurdy-gurdy houses. None had stayed at Ma's place even before Mannion had taken up residence there. Many might be flush with stolen money, but they didn't believe in paying for lodging. For a girl, yes. But not for lodging. They'd had a peaceful night. Mannion hadn't been awakened by a single shot fired.

He angled to the mouth of the side street and then tramped down the side street to the jailhouse, which seemed to still be in one piece. At least it wasn't on fire, and Sylvan Story wasn't lying in a big, fat, bloody heap at the bottom of the stoop. Two burly men in wool shirts, suspenders, dungarees, and wide-brimmed hats were at work on the gallows, a wagonload of lumber parked nearby, a mule in the traces.

He mounted the porch. Earl had been curled in sleep at the top of the steps. Instead of making a hasty retreat as before, the dog merely sat up, looked up at Mannion, and growled deep in his throat.

"Hey, we're makin' progress, Earl."

Mannion rapped on the door.

A loud, startled grunt issued from inside, and boots thumped on the floor.

Mannion winced. Sounded like he wasn't the only one who'd slept in.

"It's Mannion, Sylvan."

"Yeah, yeah."

The locking bar was removed from the brackets and was set aside. The latch was tripped, and Story opened the door, stepping back, blinking groggily.

Mannion stepped into the office, saying, "Quiet night?"

Story closed the door. "Just woke me with my own snoring. Oh, and Earl tried to join a coyote girl around three a.m. No gunfire, an' I'm still kickin', so..."

Scratching the all-but-bald top of his head, Story moved to the table by the range littered with mouse droppings and on which his coffeepot and Arbuckles sack resided. He grabbed the pot, carefully opened the door, as though expecting a bullet meant for Mannion, then went out onto the porch. Joe heard him scoop up a potful of water for coffee and then came back in, closed the door, and yawning, went to work building a fire in the potbelly stove. When he crouched down, Mannion heard the bones in his back, hips, and knees pop. Joe winced. He knew the feeling.

Old age was a strange, sad spectacle. Especially when you were a man of action. That action was almost laughable these days for both men. Joe was still stiff from yesterday.

When Story had a fire going in the stove and

sounding like a dragon's breath in the stove's firebox, he donned his battered hat, and turned to Mannion. "I'm gonna hoof it up the street and get a plate from Ma for Buzzard. He'll be howling soon and raking his damn coffee cup across the bars."

"When's the judge gonna get here?"

"Ah, hell," Story complained. "A telegram came in yesterday. He got held up in Alamosa. What I think is he tumbled for a whore an'll be holed up with her an' a bottle for a day or two. The man's been married for thirty years!"

"Well, there's the problem," Mannion quipped.

"You'll stay with Buzzard?"

"I will."

"And set the coffee on the range when the fire's goin' good?"

"I'll do that, too." It was Joe's turn to yawn. As late as he'd slept, he could have slept another hour. "Lookin' forward to a cup myself." He eased his stiff old self into Story's chair.

"Good enough."

Story tucked his shirttails into his pants, yawned again, picked up the double-barrel Greener lying over a corner of his desk, broke it open to make sure it was loaded, set it on his shoulder, said, "Stay, Earl," and lit out for the Continental.

Mannion yawned again, sat back in the chair, crossed his arms again, and fell into a light doze. He came out of it to stoke the stove and set the pot on it. He took another brief nap until he heard the water boiling. He rose with a grunt, dropped a couple of handfuls of ground Arbuckles into the pot, and when it boiled again, he removed the pot from the range, added a little water with a gourd dipper from the rain barrel to settle the grounds, then set the pot on the warming rack.

Story returned with an annoyingly aromatic platter covered with a red-and-white napkin and disappeared with it into the cellblock. He heard Buzzard whining and Story talking, voices echoing in the cellblock's bowels, then Story returned, closed and locked the cellblock door. He'd just poured himself and Mannion cups of smoking mud when hoof thuds sounded outside the office along with the wooden rattle of a wagon.

Mannion and Story moved to the window right of the door. A big, blond man with a sun-seasoned face and clad in bib-front overalls and floppy-brimmed black hat climbed heavily down from the driver's seat.

"Big Hans Kreutzer," Story said with a speculative air. "One of Mrs. Kennecott's men."

He moved to the door, opened it, and stepped out onto the stoop. Earl was just then disappearing into the brush on the other side of the street. Mannion stepped out beside the Battle Mountain town marshal.

"Hans, what can I do you for?" Story asked. "Men from town been pestering Miss Sydney again, have they?" He nudged Mannion with an elbow and gave an ironic snort.

"Nein," said Big Hans, a little breathless from climbing down from the wagon. He was Mannion's age or a little older and was wearing a tad too much tallow on his big, German frame. He spat a wad of chaw into the dirt between the hitchrail and the stock tank. "The princess is fine, but Mrs. Kennecott is madder than an old wet hen."

"That's nothing new."

Big Hans chuckled. He adjusted his hat brim and, standing at the bottom of the porch steps, planting his fists on his hips, said, "She was counting her money, as she loves to do, you know, and she came up five thousand dollars short. She thinks someone broke in and robbed her. She wants you to come and—these are her words now, Sylvan—do your job."

The German smiled.

Story cursed.

CHAPTER 16

STORY TURNED TO MANNION. "WANT TO MEET MRS. Kennecott?"

"What about Buzzard?"

Story turned to Hans Kreutzer. "Hans, you want to earn a beer and a free lunch counter?"

Kreutzer threw his arms out to both sides. "*Natür- lich.*" Of course.

Story moved down the porch steps and handed the man his Greener. "Take a seat inside. Bar the door. You're our temporary jailer. Anybody tries to get in, give 'em both barrels through the door! Mannion and I'll be listening for the shot. We'll come pronto an' add our lead to the fray."

The German seemed to love the idea. Probably a nice change of pace from being the slave-driving Mrs. Kennecott's groundskeeper and all-around handyman. He laughed heartily, accepted the shotgun eagerly, and headed up the porch steps. Still chuckling, he closed the door behind him and barred it.

Story said, "Let's go. It'll be a first for you but it's once more into the breech for me! Mrs. Kennecott always has the notion someone's skulking around the grounds of her crazy place or breaking in to rob her or molest her daughter, Miss Sydney."

He and Mannion climbed aboard the work wagon and ten minutes later climbed the steep trail leading up to the sprawling stone and wood frame castle-like house topping a red ridge that formed sort of an apron base of Battle Mountain. They followed the trail, lined with stones, across the top of the bald ridge to the house's high, stone front steps. Sitting around on the steps, smoking and chatting desultorily, were the wanted gunman Omar Sledge and the two men Story had deputized to protect Giannina Calderon the previous night— Willis Reed and the cigar store Apache, Eddie Shoots-the-Coyote.

"Well," Story said as he stopped the wagon and set the break. "Look what the cat dragged in."

All three men stared at him stonily, tolerantly.

He and Mannion dismounted and as they headed for the steps, Joe said, "All three of you work for Mrs. Kennecott."

Omar Sledge removed a quirley from his mouth and blew smoke out his nose and mouth as he said, with an insolent glance at Story, "We're backup. Just in case the local law ain't up to the job."

Story only chuckled at that as he and Mannion stepped between Mrs. Kennecott's three outlaw troubleshooters, climbing the steps to the front door adorned with a brass lion's head knocker. Story had just lifted the knocker when the door opened. Mannion assumed it was the lady of the place herself who stood scowling at them.

"I didn't think you'd ever get here. Good Lord!"

Story removed his hat, held it over his heart, and gave

a courtly bow of his head. "Mrs. Kennecott, it's always a pleasure."

"Who's this?" she said, frowning up at Mannion after glancing quickly at the badge on his shirt.

"This here is none other than Bloody Joe Mannion his ownself. We're delighted to be enjoyin' the company of such a great and famous lawman as Bloody Joe himself, who has lowered himself to spend a little time here in Battle Mountain town, assisted me in the performance of my endless and exhausting duties, don't ya know!"

He gave Mannion a furtive wink and continued grinning like a mule with a mouthful of foxtails at the regal, forty-something woman standing, gowned and bejeweled, hair carefully coifed, before him.

Mannion groaned to himself as he doffed his own hat and held it before him.

"Come in, come in!"

She drew the door open wider, and Mannion followed Story into a vast sitting area with two sets of stairs winding up into the castle's higher reaches. On a brocade sofa at the far end of the room to Mannion's left, sat a heavy Black woman in a black maid's uniform with a lacy white apron. She leaned back against the back of the sofa, sobbing. A pretty, young brunette woman in a fetching, formfitting cream day dress sat with her, holding her hands in hers. Some of the brunette's hair was wrapped in a braid that curved around the sides of her head to the back of it, where it was secured with a red bow. Her little, pink feet were bare. She cooed to the Black woman, speaking softly, soothingly.

The Black woman turned to Mrs. Kennecott and cried with desperate beseeching, "Oh, please, Missus...I didn't have nothin' to do with stealin' that money. I promise on the graves of my dear family buried in

Alabamy I wouldn't touch no money of yours and Miss Athena's!"

Miss Athena took the woman in her arms, hugging her and running both hands up and down her back. "Shhh, Lottie...oh, shh, shh, shh." She turned to Mrs. Kennecott and frowned reprovingly. "Mother doesn't believe you did. *Do you, Mother?*"

"That's enough, Lottie! That is *enough!* I simply asked you a question!"

"No, no! You said I looked over your shoulder and seen the *com'nation!*" Another bout of sobbing ensued.

Mrs. Kennecott gave an impatient sigh and then turned to her guests and beckoned haughtily. "This way, gentleman. This way to the scene of the crime!"

Mannion and Story followed the woman up two long, winding staircases and one fairly short one. When they finally crossed another large sitting room with long, deep-set arched windows, the two men were huffing and puffing as though they'd run a long way. Which they sort of had.

They followed Mrs. Kennecott into a tower that housed a large, well-appointed office. Oil paintings, book-cases, and stone and marble statues as well as several pieces of heavy, masculine, wood and leather furniture adorned the large, circular room. Through several windows from which heavy, spruce green velvet drapes had been drawn lay the wrought-iron balcony from which Story had told Mannion on the way up to the unlikely, castle-like structure that Mr. Kennecott had hanged himself when his Kennecott Mine had closed when the silver and gold had all been mined out of it.

There were fewer of the precious metals than he'd anticipated when he'd started plundering the mountain. Thus, he'd practically lost his shirt as well as his good name. Story had also told Mannion that the word was Mrs. Kennecott had remained here to reopen the mine and get her own name back. Men who were believed to be precious metals geologists had visited Battle Mountain several times over the past two years—funny, little, bespectacled, prissily dressed, luggage-laden men with strange accents that Story believed to be Canadian.

Ruth Kennecott led both men over to her desk and then pointed at a safe roughly the size of two steamer trunks abutting the wall to the left of the desk, under a large oil painting of a snow-white stallion standing on his hind legs and clawing at the sky with his forehooves. "This, gentlemen, is where I keep considerable cash since I do not trust the Gold Nugget Bank in town, as it has been robbed more times than I can count on both hands and feet in the twelve years I've resided in Battle Mountain. Practicing due diligence in overseeing my holdings, I count the money in the safe once a week, just to make sure I am not being robbed. I counted the money late last night and, having counted several times, came to the conclusion that I was five thousand dollars short. Someone has broken into my house and robbed me!"

Story looked down at the safe and whistled and then turned to Mrs. Kennecott, a not unpretty woman but one who might have been a little comelier if her brown eyes were not so severely drawn up at the corners. Her dark-brown hair showed only a few streaks of silver. She had classical features, timeworn to be sure, but some of which Mannion had seen in the face of her daughter in the few brief glances he'd gotten of Miss Athena Kennecott downstairs and whom he'd taken special interest in since he knew that the Kincaids and Mrs. Kennecott had arranged for James Kincaid to marry the girl.

"That's a pretty good amount of money, Mrs. Kennecott. I sure am sorry."

The severely featured woman arched a thin brow over an amber-brown eye that burned with anger. "That's all you have to say?"

Still holding his hat, Story flushed. Mannion intervened.

"You're sure five thousand is missing? You couldn't have overlooked it or"—he steeled himself from the obviously wrathful woman's glance—"counted it wrong?"

She regarded Mannion as though he were an underling with dung on his boots. She blinked once, pointedly, and said, "I do not count wrong, Mr. Mannion."

"Yeah, well, it's Marshal Mannion, but since you're sure you counted right, who else knows the combination of the safe?"

"Only my husband, and he is dead."

"Has anyone else been in here when you've opened the safe?"

Still haughty as a debutante, Mrs. Kennecott said, "I make it a point of being alone. That is not to say someone might have snuck in when my back was turned. That's what I suspected of my maid, Lottie, though I doubt she's capable of such subterfuge." She touched her index finger to her temple. "If you understand what I'm saying..."

"Well, you sure left her in a fit of tears downstairs," Mannion countered with a caustic chuff.

"I had every right to question the help, *Marshal* Mannion."

"All right, all right." Mannion was wearing of this insufferable woman. "What you're saying, then, is someone slipped into your house one night when you were asleep or weren't home, and cracked the safe and stole five thousand dollars."

"What else could have happened?"

"How much cash do you usually keep in the safe?"

She looked at him, eyes studying him closely and with no little paranoia. Finally, she shuttled her gaze to the safe, and said, "I usually keep right around twenty thousand dollars on hand since it's a long carriage ride to my regular bank in Pueblo. I need it to make payroll each month and for day-to-day expenses. Keeping up this place is not cheap...nor is it easy to find the right men to do it around here," she added disgustedly under her breath.

"Why would they take only five thousand and leave the rest?"

"Your guess is as good as mine, Marshal. Maybe they thought I wouldn't notice it gone."

Mannion glanced at Story and then returned his curious scowl to the woman. He canted his head to indicate the front of the house, and said, "You do realize you have three wanted men...wanted outlaws...on your payroll. Don't you, Mrs. Kennecott?"

"Of course. I run checks on everyone I hire. Besides, around here, who else am I going to get?" Mrs. Kennecott threw out her arms and let them slap back down against her side. "However, I do trust those men. They were outlaws, but I believe them to be honorable outlaws. But even if they were not, if they were going to rob me, they, as you mentioned, would have taken *everything* and lit out for *Mexico*!"

Mannion and Story exchanged glances, and Mannion said, "Point well taken."

Sylvan nodded, lips pursed, brows raised.

Mrs. Kennecott crossed her arms on her chest and

slid forward one foot clad in a black patent side-button shoe that had come out of no wish book. "They are on standby in case you can't do your job, Marshal Story. Frankly, my confidence in you is sorely lacking."

Again, Story flushed and averted his gaze like a chastised schoolboy.

"That's not very fair, Mrs. Kennecott," Mannion again intervened. "You haven't even given the man a chance."

"You have two days to find my money, Marshal Story. Two days. Then I send my men to shake down every man in every saloon in town until my five thousand dollars...or what's left of it after a good bit of gambling and whoring, no doubt...tumbles onto some sawdust-covered floor of one of Battle Mountain towns many dens of Gomorrah-like iniquity!"

"Why, Mrs. Kennecott," Story said, standing up for himself at last. "That's a good way to get a fella shot!"

"Two days. You are both dismissed. I'd have Lottie show you out, but as you saw, she is presently indisposed. I'll let her have her cry before ordering her back to work. I don't pay for tears!"

Mannion and Story let themselves out.

"How'd it go?" asked Omar Sledge, the man's feminine blond hair glistening in the late morning light.

"Fine as frog hair split four ways," Joe said, giving the man an incredulous look. "How'd you think it'd go?" He gave each man a pointed look. "You stay outta Story's way or you an' me's gonna be doin' the two-step, and I can't dance for crap. I'd love nothing more than to cash in the rewards all three of you have on your heads. Me an' the missus could use a vacation."

All three scowled back at him. That was the most emotion Mannion had seen on Eddie Shoots-the-Coyote's face since meeting the man the previous night.

"What do you think, Joe?" Story asked Mannion as they rattled along the trail back toward town.

"I think you got your work cut out for you."

"That's all you got to say? You're Bloody Joe Mannion!"

"I think the maid has it?"

Story glowered at him in disbelief as he rounded a curve in the switchbacking, two-track trail. "You serious?"

"Yep. She was carryin' on way too hard. I don't think she's nearly as soft in her thinker box as she'd like everybody to think she is."

"Well, what am I supposed to do? Mrs. Kennecott wants me to shake down the saloons."

Joe shrugged and dug his makins sack out from where it hung down inside his shirt. "Let Sledge, Reed, an' Eddie Shoots-the-Coyote do it. Hell, let the outlaws lock horns. Might cull the herd a bit, make your job a whole lot easier."

Story smiled and leaned toward Mannion. "Truth is, I got it pretty easy as it is. I steer a wide berth around them saloons. Hell, I'm gonna retire in a year, an' I'd just as soon it's to Mesilla and not Boot Hill!"

He and Mannion laughed.

They sobered when a rifle blasted four times quickly from deep in the bowels of Battle Mountain town.

A girl screamed shrilly.

She screamed again, and Mannion turned to Story, and said, "That was from the Continental. Whip up that mule, Sylvan!"

CHAPTER 17

"DON'T HAVE TO TELL ME TWICE, JOE!"

Story whipped the reins against the mule's back. The mule brayed and broke into a hard run, laying his big ears back against his head. The empty wagon rattled loudly and fishtailed in the ruts of Battle Mountain's main drag. Men had come out of both saloons to stare with mute interest toward the hotel. There were two more rifle shots. Again, the girl screamed and Mannion heard Giannina sobbing as Story pulled the wagon up to the Continental's front porch.

Boots thundered inside the place, growing louder until the little, wiry, boyish Ma Lonnigan jerked open the front door and stepped out onto the stoop, loudly cocking an old Spencer repeating rifle in her spidery, Indian-dark hands, a corncob pipe dangling from the corner of her mouth. "Who the hell's shootin' up my place?" she yelled in her smoker's whine.

She rested the rifle atop the porch rail and fired eastward, toward rocks and open desert. She fired two more rounds, the Spencer roaring and leaping in her hands.

Mannion leaped out of the wagon. Story climbed

down a little more slowly and carefully—more wisely for a man his age. Mannion ran up to the porch, yelling, "You see the shooter, Ma?"

"No!" She triggered two more rocketing blasts to the east, loudly working the Spencer's trigger guard cocking mechanism.

Joe ran into the Continental and up the creaky stairs that swung like a rope bridge beneath his thundering boots. Story mounted before Mannion gained the second story, and having two men running up the steps made the stairs creak and undulate even more severely.

"She's gotta get that fixed!" Mannion muttered under his breath, breathing hard.

At the top of the stairs, he ran forward and stopped at the first door on his right. Behind the door, the girl was sobbing, and he could hear a man—likely James—groaning. Mannion tried the door. Locked.

"Giannina, it's Joe Mannion. Unlock the door!"

A loud, startled gasp and then Mannion heard someone turning the key in the lock. The lock was rusted, so it took some doing. Giannina kept sobbing and then the latching bolt clicked as it retreated into the door. Mannion shoved the door open to see the girl, clad in one of Ma's nightgowns, staring up at him with large, brown eyes bright with tears. More tears streaked her olive-colored cheeks.

Behind her, most of the glass in the window had been shot out. Beyond was the roof of one of the boarded-up shops. That was probably where the shooter had fired from.

Giannina shuffled back and looked down and to Mannion's right.

Mannion saw James sitting on the floor, his back against the wall. The young man was holding his right hand over his upper left arm. Blood stained his shirtsleeve.

As Story shoved into the room behind Mannion, Joe dropped to a knee beside James. He pried the young man's hand off his arm. "How bad you hit?"

James stretched his lips back from his teeth and writhed, moving his legs. "It's just a graze but it burns like the blazes." He chucked ruefully. "I never been shot before!"

Mannion straightened and turned to Giannina. She stood staring down at James, a hand over her mouth, shoulders jerking as she sobbed. Mannion took her arm and pulled her away from the window. "Don't get in front of the window. Keep low, pour some water over that burn in his arm, and wrap it—all right?"

She looked up at him in shock. He shook her none too gently. It was time she came out of this, took her life back, away from those—whoever they were—who wanted her dead. "Giannina, do you understand?"

"Si, si, si!" she cried.

Mannion turned to Story. "Stay with them, Sylvan. I'm gonna run down that damn dry-gulching son of Satan!"

"You got it, Joe!"

Mannion negotiated the creaking stairs again, crossed the lobby, and walked out onto the stoop. Ma was out in the middle of the street, beyond the mule and parked wagon, aiming down the barrel of her cocked Spencer toward the east end of town. The old rifle had to weigh at least half what she did, but she held it steadily in her skinny arms, up which she'd rolled the sleeves of her man's checked wool shirt.

"Anything?"

"I don't see him, Joe. I don't see him. But I'd sure like to!"

"Lower the rifle, Ma. I'm gonna mosey down there."

Mannion slid his Yellowboy out from beneath the wagon's seat. He removed it from the sheath, tossed the sheath back into the wagon, racked a round into the Winchester's action, and setting the hammer to half-cock, began striding down the rutted, sage-stippled street toward the high New Mexico desert opening roughly a hundred yards beyond.

"Don't shoot me in the back, Ma."

"Don't insult my marksmanship, Joe."

Mannion gave a wry chuff and kept walking, holding the Yellowboy straight out from his right hip. He shuttled his gaze from the scraggly, abandoned, boarded-up, and brush-overgrown buildings and pens and privies and derelict wagons on the left side of the broad street to those on the street's right side. A breeze shepherded tumbleweeds along the street to either side of him, lifting little dust tornadoes and nipping the broad brim of Mannion's high-crowned Stetson.

He kept his wolf-gray eyes narrowed, keenly, cautiously scrutinizing every nook and cranny and every bit of cover that might conceal a spineless devil of a dry-gulching son of Ol' Scratch.

"Where are you, you devil?" he growled, holding his gloved right index finger taut against the trigger.

He moved up to a narrow, brush-overgrown gap between the barn with the caved-in roof and a log cabin with a badly rusted corrugated tin roof. A sign stretching into the street on crooked pine posts was badly weathered and faded, but Mannion could still make out the lettering. In smaller letters beneath *FINE FURNITURE* were the words *TOOTH EXTRACTIONS 5 Cents*. To the right of that was a crude drawing of a tooth.

Mannion stopped when he heard what sounded like a horse whicker. It had come from somewhere in the gap between the barn and the furniture maker/dentist's place. He swung left and gazed into the gap, which was about thirty feet wide and a hundred feet deep. A small side shed of rotting gray boards protruded from the side of the barn near the rear.

Mannion stared, scrutinizing the brush and old trash and a wheelless wagon rotting in the sage, a spindly ponderosa pine growing up between the boards of the wagon's bed. A chickadee sat atop the bending seedling, cheeping at Mannion. It swung around fleetly, again planting its little feet atop the seedling, looking toward the rear of the barn. It cheeped again, three times, shrilly, then lit from the seedling and caromed over Mannion toward the brush and abandoned structures on the other side of First Street.

Mannion moved forward slowly, keeping his index finger drawn taut against the Yellowboy's trigger, his thumb caressing the hammer. He moved straight down the middle of the gap between the buildings, stepping over and around obstacles. When he was halfway between the mouth of the gap and the rear of both buildings, he angled closer to the barn and then walked with his left shoulder about six feet off from the side of it.

He slowed his pace further as he neared the side shed.

When he came to the shed, he brushed his left shoulder against it, slowly approaching the far end.

The rear corner inched toward him.

He was four feet...then two feet away.

When he was inches away from the rear corner, he

paused and then took one more step forward, and swung sharply left, bringing the Yellowboy around.

His heart jolted, and his eyes widened in surprise when a big buckskin horse filled his vision, and a man with long, dark-brown hair and clad in an ancient three-piece suit grinned down at him. The horse whinnied shrilly, deafeningly, rising off its front hooves. The rifle in the man's right hand roared and then the buckskin dropped back down to its front hooves and shot forward as though from a cannon. Mannion fell and rolled to his right. One of the horse's pounding hooves clipped his left thigh as horse and rider swung sharply to their right and galloped hard toward the front of the gap.

Mannion had lost the Yellowboy in the fall.

He clawed his left-hand .44 from its cross-draw holster, cocked it, and sent a single bullet hurling toward the fleeing dry-gulcher. The man slumped forward sharply as the horse barreled straight toward Ma Lonnigan, who was raising her rifle to her shoulder, bellowing, "Ah, ya mangy son of Satan—shoot up my place will...*oh-ahhhh*!" Ma cried as the horse rammed into the little woman, sending her flying backward.

She triggered the Spencer skyward just before dropping the rifle and rolling in the dusty street.

Mannion triggered another shot, but his slug flew wide as his dry-gulcher reined the buckskin sharply left and crouching low in the saddle, favoring his right shoulder, galloped eastward, disappearing behind the furniture maker/dentist's boarded-up cabin.

"Ohhhh, you devil!" Ma cried, flopping around in the street, partly obscured by the rider's sifting dust.

Mannion sat up with a grunt, taking silent inventory of his battered person. He didn't think anything was broken. With another grunt, he heaved himself to his feet, collected his hat and rifle and tramped, limping on his already aching ankle, back out of the alley. He glanced to the east, toward the open desert. The bushwhacker and his buckskin were gone. The sifting dust was all that remained of them. And the aches and pains in Mannion's battered frame. And the echo of the buckskin's high-pitched whinny in his ears.

He walked over to the howling Ma Lonnigan.

"How bad you hurt, Ma?"

"Oh, I ain't hurt bad!" She extended her hand to Mannion, and he set his boots and pulled her to a sitting position.

He dropped to a knee beside her. "You sure? That buckskin kissed you good."

"No, no. It's my pride that took the brunt of *that* blow. I had a shot at the SOB, an' I missed him clean!"

Mannion glanced along the street to the east. He wished Red was here. If he was, he'd be hot on that dry-gulcher's trail.

"I think I winged him," Joe said. "Did you get a look at him?"

"Not a good one. All I seen was hoss!"

"Yeah—me too," Mannion admitted. "If a man needs a bullet dug out of his hide, who'd he go to?"

"Prob'ly Ernie Kellerman. Bartender at the Red Light All Night hurdy-gurdy house on the north end of town. Nothin' out there but the house—three-story wood frame place. Gone to hell now, but the fella who once owned the lumberyard built it for his family. Abandoned it when the gold and silver played out in Battle Mountain and the rest of the town went belly up."

"Thanks. I'll keep an eye on the place." Mannion fingered his ear. "Damn, damn, damn!"

"What is it?"

"Someone still wants Giannina dead. Someone is obviously almighty determined to turn her toe down along with the rest of her family."

"Looks like."

"Who, Ma? Who?"

Again, Ma extended her hand to him. He pulled her to her feet. She stood before him, her wizened head coming up only to the middle of his chest. "I wish I knew, Joe. I wish I knew. Uh...sorry about...you know... before..."

"Not tellin' me who she was?"

"Yeah." Ma lowered her chin and flushed, incredulous. "I reckon I figure you was just passin' through an' why incriminate most of the town? I have to live here with those men, too."

"Yeah," Mannion said accusingly. "Why incriminate most of the town for just a simpleminded Mescin girl?"

"Ah, hell, Joe."

"Come on." Mannion turned and started tramping back in the direction of the Continental. "I gotta get that girl somewhere safe while I try to figure out who's tryin' to perforate her hide. By god, I'm gonna perforate *theirs*!"

"Yeah, well, that's why you're Bloody Joe, Bloody Joe," Ma said, having retrieved her rifle and falling into step beside him. "Just hope you can do it before one of these outlaws gets tired of havin' you around."

Mannion chuckled dryly.

She'd taken the words right out of his mouth.

CHAPTER 18

MANNION HAD TAKEN ONLY THREE STEPS BACK IN THE direction of the Continental when he stopped suddenly.

Three riders sat three horses in front of the hotel.

James stood on the Continental's front porch, a defiant set to his shoulders.

Voices were raised contentiously, but Mannion couldn't quite make out what the four were saying.

"Now, what?" Ma said.

Mannion just sighed.

He continued forward, quickening his pace despite the additional grievances in his over-the-hill carcass. As he closed on the Continental, he quickly scrutinized the three riders, two set back a little to each side of the one, who was obviously their leader—a stocky man with sandy blond sideburns, brushy mustache, and goatee. He appeared to be in his late twenties, early thirties. Even from the side, Mannion thought his face could have been chiseled out of granite, with heavy brows and a long, strong jaw.

The other two were the same height but one was tall and lean, the other tall but thicker and broader through the waist and shoulders. They sat slouched desultorily in their saddles, grinning, while the sandy blond man did the talking, one fist on his hip. He leaned slightly forward in his saddle, and his voice was both commanding and jeering.

"...old man said to ride into Battle Mountain an' fetch his son, an' that's what we're here to do. I do have to thank you for the promotion, though, James. Never woulda got it if you hadn't drilled that pill into Wayne Cord's shoulder. Howled all night long. Him an' Coffee. Quade couldn't quite get comfortable due to..."

The lead rider let his voice trail off. In the corner of his right eye, he'd spied the approaching Mannion and Ma Lonnigan. He turned to Joe now, as did the other two.

He jerked his chin up sharply, angrily, and said, "You Mannion?"

"Yep. Who're you?"

"Pat Winslow. The new foreman of Horsehead. These two are C.J. Harriman an' Tyrell Brand. Also from Horsehead."

Harriman was the tall one who also had a mustache and chin whiskers, though his were dark brown. He appeared to have one unmoored, dark-blue eye. Brand was the thicker one. A knotted white scar ran down through his lips to the nub of his chin. He had a big, square face like their fearless leader, Winslow, only his was more deeply tanned, and his eyes were set closer together, giving him a naturally pugnacious appearance. His dark-brown hair hung down his back in a long queue held together with braided rawhide.

As Mannion approached, Brand either consciously or unconsciously set his right, black-gloved hand on the walnut grip of the Bisley revolver sitting up high on his right hip.

"Get your hand off that gun!" Mannion barked as he drew within ten feet of the three Horsehead riders and stopped, raising his Winchester straight up before him and loudly levering a fresh round into the action.

Brand scowled, his dark brows ridging heavily over his deep-set, too-close-together eyes. "Says who?"

"The fella who just jacked a live round into his Winchester's breech, you dunce!"

Brand's scowl grew more severe. He curled his upper lip and flared his nostrils.

Pat Winslow glanced back at him. "Now, now. Keep it pouched, Tyrell. We didn't come to town to tangle with Bloody Joe Mannion. We came to town on Horsehead business." He shifted his gaze to the lawman. "Which ain't any of yours, Mannion." He pointed at Joe with his brown-gloved right hand. "This is Horsehead business an' Horsehead business only."

Mannion turned to James, still standing on the Continental's stoop. "James, are you riding back to Horsehead with the new Horsehead foreman here?"

James wagged his head. He had one boot cocked forward, his thumbs hooked behind his cartridge belt. A red cloth was wrapped tightly around his upper left arm. "No, sir, I'm not." He turned to Winslow. "I aim to find out who murdered my girl's family and ran her into the ravine, scared her so bad she lost her memory. Till last night," he added, glancing at Mannion.

Joe gave a relieved half smile and nodded.

Winslow shook his head darkly. "Don't encourage him, Mannion. I don't know where his spine suddenly came from, but it's not the right time. My orders are to bring him back to Horsehead. Believe me, it'll be far better for him if he comes. The boss is hoppin' mad over what you an' Junior did to Cord, Coffee, and Quade. He had to fire 'em, an' that was the last thing he wanted to do." He shrugged and added, "Not that I can't fill Cord's boots, but..."

"I'm sure you'll do a swell job, Pat," Mannion said, smiling benevolently.

"Why, thank you, Bloody Joe."

"Go home, Pat. Tell Pa I'll return when I'm good 'n' ready," James said. "You can also tell him he better not have had anything to do with murdering Giannina's family." He shook his head darkly.

"James, you damn fool!" Winslow intoned in exasperation. "She's a damn Mescin whore. A *puta!* Get your damn head on straight! You don't wanna be burnin' bridges here, boy!"

"I'm not the one burnin' 'em, Pat. In fact, I'm tryin' to put the fire out. But I got a feelin' that just before you fellas rode into town, Pa sent someone else to kill Giannina. Probably thought it was her in the window. That's why I got this." James brushed his thumb across the wrapped wound in his arm.

Pat straightened in the saddle and sighed.

He glanced from Harriman to Tyrell Brand, darkly.

"What?" Harriman said. "We ride back to Horsehead an' tell the boss we couldn't get 'er done? Hell, we'll be fired just like Cord, Coffee, an' Quade!"

Mannion aimed the Yellowboy straight out from his right hip. "It's either that or die right here."

James hooked a lopsided smile. "You fellas don't wanna shoot it out with Bloody Joe."

Ma Lonnigan had been standing one step back and to Joe's left. Now she stepped forward, ramming another

.56-caliber cartridge into her Spencer's chamber, snarling, "Nor 'Deadeye' Ma Lonnigan!"

Mannion glanced at her. She glanced back at him and shrugged.

The three Horsehead men stared at James grimly. They shuttled their gazes to Mannion and Ma Lonnigan, who, in contrast to Joe's six foot four, appeared a child, albeit an old and wizened one.

Winslow snarled and then neck-reined his mount around, and said, "Come on—I've done better talkin' reasonin' to mules!" He stopped his horse and hipped around, red-faced, to growl at Mannion. "Next time you see a Horsehead rider, I got me a feelin' you're gonna see the whole damn roll!"

He put steel to his mount, which lunged off its rear hooves and broke into a hard run to the west. The other two followed suit, and soon, all that remained of them was their dust sifting over the quiet, brightly sunlit, deeply rutted main street of Battle Mountain. Men holding frothy beer mugs even at this early hour, standing out in front of the town's two remaining saloons, stared after them, muttering among themselves.

James drew a deep breath and let it out slowly. He unknotted his neckerchief, removed his hat, and mopped the sweat from his forehead. Setting his hat back down on his head, he turned to Mannion.

"What're we gonna do now?"

"Get the girl ready to travel," Mannion said. "We need to get you both out of town for a spell. Can Gian-nina ride?"

"She can ride."

"You know of a place you won't be found?"

James stared at him, pondering. Then he nodded, and said, "I think so."

"How far?"

"Only about an hour's ride."

"Perfect. I'll fetch our horses."

He glanced at Ma Lonnigan. "Thanks for backin' me, Ma."

She scowled at the big lawman. "Who was backin' *who?*"

Mannion depressed the Yellowboy's hammer, lowered it to his side, and strode down the street to the west, heading for the livery stable. As he walked, hearing the hammering as the two construction workers continued work on Buzzard's gallows, he scrutinized every nook and cranny around him, every rooftop, every shadow that might conceal Harry Marcum or some other weak-livered, dry-gulching son of the devil.

Yessir, he'd never felt quite so much like a cat in an attic full of rocking chairs as he did here in Battle Mountain town.

A half hour after he'd set out from the Continental, he reined Red down in front of the jailhouse, James's mouse-brown dun and a rented paint horse in tow. Sylvan Story came out of the jailhouse, setting his double-barrel Greener on his shoulder. The intermittent hammering of the men building the gallows echoed.

"Heard shootin'," he said with a grim wag of his head. "Thought you might've bought the farm this time, Joe."

"Oh, hell. Sylvan, you talk like a young widow afraid o' the lightnin'."

"When you waltz around out in the open like you do, Joe, you're liable to get struck one o' these times."

"I'm gonna take the kid and the girl out of town, put 'em up somewhere safe. His old man just sent three more men for them. After someone tried to plug the girl again."

Story grimaced and shook his head. "Why is it I feel like I'm sittin' on a keg of dynamite with a lit fuse?"

"Can you send for Reed and Eddie Shoots-the-Coyote? You're gonna need help if Buzzard's gang comes calling. I got a feeling they're likely sleeping off last night with some comely whores, but as soon as they get a beer and a shot and a big breakfast in 'em, they're gonna feel right industrious, try to relieve you of their fearless leader."

"Six of 'em, you say?"

"Six, yes."

"Ah, hell, six used to be nothin' to me, Joe. I could take out two at a time with each barrel." Story glanced at the Greener resting on his shoulder. "Another two with my old Colt."

"I hate to tell you, Sylvan, but you an' that Colt are both old now. I feel it myself, and I don't like to look at it, but sometimes you have to."

Story grimaced again and sighed, scratching his neck. "I got Buzzard in the office, chained to a post. If'n his gang shows, I'll let 'em know if they try to bust in here, I'll blow his head off an' they'll have made the trip for a headless corpse."

"That *might* work."

"I'll send for Reed an' Eddie. Looks to me like all they're doing for Mrs. Kennecott is litterin' her front step with cigarette butts."

Mannion reined Red and his two extra horses away from the jailhouse. "I should be back in a couple of hours to help you hold down the fort if the gang decides to carouse another day and strike tonight."

"I'll be here, Joe." Story raised his voice as Mannion trotted his horses back up the side street toward the

Continental. "Keep a finger on your trigger an' one eye on your back trail!"

Mannion glanced back, pinched his hat brim, and continued to the hotel, reining all three horses up before it.

He'd started to swing down from the saddle when the Continental's front door opened. James stepped back, glancing to his side. Giannina stepped into the opening. She wore a round-brimmed butterscotch hat, which Ma had likely supplied along with the denim trousers, dark-blue work shirt, suspenders, and boots. A red bandanna was knotted around the girl's neck. She raised her hand to shade her eyes from the bright morning sun. She looked cautiously up and down the street, as though for more men who might want her dead, before settling her gaze on Mannion.

"Is it all right, señor?"

Mannion nodded. "It's all right. I know I told you you'd be safe here, but James and I think we know where you'll be safer."

"You will protect me..." She glanced up and down the street once more before returning her brown-eyed gaze to Joe. "From them...the men who killed my familia?" Tears glazed her eyes, but there was a stubbornness and anger there, as well, Mannion was glad to see.

"Yes," Mannion said, though he wouldn't blame her if she didn't believe him. He'd nearly failed twice before. "Going to take you somewhere safe. James will stay with you. I have to get back to town and find out who sent those men in the first place and to take care of some other business." Namely, Harry Marcum and Buzzard Lee's cutthroat gang.

Tentatively, the girl walked out of the hotel.

James came out, then, as well, holding his rifle in his right hand, his saddlebags draped over his right shoulder. He followed Giannina over to the horses, slung his saddlebags over the back of his gelding, shoved his rifle into its boot and then helped the girl into the saddle of the horse Mannion had rented from the livery. It was a short, stocky mount with a broad barrel and good legs. He'd picked out a mount he thought would be good for a hard run in rough country, if needed. He hoped it wouldn't be needed. He would join James and the girl in case they were followed; they needed their back trail scoured of more would-be assassins.

"Feel good?" James called up to her, giving her the reins.

She looked at her feet in the stirrups. Mannion had adjusted them, guessing at the length, but it appeared he'd gotten it right. She nodded.

James swung up onto his own mount's back. As he did, Ma Lonnigan stepped out onto the porch, stood at the top of the steps, and crossed her skinny arms on her chest.

"Farewell, darlin'," she told the girl. "I got a feelin' everything's gonna work out for you. I just got a feelin'." She smiled, deep lines spoking around her eyes and at the corners of her thin-lipped mouth. Her corncob pipe poked up out of the breast pocket of her shirt. She glanced at Mannion, and there wasn't so much optimism in her eyes as hope.

Mannion pinched his hat brim to her. "I'll be back later, Ma."

"I'll keep a lamp burnin', Joe."

The three of them reined their horses away from the hitchrack. Mannion led them on a circuitous route out of town, making sure they wouldn't be followed. At least, trying hard not to be, constantly hipping around in his saddle to make relatively certain they weren't. When they were well west of town, he let James take the lead. They headed up into rough, pine and cedar country, and then it was just firs and pines, and the air cooled as they gained altitude.

As they crossed a windy pass, Mannion, riding behind both James and Giannina, halted Red.

A mare's tail of dust rose down in the desert country below, along their back trail.

Anger rose in Mannion.

Despite how carefully he'd chosen their route, they'd picked up shadows.

He half turned his head to call to James and Giannina, who were riding down the opposite side of the pass. "You two go on ahead. I'm gonna wait here a spell."

James threw out an acknowledging arm.

Mannion reached forward to loosen the Yellowboy in its scabbard.

CHAPTER 19

MANNION PUT RED A HUNDRED FEET DOWN THE SIDE of the pass and then swung from the leather.

He ground reined the mount and patted the loyal bay's right wither as he shucked the Yellowboy from its sheath. "You stay, hoss. I'll give you some water soon. First, I'm gonna see who our shadows are."

The horse whickered and lifted his snout to give Mannion's left ear a playful nip. Mannion chuckled and shoved the long, fine snout down.

Ten feet from the top of the pass, he doffed his hat and crawled on hands and knees until he could edge a look over the top and down the other side. Resting his chin on the ground, he studied the trail dropping down through pines and firs, a cool breeze jostling columnar shadows across the rocky, two-track trace likely carved by a prospector's wagon hauling supplies to the cabin James had told Mannion about. The cabin was known by few. James had come upon it accidentally during a previous roundup, and he'd taken Giannina there to be alone with the girl, away from Battle Mountain town's prying eyes.

Chin resting on the pebbly, pine-needle-littered

ground, Mannion stared down the trail toward the flat-bottomed, sage-peppered valley below, where the sun shone more brightly. He frowned. He could no longer see that mare's tail of rising dust. If his shadowers were still coming, that dust tail should have grown more visible, not less so.

He shuttled his gaze to his left and then back across the trail and up the steep, forested rise over his right shoulder.

Had they gotten around him?

He doubted it. He would have seen them, or Red would have winded them. They'd have made more noise in the forest on either side of the trail. No, if they were shadowing him and James and Giannina, they'd have stuck to the trail. They might have spied him sitting Red atop the pass and gone to ground.

Or...they might not be shadowing him at all. They could just be riders from one of the area ranches riding out to look for herd quitters, those cattle who'd strayed from the larger herds into the remoter areas of the mountains.

Mannion waited.

Five minutes passed.

Ten.

Fifteen.

Joe sighed. "Well, that tears it."

No point in waiting any longer. Deciding whoever had been on his back trail was there for innocent reasons —or that at least they weren't following him and his two charges—Mannion rose and strode back down the slope. He gave Red a good drink from his hat and then slid the Winchester into its scabbard, mounted up, and continued down the trail.

He was riding down the side of another forested ridge

twenty minutes later when a small log cabin came into view below, in a crease between ridges and fronted by a narrow, winding stream running down the crease's middle. Birds piped and squirrels chittered. The breeze made a soft, rushing sound in the pine crowns, and the stream chimed softly as it rippled over rocks.

Mannion drew rein and sat gazing over the long, narrow valley at the mossy-roofed cabin on the other side of the stream—a former trapper's cabin, long abandoned. James and Giannina's horses were both tied to the worn hitchrack off the cabin's small, crude, plankboard stoop. James had stripped their tack and set it on the ground. A log cut to form a chair sat to the right side of the cabin's open front door. James was on the roof just then, removing a coffee tin overturned atop the rusty stovepipe.

Mannion rode on down the ridge. As he crossed the stream, he saw Giannina standing in some shrubs to the left of the cabin. She turned to Mannion and smiled as she popped a blackberry into her mouth and chewed. Her lips were stained purple.

Mannion smiled. It was nice to see the girl smile. He hadn't seen her smile before. He liked the way it spread her full lips and drew the corners of her dark-brown eyes up slightly and made them flash.

As Mannion drew rein before the cabin, James walked carefully down the slightly pitched roof to the edge. He paused, looked down at the ground, then threw his arms out to both sides, and stepped over the edge. He struck the ground, bending his knees to absorb the shock. Straightening, he smiled at Mannion.

"Want to stay for coffee and blackberries?"

Mannion glanced back up the ridge he'd just descended, on the scout for his shadowers. If the riders had, indeed, been shadowing him. He'd stick around awhile, make sure no one with nefarious intentions showed up.

Turning back to James, he said, "Why not?"

James headed for the cabin's open door. "There's dry wood inside. I'll get a fire going."

Mannion swung down from the saddle and stripped the tack from Red's back. He was rubbing the bay down with a scrap of burlap when he smelled the burning pine issuing from the stovepipe. James emerged from the cabin with a white-speckled black coffeepot. He walked down to the stream, crouched to fill the pot with water, then returned to the cabin.

Mannion was just finishing rubbing Red down when he smelled the enticing aroma of coffee, lacing the smell of the burning pine and fir.

Ten minutes later, he sat at the small wooden table inside the cabin, lifting a smoking tin cup to his lips. His rifle leaned against the wall near the door; his hat was on the table. He sat facing the sashed window in the wall before him, watching Giannina wade in the stream, her denims rolled up to her brown knees. James sat to Mannion's left. His hat was hooked on a wall peg; his hair showed the indentations of it. His face was red with recent sun and windburn. The younger man lifted his own steaming cup to his lips.

His eyes looked more certain, more confident than when Mannion had first seen him up close, when he'd saved Joe's bacon from Cord and the two other Horsehead toughnuts. He looked like a man coming into his own.

But at what cost? Joe vaguely thought.

"How much does she remember?" Mannion asked him.

James sipped his coffee. He had his head turned so he could watch Giannina frolic in the stream like a chocolate-eyed, brown-skinned forest sprite, the breeze blowing wisps of her dark-brown hair against her cheeks. He watched her with a somber air, but with amusement and affection, as well.

"She remembers most things about her life clearly." James turned to Mannion and shook his head. "But about that night, hardly anything at all. She remembers some shooting and screaming and about being afraid and running, hearing men riding after her. But then everything goes dark."

"Right."

Again, Mannion sipped his coffee, set the cup down, and stared down into the hot, steaming liquid. He looked at James. "What's your plan, son?"

"I have no idea. Beyond finding out who killed her family, that is."

"You do realize that most indications point to your father, don't you?"

James pulled his mouth corners down and nodded. As he did, Giannina stooped over to pick a rock up out of the stream. She held it up to the clear, high-country light, squinting as she inspected it closely, reaching up with her other hand to brush something off it.

Slowly, James turned to Mannion. "It's time he was stopped. I wish I'd had sense enough to defy him long ago. And left there." He shook his head. "I didn't have the spine. He took that away from me. Early on, he took my courage and all sense of myself. Ma fell into lockstep with him. I think they were afraid, deep down, of me possibly becoming more of a man than Pa was.

"Men like Pa, you see, Marshal Mannion, are really little men inside. They're afraid and angry. That's why they feel the need to suppress others. Even their sons. Their sons are their biggest threat. So he took away that threat and turned me into an unconfident, simpering thing, afraid of his own shadow. Afraid his shadow might slip out away from his father's shadow and be out there all alone."

James sipped his coffee and glanced out the window once more at Giannina, who was squatting down in the stream, brushing off another rock she'd plucked from the bottom. The sunlight glinted off her upraised knees, and it shone gold in her hair—flame red at the very edge of it.

James turned back to Mannion. "I'm out here now. Alone. Just me an' Giannina. And I like it." He chuckled dryly and took another sip of his coffee. "I may not survive it. No one crosses Pa an' gets by with it. Not even his son. Not that I'd think he'd kill me, but he'd try to enslave me again." He shook his head quickly. "But I won't have it."

He stared at his thumb caressing the rim of his half-empty cup for a time.

Mannion kept a close eye on the ridge above and beyond Giannina, who'd gone back to kicking around in the stream again.

James continued with, "When I shot Wayne Cord, I didn't hesitate. It was almost like I was watching myself from outside my body. I knew what had to be done. I knew who Cord was. I knew what he meant to my father. But I knew that I couldn't *not* shoot him. It was the right thing to do, to keep him from shooting you. In that instance, just before I pulled the trigger, I realized he wasn't the big monster I'd been so afraid of. That big giant of a monster had only lived in my mind. He was just a man like everyone else. And he needed to be stopped."

He glanced at Giannina, who was inspecting a leaf on

one of the shrub branches leaning over the water, then turned back to Mannion again. "You know what I felt after I shot him?"

"What?"

"I felt I should've done it long ago." James smiled. His eyes were clear and deep. They were a man's eyes.

Mannion was a little off-put by the look the younger man gave him. It worried him. There was such a thing as being overconfident, of feeling you have to prove too much too soon. He didn't voice this feeling, however. The young man was coming into his own, and sometimes that meant paying the price for it, too. No other man could help you with that. Mannion learned that lesson the hard way when his first wife, Sarah, had hanged herself from a cottonwood in their yard in Kansas, when Vangie had been only a few months old.

He'd come into his own too quickly, had spent too much time proving himself a worthy town-taming lawman, spending too much time away from home even though his wife had a sensitive nature, and she'd just had a baby and had gone to dark places in the wake of the delivery.

Apprehension about the younger man's future nettling him, Joe threw back the last of his coffee. "I should go." He went to the door, which was propped open with a rock, and tossed his coffee dregs into the yard. He strode back into the cabin. "I was worried we might've been followed, but I don't think we were." He set his cup on the table and set his hat on his head. "Still..."

"We'll be fine. This cabin's only an hour from town, but few know about it."

Mannion picked up the Yellowboy and set it on his shoulder. "I'll do some investigating in town. I'll ride out here again in a few days. I have a feeling I'll have news by then."

He stretched his lips and lifted his cheeks as he studied the floor, troubled.

"Look," he said, "if your father is the one responsible for killing Giannina's family, don't try to take him on. He has the entire Horsehead roll behind him. That would be foolish."

"What do you propose I do, Marshal?"

"Leave. Take Giannina and leave here. For good. If I have evidence your father is guilty for the killings, I'll wire the chief U.S. marshal in Denver. He'll send a team of deputies out here to arrest your father and the men whom he sent to perform the barbaric deed."

James drew a breath and shrugged. "I reckon we'll just have to see how it shakes down."

Mannion stepped forward. He leaned toward James, one fist on the table. "Don't do that girl out there the added injustice of getting yourself killed, too."

James stared back at him. He pursed his lips and slowly nodded.

Mannion was skeptical his advice had really reached him, but he'd done all he could do. For now. He was glad James and Giannina were out here, well away from town. Out here, they just might have a chance. Meanwhile, Mannion might be able to run the culprits down himself, though he'd meant what he'd said about the marshals. That was what they were for.

He swung around and headed outside.

He rode Red down the bench and into the stream.

"Look!" Giannina said, holding up something in her dripping right hand. She smiled. "A spearhead, I think, no?"

Mannion leaned out from his saddle to get a closer look.

Then he smiled. "I think so, yes." He pinched his hat brim to the girl. "I'll see you again soon, darlin'."

"*Hasta luego. Viaje seguro.*" Travel safe.

Mannion booted Red out of the stream and up the ridge.

CHAPTER 20

A WHICKER FROM INSIDE THE STABLE FLANKING THE cabin woke James from a doze.

Sitting in the log chair outside and to the right of the cabin's door, he lifted his chin, which had sagged nearly to his chest—how long ago, he wasn't sure. He'd come out here at ten, after he and Giannina had finished playing several games of cribbage, using the board and a deck of cards that had been in the cabin for as long as James could remember. He'd had Giannina drop the locking bar into the brackets on each side of the door-frame before she'd gone to bed.

She'd looked up at him, worried. They'd been having such a good time, playing together and laughing as they'd done before the trouble, before James's parents had forbidden him from seeing her again. They'd been having fun together, boxing out the worlds each of them had had to endure when they were apart. But telling Giannina to lock the door behind him had put a pall over everything. She'd looked up at him, remembrance and grief glazing her eyes.

He'd lifted her chin, tipping her head back to face him.

He'd kissed her lovely, swollen lips, and he'd said, "We are going through a tough time here, Giannina. Neither one of us is a kid. We can have our fun, but we have to be tough to match the times we're in. We can survive this, but we can't deny what's happening. I don't want you to be sad. I don't want you to grieve forever. I want you to enjoy the times when we are together. But we must be grown-ups now, and fight for our survival. Do you understand?"

She'd stared up at him for a long time. Gradually, the sadness had left her eyes. The sheen cleared. The emotion had been replaced by a slow-growing, mature determination. Finally, she'd pursed her lips and nodded slowly. "Si. We need to survive. The children stuff in its own time. Now, you must do what you have to do, and I will help you, James. *Mi amore.*"

She'd risen onto her bare toes and returned his kiss with a passionate one of her own.

James smiled at her.

Then he'd gone out and stood on the small wooden stoop. When he'd heard her drop the locking bar into place, he'd gone around behind the cabin to check on the horses in the small log stable with its connecting, unpeeled pine pole corral surrounded by pines.

The horses had been fine, dozing on their feet, heads hanging.

He'd investigated the area surrounding the cabin and stable, moving slowly, looking and listening as his father had taught him to do when they'd gone out hunting together. Hunting trips were the only times James had ever felt close to the man, but even then, if he'd missed a shot or had not shot the deer or elk or bear right where his father had instructed him to, the old man would regard him with disgust and shake his head, as though deeply disappointed in the only son his wife had been able to give him.

There should have been many more, that repelled look had said, that grave look of deep, existential disappointment. So many more boys, strong boys who'd make good men worthy of carrying on the Kincaid name, of taking Grant's place behind the brand when Grant had passed.

When James had satisfied himself that he and Giannina were alone, he'd returned to the cabin stoop and taken up his post in the log chair. He'd kept his eyes and ears skinned, listening and watching intently. The moon was waning and partly concealed by scalloped cloud edges, so the night was dark. Save the howling of a couple of distant coyotes and, at one point, the angry snarl of a hunting wildcat, it was quiet, as well.

James had felt his eyes grow heavy. His chin, as well. Now, as he lifted it, all his senses came alive once more. Again, came a whicker from the stable. A shod hoof struck a stable partition.

A wolf howled mournfully from a ridge to the west.

To James's left came the soft, almost silent crunch of a stealthy foot coming down on pine needles. A man's whisper touched James's ears.

James rose from the pine log chair and slipped quietly, keeping low, around the corner of the cabin. Abutting the cabin's east wall was a pile of moldering stove wood roughly six feet high. He went to the far end of it and crouched down beside it, in the deep shadows on that side of the cabin.

He held his Winchester straight up and down in his hands, the butt on the ground. He thumbed his hat up onto his forehead and leaned forward on the rifle, staring up the dark forested slope rising toward the star-filled sky before him, roughly fifty yards away.

His heart beat slowly, purposefully.

His hands were not shaking. His knees were not quivering.

He was strangely calm. It was like when he'd hunted alone. He'd felt a welcome calm. When his father had joined him, he'd been jumpy from start to finish, wanting to please the man, wanting to gain his respect while knowing it was impossible.

He was alone now. And calm. His mind filled with grim purpose.

He could hear the footsteps clearly now. The soft thuds and crunching sounds grew louder as the stalkers came down the forested ridge. Occasionally, a furtive whisper touched his ears. The soft snap of a twig under a boot.

He stared at the ridge. Presently, he saw shadows move among the dark velvet blanket of the trees. Then three shadows, one after another, slipped out of the blanket of the forest and came out on the flat, sage-peppered clearing—three men crouched low over the rifles in their hands. They made for a large rock ahead of James and to his right, maybe a hundred feet from the cabin.

The lead man was an indistinguishable silhouette, but there was a patch of something pale on him. Then, as he and the others continued to approach, heading for the rock, scurrying rat-like, single-file, James smiled. The patch of white was an arm sling likely made from a torn sheet or a pillowcase.

That would be Wayne Cord. The bunkhouse cook at Horsehead had made him a sling for his right arm. The big, lumbering man behind him would be Max Coffee. The smaller man behind Coffee was Neil Quade.

One by one, they scurried behind the boulder.

Silence. No movement for a time.

Then James saw part of a head slip out from behind the boulder as a man edged a look around it toward the cabin. The man's hat was off. Under the cap of dark hair was the pale oval of a face and a dark mustache mantling the man's upper lip.

Cord.

The head disappeared behind the rock.

Thirty seconds later, Cord stepped out from behind the rock, setting his hat on his head, moving at a crouch toward the cabin, holding his rifle down low in his right hand.

Coffee moved out from behind the rock and fell into step behind him.

Then came Quade, bringing up the rear.

Cord was thirty feet away from James, ahead and to his right, heading for the cabin's front door, which he likely planned to kick open, run in, Quade and Coffee behind him, and begin shooting, filling James and Giannina with hot lead as they slept.

When Cord was twenty feet away from James, James straightened, stepped out away from the stacked stovewood, cocked his rifle loudly, and said, "Nice night fer a killin', eh, fellas?"

They froze and then swung toward James.

Quade gasped, cursed.

"Don't aim them rifles at me, fellas," James warned.

Cord glanced at the men behind him and then turned his head back to James and lowered the barrel of the

Winchester in his hands. Coffee did the same with his Henry. Quade removed his right hand from his carbine's forestock and let the rifle hang straight down against his left leg.

James stared at them over the barrel of his rifle, which he aimed straight out from his right hip. He remained silent. Inwardly, he smiled. He thought he could hear the drumming of the men's hearts from here. He'd let one of them speak next. He was done talking.

They didn't say anything until a minute or so had passed.

Cord cleared his throat and said, "You're makin' a big mistake, James."

"Nope." Smiling with feigned benevolence, James shook his head slowly. "You're the ones who made the mistake comin' here to kill me an' my girl. That was just plain suicidal, Cord."

"Listen to yourself, James!" Cord said, stretching his lips so that James could see the pale line of his teeth in the darkness. "You've gone mad!"

"Doin' what a man has to do ain't madness, Cord. And killin' you three—I see now you aren't gonna let it be any other way. If I don't kill you now, you'll just come after me again. Me an' Giannina. You ain't gonna be able to let it go."

"I can let it go," Neil Quade said quickly. "Hell, I can...I can let it go."

Cord jerked his head to one side. "Shut up, Neil, you yellow-livered dog!"

Coffee, who had a bandage over his nose—a white one but darkened with blood—said, "Cord, now, maybe... maybe..."

"Shut up!"

Cord turned to James. "You've gone wrong, kid. Way

wrong. You let us ride out of here. No need for more shootin'."

James's smile widened. He enjoyed hearing the pleading in the savage man's voice. In the voice of the man who once harassed him terribly, who took great pleasure in harassing the boss's son, knowing that the boss not only allowed it but approved it.

"Nah," James said, again slowly shaking his head. "I don't like you, Cord. Never have. I should've gunned you a long time ago, the first time you ever laid into me, the first time you ever beat me with a coiled lariat. Here tonight, I'm gonna make good on that mistake. You're gonna die, and there's not a damn thing any of you can do about it."

He smiled again.

"You think you're that fast?" Cord said.

"We'll see."

Quade took one step forward, holding up his right gloved hand in supplication. "Kid, now...James..."

"He done killed you, Quade," James said, glancing at Cord. "What do you think of that?"

Quade opened his mouth, but he seemed unable to form words. He stared at James, his eyes glinting fearfully in the darkness.

Silence.

The wolf gave another long, mournful complaint from a distant ridge. It was like a dirge for the man or men who would die here tonight.

The wail seemed to snap the nerves in Coffee. The big man yelled suddenly and snapped his Henry to his shoulder. Flames and smoke spewed from the barrel, drilling the bullet into the dirt halfway between Coffee and James an eighth of a second after James had drilled the big man in the chest.

Cord jerked up his own rifle, which roared, flames lapping from the barrel. The bullet slammed into the log wall behind James, who shot Cord next and Quade after that, as the shorter man held his own rifle straight down and, holding up his supplicating hand, yelled, "No! No! N—"

He crumpled.

Cord was still alive. He lay on his back, breathing hard.

James walked toward him.

Cord stared up at him, chest rising and falling sharply. His wide black eyes glared up at James. He stretched his lips back from his teeth and tried to say something, but he died before he could get any words out, his chest falling still, his body slackening, his head turning to one side. He shivered once, and that was the end of him.

Coffee lay on his side, dead.

Quade stared up at James. "No," he said. "No...I... never...never even raised my gun..."

"You should have," James said, and finished him.

He heard a gasp behind him. He wheeled, levering another round into the Winchester's breech. Another gasp. He saw her standing at the corner of the cabin, a small, slender silhouette against the starry sky behind her.

James let out his held breath, depressed the Winchester's hammer, and lowered the rifle to his side. He moved to Giannina. He took her in his arms and squeezed her reassuringly.

"It's over," he said. "At least for now, it's over." He continued hugging her, his chin on her head. "Tomorrow, I'm gonna teach you how to shoot. All right? How does that sound?"

He smiled down at her.

She gazed up at him, uncertainly. Maybe a little fearfully.

"How does that sound, honey?"

She blinked once. The apprehension remained in her gaze as she said tonelessly, "All right, James."

CHAPTER 21

KATHERINE KINCAID SQUEEZED HER GLASS OF COGNAC so tightly in her hand that Grant was afraid she'd shatter it.

They'd started out this morning drinking only coffee but after Kincaid had gone out to the bunkhouse to give his men their orders for the day, and returned to the house, he'd seen that Katherine had started spiking her post-breakfast coffee with the cognac she'd brought back after her last trip to France.

When they'd finished the coffee and cognac, they'd gone straight to unadulterated cognac, continuing their heated discussion in the parlor of their grand lodge at Horsehead headquarters.

"We simply must do *something* about that boy, Grant. He's become an *abomination*!" She turned from the window, took a quick sip of the cognac, and looked at her husband seated by the cold fireplace in an overstuffed leather chair. "He shot your foreman? His boss! My god! What if the Ramses find out. The Hermans. My god—what if the DuPonts found out. What an embarrassment. Why, I'd be downright mortified if any of our friends from back east learned what our son had become!"

Katherine Kincaid drew a deep, exasperated breath, eyes growing even wider. "What if the senator and Mrs. Buchanon find out, Grant! They'll think we're running an *outlaw* ranch out here!"

Kincaid wasn't sure how to confront this onslaught. The fact was, Katherine was only giving voice to most of his own terrors, which had been lurking around in his semiconsciousness for the past two days. He felt as though he must be asleep and dreaming. No. Having a nightmare like no nightmare he'd ever endured before.

James was supposed to marry Athena Kennecott in one month. Over two hundred guests had been invited. Guests from neighboring ranches, from Denver and Leadville, guests from back east as well as Europe!

Grant wanted to reprimand his wife, as he usually did, for overreacting. But he knew this morning his words would sound hollow. The fact was, Katherine was not exaggerating James's possible damage to the Kincaid name, to the family's reputation. One problem she had not given voice to was the possibility of this problem getting so out of control that they'd never be able to find a worthy husband for Sydney.

Grant took a deep sip of his brandy, tamping down the growing rage and desperation inside him, and quickly refilled his glass.

"Grant!" Katherine said, stirred to an even keener anger by his brooding silence. "What are we going to—"

She was interrupted suddenly by a loud voice clearing.

Grant turned to see his blond-haired, brown-eyed daughter, Sydney, standing in the parlor's arched doorway, brows arched, hands entwined down low before her. She'd been giving her horses a workout and was dressed accordingly so that from a distance, you'd think she were one of Grant's cowpunchers, albeit one especially handy in the saddle, and slender, and one with long, curly blond hair bouncing on her slender shoulders. "Father...Mother," she said in her mock-prim, insouciant way, blinking slowly, "your new foreman is here. Lottiis in the garden, so I let him in."

She wheeled, extending her hand as though introducing an English nobleman to the Kincaid parlor. She canted her head to one side, smiled up at the man with the melodrama of a bad actress, closing her eyes to slits, then tramped back down the hall toward the foyer, her spurs chinging loudly.

Pat Winslow stood in the arched doorway, his hat in his hands, chin down, as though he were a schoolboy summoned by a schoolmarm after an especially raucous recess.

"What is it, Pat?" Kincaid prompted.

"Sir, I think you'd better have a look for yourself."

"A look at what?" both Kincaid and Katherine said at the same time.

Keeping his chin down, looking at Kincaid from beneath his brows, the foreman wagged his head once, wincing, and said, "Uh...think you better have a look for yourself, sir."

Kincaid glanced at his wife. She beetled her brows uneasily.

"Gonna have to take a ride," the foreman added.

"Ride?" Kincaid said. "To where?"

Again, the foreman winced and gave his head a single shake. "Best wait an' see for yourself."

Again, Kincaid and his wife shared an uneasy, incredulous glance.

Kincaid stared at his foreman. Then he said, "All

right, all right." He threw back the last of his cognac and rose from his chair. The foreman turned and led him down the meandering corridor to the foyer, not knowing that Sydney was in the kitchen, her back to the wall opening onto the foyer, eavesdropping.

Her quickening heart skipped beats.

———

IN THE FOYER, WINSLOW INFORMED KINCAID THAT he'd have to ride out with him and C.J. Harriman and Tyrell Brand to see what Winslow wanted him to see.

The incredulous rancher retrieved his shell belt and pearl-gripped .45 Peacemaker and high-crowned gray Stetson from his study. Wearing the gun and the hat as well as a light denim jacket against the midmorning chill, he followed the foreman outside where both Harriman and Brand sat their mounts, leaning forward against their saddle horns, dark looks in their eyes.

Kincaid removed the reins of his big lineback dun from the hitchrack and scowled at Winslow. "What in holy blazes are you about to show me?"

"Like I said, boss," Winslow said, swinging up onto the back of his own horse and settling himself. "Best if you see—"

"Yes, I know, I know," Kincaid said, climbing into his own saddle with a grunt. "Best if I see for myself."

Winslow led the way out of the Horsehead headquarters, several men eyeing them bleakly from various points around the ranch yard. Once through the portal and out of the yard, Kincaid rode up beside Winslow at half a gallop. Harriman and Brand rode behind them. They followed the two-track trail out toward the main trail that led to town, but well before they reached the trail to town, Winslow slowed his mount to the left of Kincaid's.

The rancher turned to the man, frowning.

Then he turned his head forward and let the question he was about to ask die on his lips.

Winslow checked his mount down to a walk. Kincaid did likewise.

Slowly, they approached a large cottonwood that stood at a fork in the trail, one tine jogging off toward the Horsehead's western range, the other tine leading to the Horsehead's southern range. From one of the cottonwood's stout branches, three hanged men twisted and turned slowly in the morning breeze.

At first, Kincaid assumed the three were rustlers, as it was his policy to hang rustlers as a warning to others who might have the same idea.

But then, as the lineback dun brought him closer to the tree, he began to make out the features of the three men, including the long, broad-shouldered body of his former ramrod, Wayne Cord, whose small, black eyes and dragoon-style mustache were unmistakable. The points of a green silk neckerchief fluttered in the breeze around his neck, poking out from behind the stout rope knotted around the same. The other two were the big, red-bearded Max Coffee and the shorter, stocky, square-headed blond, Neil Quade.

Kincaid nudged the dun up close to the tree for a thorough appraisal.

The three former Horsehead hands almost looked like they could have been sleeping, hanging there, Cord's and Quade's heads canted to one side, Coffee's chin dipped nearly to his chest.

Only, their eyes were open, and cast with the same terror with which they must have regarded the man who'd killed them. Especially the eyes of Cord and Quade, who each had the puckered blue holes of bullets in their foreheads. Finishing shots likely delivered at close range, judging by the powder burns around the wounds. Blood stained their shirts and vests, as well. Coffee had apparently died from the single wound to his chest. There'd been no need to waste a second bullet on the big man.

The ropes creaked softly as the breeze nudged the bodies.

Already, the birds had been at them, pecking at their faces, at Quade's right eye.

Kincaid jerked with an embarrassing start when Winslow cleared his throat only a few feet away on his left. Preoccupied, the rancher hadn't realized his new foreman had moved that close to him.

Winslow said, "Any idea who might've done this, uh, Mr. Kincaid?"

Kincaid turned his hard gaze to the man, who flushed a little, the blood rising in his fair cheeks above his sandy blond mustache and goatee. The man's pale blue eyes acquired a sheepish cast. He knew as well as Kincaid did who had shot and then hanged these men on Horsehead range, likely as a warning of sorts.

Imagine James Kincaid warning his father while at the same time mocking his practice of hanging rustlers.

Warning him of what?

James.

James!

Kincaid stared back at his foreman, his steady stare belying the turmoil in his heart, the apprehension and incomprehension that was tying his insides in knots.

"Cut them down. Haul them over to Crow Canyon and toss them in. The wolves and wildcats will take care of them." Kincaid paused, glanced at the other two men flanking him and his new foreman, then returned his gaze to Winslow. "Not a word of this to anyone. Understand? Not to the rest of the men, not to anyone." Through a grimace, emotion sparking his otherwise stony eyes, he added, "Not for the rest of your days. Do you understand me?"

The others regarded him gravely.

"Right," Winslow muttered, nodding, then sliding his gaze to the other two. "Of course, boss. Not a word."

"*Not one word!*" Kincaid barked, startling all three horses.

"Of course, boss," said C.J. Harriman, holding his reins back taut against his chest. "You got it."

"Get it done. I'm heading to town. Got business to take care of."

Kincaid put the dun around the tree and continued toward the main trail to town.

———

An hour later, just after entering the raggedy outskirts of Battle Mountain town, Kincaid put the dun up the steep, switchback trail that led up to the formidable Victorian mansion that always appeared to him more like some misplaced medieval castle or maybe some fort—a bastion against the savages that had once populated this isolated country—that the conquistadors had left behind.

"The savages that had *once* populated this country."

Kincaid laughed as the dun topped the ridge and rode across the broad, deep, hard-packed yard toward the front of the sun-splashed dwelling. He had enough self-awareness to know that he was one of those savages. He stopped the dun and stared up at the tower from which Hayward Kennecott had hanged himself when his mine had gone belly up. "And she was, too...from the tips of her shoes, custom made in Italy and sent here via clipper ship, train, and stage...to her carefully cut and styled hair, usually done by someone she brought in from Boston... despite that, she was a known recluse and hardly ever staged the balls and parties she'd so pined to do when Hayward had been alive.

Yes, they killed men easily, though they always hired it done, of course. No blood on their hands.

Ha!

Kincaid and Ruth Kennecott were savages. Every bit as savage as those Red Men who'd once called this wild, stark, up-and-down country home. She may not have seen herself that way, but he was seeing himself that way now, having stared up at the terrified, infuriated eyes of the three men his own son had shot and hanged on his, Grant's, own land as trophies of sorts.

Mocking how Grant had raised him. Hadn't Grant wanted James to be the son, the kind of *man* who could hang men on Horsehead range as a warning to others? Without so much as flinching or batting an eye?

Well, he'd accomplished that task, all right.

But now Grant was the one being warned. Mocked. Threatened.

"Grant?"

Kincaid shuttled his gaze back to the high, stone tower. Ruth Kennecott stood on the balcony that ringed it a hundred feet above the ground. Her dark hair was neatly coifed and secured tightly behind her head. She wore a dark-blue gown trimmed with black lace and scalloped white edges at the neck and cuffs. The breeze buffeted the long, pleated skirt around her legs. Her pale, beringed hands rested on the balcony rail from which her husband had hanged himself early one morning for all the town to see.

She canted her head to indicate the office behind her and then turned and strode through the two open French doors flanking the balcony.

Kincaid gigged the lineback ahead, toward the plump Black woman holding open one of the two thick oak doors above the stone steps, smiling broadly.

"Well, good mornin', Master Kincaid. Good mornin', sir. Mighty nice one, I would say. The missus—why, she'll be delighted to see you. You're just in time for lunch. I'll send for big Hans to put up your horse!"

CHAPTER 22

A HALF-HOUR LATER, LOTTIE REFILLED KINCAID'S WINE glass.

She refilled Ruth Kennecott's glass where the lady of the house sat in all her prim, moody refinement at the head of the table, to Grant's left. Apparently, Miss Athena did not take meals at the table. At least, she wasn't today. Kincaid had heard Lottie climbing the stairs; he assumed Miss Athena was taking her noon dinner in her room somewhere in the high reaches of the oddly structured, coldly elegant house.

Possibly, Athena was too embarrassed to be in Grant's presence. Since her and James's marriage, which had been in preparation for over a year, had been postponed, though not officially so, her humiliation was likely too keen to share a meal with the father of the boy who was on course to leave her at the proverbial altar.

Kincaid didn't blame the girl.

He didn't blame her mother for the chilly reception he'd so far received today, either.

Grant glanced at the woman as she primly cut into a thick chunk of exquisitely roasted beef. Ruth Kennecott reminded him so much of his wife in the hard outer shell she'd had to acquire to survive here on the savage frontier, running a household and keeping a business solvent, that their likenesses never ceased to amaze him. He was sure that if he died before she did, Katherine would have no trouble comfortably slipping into the rugged hide of owner and operator of the Horsehead.

Already, having kept their books since he'd married her twenty-five years ago, she knew more about their investments and finances than he did. She didn't get out of the house often—usually just when socializing at neighboring ranches—but when she did, she almost always offered sound advice on some practical element of rangeland management or animal husbandry: "Grant, don't you think that big Galloway bull should be paired with those cows with longhorn blood that you pushed onto the home pasture last week? I think their calves might turn out far heftier than the spindly little urchins they'd dropped so far, afraid of their own shadows!"

Kincaid drew a deep breath, let it out slow as he ladled dark-brown gravy onto his mashed potatoes and then returned the ladle to the silver boat on the white-clothed table before him. He just forked up a mouthful of the potatoes and gravy when Ruth sipped her wine, set her glass back down on the table, and said, "So, Grant, are we going to be so civilized as to not breech the subject of what's eating you until we've finished the meal?"

Kincaid halted the fork halfway to his mouth. He turned to her and said, "It be best. What's eating me is rather, uh...well...it's rather distasteful, Ruth." Of course, he'd hanged enough men that to have recently seen three more—even if they had been men he'd known and worked with for several years—had done nothing to sour his appetite. Ruth was as tough as Katherine. Tough as whang leather. Still, the hanged men were not for the dinner table. Unless he cut down on the details, but he thought she should know it all.

He wanted her to know it all. After all, she'd instigated it. He was sure of that.

Not that he'd been compelled to carry out the dirty deed himself. Of attacking the Calderons. But Ruth had actually gone through with it.

She studied him closely, thin brows mantling her light-brown eyes. "Are we going to call the marriage off, Grant? Is that what you came to tell me?" Of course, doing so would be as uncomely for Ruth Kennecott as it would be for the Kincaids, for she'd sent out her invitations, as well. Locally as well as far and wide.

Still, who did she have to blame but herself?

Trying so hard to get ahead in a man's world had caused her to go too far. Way too far, indeed.

"I don't think we have to go that far just yet, Ruth." Kincaid set his fork back down on his plate and wiped his mouth with his napkin. He sipped his wine. "At least, not yet. I can track down my son, and I might be able to talk some sense into him. I might be able to make him understand you made a mistake. A terrible mistake. But one made out of—"

"What?" Ruth's brows beetled more severely than before. She chuckled with deep incredulity and said, "What mistake did *I* make? It was *you* who attacked the Calderon farm!"

Now Kincaid felt his own, shaggy brows beetle over his eyes. "What? I did no such thing, Ruth. It had to be you. You're the only one—other than myself, that is— who had reason to make sure that girl was out of James's life." He paused, parrying Ruth's stupefied gaze with one of his own. "So he could marry Athena, and our families would be joined by marriage as well as..." He'd gradually let his voice trail off to bewildered silence.

Slowly, the woman shook her head. "I did no such thing, Grant. Further, I never would have even *considered* such a thing. My god. What kind of barbarian do you think I am?"

Anger rose in him. "What kind of barbarian do you think *I* am, Ruth?"

"Hah!" She sat back in her chair, laughing, wiping her mouth with her napkin. "Everyone within a thousand square miles knows what a savage you are. You don't do a very good job of covering your tracks, Grant!"

Kincaid's anger turned to rage. He slammed his fist down on the table, rattling the silver and china, and rose from his chair so quickly he almost knocked it over backwards. He strode to a window, laid one arm across his chest, lifted his other hand to his mouth, and ran his index finger across his upper lip in deep consternation.

"If not you," he muttered, "who?"

His mind swirled like a flooded arroyo in the middle of a mountain storm.

Ruth got up from the table, tossed her napkin onto the chair and strode to him, concern darkening her eyes. "Grant, if not *you*, who?"

Grant kept his gaze to the north, toward where the Sangre de Cristos humped up darkly in the far distance, the San Juans beyond them to the northwest. He saw neither range, however. His attention was riveted on the problem at hand.

Had someone else, some other area rancher, perhaps, wanted to destroy the chances of the Kincaids and the Kennecotts coming together through marriage as well as business?

If so, they likely couldn't have imagined what a keg of dynamite they'd set a match to in Kincaid's own son, the previously spineless, gutless James!

They were probably laughing into their hats.

"Grant," Ruth said, standing before him, hands hanging straight down at her sides, "where is James?" She took one step closer and to his left, trying to get him to look at her. "You have to talk to him. You have to convince him that neither I nor you—if your denial is true—had anything to do with the cold-blooded murder of that...that...that *girl's* family. You must also convince him that that girl is not marriage material. My god—what is he thinking? Does he not have any idea what it would do to our reputations, not to mention to both of our future business ventures, if he..."

"I know! I know, Ruth!" Kincaid said, finally shuttling his attention from the window to the woman standing in desperate beseeching before him. "Believe me, I know what it would do."

"I knew he was weak," Ruth said, wheeling, giving Kincaid her back, taking three steps away from him and crossing her arms on her chest. "I thought that meant he'd be...he'd be, well...*malleable*. I also thought he'd make a good father." She glanced over her shoulder at Kincaid. "Not domineering, like you. Or like myself, for that matter, if you must know."

"Oh, I know!" Kincaid laughed drolly.

"Can you find him? Can you talk to him? Can you *reason* with him?"

Kincaid drew a deep breath and returned his attention to the window. Again, he raised a hand to his mouth, squeezing his lower lip worriedly between index finger and thumb. "I don't know. Doubtful, actually, after today."

He hadn't intended to say that last part aloud. He'd decided to not tell her about the especially tart bit of nastiness he'd witnessed earlier on Horsehead range. The ripe fruit hanging from the cottonwood.

But why not? Let her hear it and let her make up her own mind about what may or may not be able to be done about his obviously mad son.

"Earlier," he said, staring out the window again, worrying his bottom lip between thumb and index finger, "my men showed me three men. Three of my own former hands including my foreman, Wayne Cord, hanging from a cottonwood where the trail to the Horsehead leads to the main road to town. That's where I've hung rustlers in the past, I don't mind admitting. Hey, it works...at least for a time, at least for all but the especially tough and defiant long-loopers, those that figure they have bones to pick with the Horsehead."

"Who hanged those men, Grant?"

He lowered his hand and turned to her, smiling. "Why, James did, of course. Who else?"

She opened her mouth nearly a full minute before any words slipped between them. "Are you sure? I mean, how can you be sure it was James?"

"It was James. Take my word for it, Ruth. The previous day, he shot and wounded Cord. Cord had been about to shoot Bloody Joe Mannion. James had saved him. Now I've been told the two are riding together. Protecting the girl over at Ma Lonnigan's Continental Hotel."

"I heard they were at the hotel."

"After what he did last night, I doubt they still are."

"Where, then?"

Kincaid shrugged and shook his head.

She moved to him again, wrapped her fingers around

his wrist and squeezed. "You have to find him. Reason with him."

"If he can be reasoned with. I'm not sure at this point."

Ruth studied him darkly. "My god, Grant. What did you do to that boy?"

Again, anger rose in Kincaid. He bunched his lips and hardened his jaws. "What I did was try to make a man of him. From an early age, he was timid and weak. He let the men make fun of him because he walked funny and couldn't sit on a horse for more than a few seconds before bawling. Hell, Sydney at twelve years old was twice the man he'd ever be!"

"Or so you thought."

He had no response to that.

"Now he's gone wild on you."

Kincaid looked out the window again, filled his lungs with air and let it out slowly.

"I think we're going to have to bite the bullet, Grant."

He glanced at her, frowning. "What do you mean?"

"We're going to have to cancel the wedding. Send out all those humiliating letters and cables." She lowered her chin and pressed the heels of her hands to her temples.

A knock sounded on the dining room door.

Clearing her throat of the emotion lodged there like a prune pit, Ruth turned, lowering her hands and smoothing her skirt down against her thighs. "Come, Lottie."

The door opened. It was not Lottie who poked her head into the vast dining room, which seemed all the vaster for there being only two place settings and only a few dishes on one end of the table. Athena frowned beautifully. She made every expression beautiful, Kincaid thought. Oh, to have some of her blood in his family, in his grandchildren. He couldn't wait for Sydney.

The girl's blue eyes glinted in the sunlight angling in over Kincaid's shoulder.

"Athena..." Ruth said, haltingly.

"Is everything all right, Mother?" asked the young lady clad in a fetching, light green skirt and a light tan blouse that accentuated her chestnut hair. "I heard... raised voices." She shifted her clear, intelligent gaze between the two people standing on the opposite side of the table from her.

"Everything is fine, dear. You know how I and Grant are. Passionate about our endeavors." She smiled. "Did you finish trimming the roses?"

"No," the girl said, smiling then herself. "But I will."

She withdrew her head and closed and latched the door.

Kincaid turned to Ruth. "Does she know?"

"God, no. She thinks we'll be having you and Katherine and James in for dinner one of these nights to start making the *final* preparations."

"She knows nothing. Even about...the girl..."

"I shouldn't think so. She lives in a sealed world up here. One sealed for her benefit. She knows that. The only time she gets away is to go riding with your Sydney. I'm so thankful Sydney has taken Athena under her wing. It's good for her to go out for a ride, to learn about horses, to have a friend in Sydney. By the way—thank you for the horse, Grant."

"Oh, it was nothing, nothing. Glad to help. I'm sure Sydney hasn't told her. We've discussed Athena's delicate nature, Sydney and I and her mother."

"My god, if she did know, it would...it would...well, I don't know *what* it would do to her."

Ruth's eyes acquired a speculative cast. She slid them toward the door, pensive.

"What is it?" Kincaid prodded.

She held her gaze on the door for several more stretched seconds, unblinking. Then she blinked and shook her head. "Nothing. It's nothing. Just foolishness. This entire charade has me fit to be tied."

"Me too."

"What are you going to do, Grant?"

"I'm going to talk to Mannion. I have a feeling he might be the instigator, the *puppet master* behind all of this. Ol' Bloody Joe!"

Ruth stared at him, her eyes hard, commanding. She moved toward him again and gazed up at him. "He's gone rogue on you, Grant, I think. You know what happens when they go rogue...men as well as animals."

Grant just stared back at her, again finding no words with which to respond.

"If they can't be brought to heel..." Ruth nibbled a thumbnail and arched a brow. Her eyes hardened, showing the savage lurking behind the isinglass of her cool, intelligent gaze. "They must be hunted down and..." Again, she let the sentence trail away to silence.

She almost smiled.

My god, Kincaid thought.

She wants revenge.

CHAPTER 23

MANNION HAD RIDDEN BACK INTO BATTLE MOUNTAIN town in the midafternoon of the previous day. He'd checked on Sylvan Story and the man's prisoner, Buzzard Lee. Finding them both in their rightful places, he had an early supper before taking a swing through town, looking for Harry Marcum. Seeing no sign of the man, and not seeing the six horses he figured belonged to Buzzard's bunch at either of the hitchracks fronting the saloons, he stabled Red, went to bed, and took another swing through town early the next morning.

Still spying no sign of the dry-gulching Marcum nor the six toughnuts he presumed were Buzzard Lee's bunch, he took a ride into the desert west of town, hoping to draw out Marcum. Story didn't need his help, as when Mannion had checked on him, Sylvan had Willis Reed and Eddie Shoots-the-Coyote as well as the top dog in the threesome, Omar Sledge, taking up desultory positions on his stoop—all three deputized in case Buzzard's bunch came calling.

In the desert outside town, Joe saw no sign of

Marcum. Not so much as a mare's tail of dust drifting across his back trail.

In the midafternoon, he rode back to town in frustration.

As had become his habit since visiting the dying former boomtown which had now become a cauldron of howling, feasting, drinking, and carousing devils, though the streets were deserted this time of the day, he raked his gaze across the rooftops on both sides of the main street, and in the shadows angling out from the town's east side as the sun angled down in the west.

As he approached the Blue Dog Saloon on the street's right side, cloaked in shadows, he noted the dozen saddled horses tied to one of the hitchracks fronting the place. At the hitchracks of the other saloon a little farther up the street and on the street's left side, the Holy Moses, only four horses stood, heads drooping.

The Blue Dog was doing a better business.

Hmm.

As he put Red on past the place, Joe scratched his neck and scrunched up his freshly sunburned face, the deep lines around his gray eyes and his mouth crusted with trail dust. He couldn't help being curious about the Blue Dog's clientele. Possibly, Buzzard Lee's bunch was there.

He neck-reined Red around sharply and put him up to the hitchrack with the fewest horses tied to it. He had to admit that after the ride up to the old trapper's cabin the day before and his frustrating ride into the country again today, he was dying for a drink, though he knew he should wait at least until five o'clock. But, hell, he was on a vacation of sorts, he told himself, despite knowing that wasn't true—he was in Battle Mountain on business that turned out to have become prolonged due to unforeseen complications—namely, James Kincaid and Harry Marcum.

He wondered if Marcum might be milling among the men who belonged to the horses tethered to the hitchracks fronting the Blue Dog. Sometimes, the best place for a man to hide was among other men. Joe was sure that if Buzzard Lee's pards had busted him out of Sylvan Story's jail, he'd have seen some indication of it by now—some scurrying among the more law-abiding residents of Battle Mountain, possibly even a makeshift, reluctant posse being formed to go after the varmints. Some of the lawless might even go after the bunch, since several, including Buzzard Lee, had considerable bounties on their heads.

Mannion snorted as he wrapped Red's reins around the hitchrack.

Men with bounties on their heads going after men with bounties on their heads.

What was the world coming to?

Ah, hell, he thought, stepping up onto the boardwalk and batting his hat against his black denim trousers, making dust billow. The world had gone to hell in a handbasket a long damn time ago. It was just so bad it always *seemed* worse.

Mannion chuckled at his dark turn of mind, knowing his thoughts had soured and were growing even more sour knowing someone was still out to kill the lovely young Giannina Calderon. Why, he had no idea.

He pushed through the batwings and stepped to one side, quickly scanning the room.

All faces turned to him.

A few he recognized.

Six shaggy, bearded men clad in ragged trail garb sat at two round tables pushed together, drinking whiskey and playing poker. Mannion was sure they were Buzzard's men, but he couldn't be sure. A big, shaggy-headed, shaggy-bearded man had a patch over one eye. Pistols bristled on their hips. A sawed-off, double-barrel shotgun lay across the seat of an otherwise empty chair beside one of the men—a tall, yellow-haired albino who would be Victor Sanchez, who hipped around in his chair, staring at Joe. He looked Mannion up and down with his odd, colorless gaze, then grinned, showing a mouthful of chipped, crooked, tobacco-rimmed teeth.

Sanchez turned forward in his chair, and the poker game resumed.

When the other drinkers in the room had gone back to drinking and chinning, Mannion saw that the room was being served by a big, buxom woman in a black skirt and plain white blouse, the sleeves rolled to her pale elbows. Mannion headed for a table on the room's far side and sat down with his back to the wall.

With a sigh, he tossed his hat on the table and scrubbed his fingers through his hair, scratching his sweaty scalp. He dug his makins sack out of his shirt pocket, leaned forward, resting his elbows on the table, and built a quirley. He'd just fired the cigarette to life, smoke billowing around his head, when the big-serving lady, small dark eyes buried in the pale suet of her face, stopped at his table and said wearily, "What's yours?"

"Gimme a double shot of whiskey and a beer, honey."

"I ain't your honey," she said, again wearily, turned, and began ambling toward the bar.

When she'd brought the whiskey and the beer, Mannion threw back half the shot and sipped the beer to wash down the burn of the tarantula juice—which was so bad that to Mannion, a true connoisseur of rotgut, it was good—then leaned back in his chair with a sigh. He was silently, half-amusedly appraising the saloon, which was again filled with enough bounty money to paste a great, big coyote grin on any bounty hunter's greedy mug, when he saw Sylvan Story walk past the large, dirty window on which *BLUE DOG SALOON* was stenciled in blocky, black lettering, facing the street.

Story passed from Mannion's right to his left, heading for the batwings. He'd likely come from the jailhouse. Worry nipped at the edge of Mannion's consciousness. He hoped Buzzard Lee, whose unwelcome company he'd had to endure all the way down here from Del Norte, hadn't somehow gotten himself sprung from Story and the town marshal's three part-time deputies. Mannion wouldn't put it past those three to throw in with Buzzard.

Story pushed his big, ungainly frame through the batwings. He was flushed and breathing hard and Mannion hoped it was only from the long trek—for a man of Story's size—from the jailhouse. Story's squint-eyed gaze swept the room. The outlaws regarded him only in passing, with no interest whatever. They apparently were not only unafraid of Battle Mountain's lone lawdog, they had no respect for him, either. That was all right. Sylvan didn't require respect. He just wanted to remain on this side of the sod until he could retire and fish in the mountains until the angels called him home.

Story's gaze settled on Mannion, and he ambled forward, weaving through the tables.

"How'd you know I was here?" Mannion asked as Story kicked a chair out from his table, across from Joe.

Story slacked into the chair and gave a wry grin. "Oh, I know everything that goes on around here, Joe. I might not do much about most of it, but I know, all right." He winked and added proudly, "I got my spies. Besides," he added, dryly, "I seen you ride in when I was over at the Western Union office."

Joe chuckled.

"What happened?"

Story frowned. "Huh?"

"What're you doin' here? I figure somethin' must've happened."

"Oh, nothin'. Nothin' happened. Except the judge is on his way here. In fact, he should be here by now. There was some trouble with the telegraph lines, and I didn't get the cable until a few minutes ago, but it was sent early this morning from Cosmo, only about thirty miles southeast of here. The judge was just then pulling out with his team. He should be here anytime. I still got Reed and Eddie-Shoots-the-Coyote guarding Buzzard. Don't know where Sledge took off to. He's peculiar, that one."

"I see." Mannion threw the rest of his whiskey back. "I thought maybe somethin' was wrong."

"No, no. Nothin's wrong." Story leaned forward, resting his arms on the table and entwining his fingers. He crumpled his face up as though with concern, and said, "That's sort of the problem."

"What is?"

Story glanced over his shoulder at the six men, including Victor Sanchez. He turned back to Joe, and said, "They'd been around town for the past two days. Ain't made a single move to bust Buzzard out of the hoosegow."

"You're sure those are Buzzard's men? I think the albino's Sanchez, but I only know him from his likeness on a wanted dodger from a long time ago."

Story smiled wolfishly. "Like I said, I got my spies... an' informants. They scratch my back..."

"And you scratch theirs."

"How'd ya know?" the town marshal of Battle Mountain said through another wolfish grin.

He glanced over his shoulder again and when he turned forward, he was frowning again, incredulous. "What do you suppose they're waitin' for? I hate waitin' for trouble. Just makes my nerves raw." He was squeezing his hands together as though he were trying to crack a walnut between his palms. He glanced at the big clock over the bar. "I wish the judge would get here. He'd hold the trial over in the old church and since the gallows is all but knocked together, he could hang Buzzard before the sun goes down."

"I'm sure he'll be here soon, the judge," Mannion said, taking another sip of his beer. "Rough country between here and Cosmo."

"Yeah, yeah—I'm just edgy, that's all."

"Oh, oh," Joe said.

He'd caught sight of a big man with a broad, red, severely weathered face pull up to one of the hitchracks fronting the Blue Dog, on a rangy, lineback dun.

"What is it—they stirrin'?" Story said, casting another, more cautious look behind him and lowering one hand beneath the table.

"Nah, nah. It's Grant Kincaid."

As his own dust swept over him from behind, the tall, middle-aged but still sturdy-looking rancher swung down from the leather. He blinked against the dust and slapped his hat against his whipcord trousers, making even more dust rise. His horse was blowing hard and glistening with sweat from a long, hard ride.

"Now, how in hell does everybody know I'm here?" Mannion asked.

"Oh, don't worry." Story leaned low across the table,

again grinning. "He's got his spies, too. I only got 'em in town but he's got 'em all over the county an' he even has a good many in Denver. Or maybe he just recognized ol' Red." He gave a mulish laugh, heavy shoulders jerking, then pushed to his feet. "I'll let you two palaver in private."

He winked at Mannion and added, "Good luck, Joe."

Story retraced his route through the saloon and reached the batwings just as the rancher pushed through them. Story stepped to one side, grinning like the cat that ate the canary. Kincaid looked him up and down, scowling, then surveyed the room before resting his gaze on Mannion on the far side of the room. He took one more look of vague disgust at Story, flaring a nostril. He regarded the unscrubbed, gun-hung, obvious outlaws populating the room as though he'd found himself in a rattlesnake nest—which, in a way, he had...a nest of human rattlesnakes—then made his way to Mannion's table.

He gazed down at the lawman with an expression similar to the one he'd given Story and then removed his gray Stetson, set it on the table, and slacked into Story's chair. He ran a hand back through his hair, slid the chair up close to the table, and rested his elbows on the edge of it.

"Where's my son, Mannion?"

With the thumb and index finger of his left hand, keeping the right one free, Mannion absently turned his half-empty beer schooner on the table, in its circular water ring. "Can't tell you that."

"Can't or won't?"

"Won't."

Kincaid gritted his teeth. "He's my son!"

"The way I see it, I'm doing you a favor. You turned

that kid against you. He's as likely to shoot you as look at you."

Kincaid sat back in his chair. When the barmaid sidled up to the table, tentatively, he waved her away without ordering anything, keeping his scowling gaze on Mannion sitting on the other side of the table from him. "You did this to him. It was you. He was never like this before you showed up, *Bloody Joe!*" He added that last with a darkening of his gaze and curling of his upper lip. "Before you came, he..."

"Was a dog you laid into pretty good with a short stick. You and your foreman."

Kincaid sat glaring at Mannion, his broad chest rising and falling slowly, heavily. His lips were pursed; Joe could hear him breathing through his nose.

"He killed Cord, Coffee, and Quade—didn't he?"

Mannion frowned. "I don't know—did he?"

"He shot all three, hauled them onto Horsehead range, and hanged them where he knew I'd find them."

The information surprised Mannion. But then he remembered the riders he thought he'd spied on his back trail the day before.

Joe couldn't help giving a wry half smile at the irony, of the poetic justice the kid—who was no longer a kid, to Bloody Joe's way of thinking—had delivered to his old man on a steaming platter. On the other hand, James worried him, also. He was mad. Fighting mad. Running off his leash. He may have gone too far. Around here, that was likely to get him killed. The girl, too.

Kincaid leaned forward again. "Did you put him up to that?"

Apparently, Kincaid hadn't sicked the three now-dead hands after James. They must have trailed him, the girl, and Mannion to the cabin all of their own, likely vengeance-seeking accord.

Joe shook his head. "You did, Kincaid. You did." He took a big drink of his beer, set the schooner down, and added, tightly, "You may know how to raise horses and cattle, but you know nothing about raising sons."

Kincaid bunched his lips and slammed the edge of his fist down on the table. "I tried to make a man of him, dammit!"

Ignoring the incredulous, curious glances being sent his and the rancher's way from around the room, Joe said, "Well, you did that. You made a man of him—one with one hell of a big chip on his shoulder."

Again, the red-faced rancher slammed his fist down on the table in fury. "I didn't kill the Calderons, dammit!"

"Don't matter. He thinks you did. Now, you might just as well have." Mannion narrowed his calm, brooding, gray-eyed gaze at Kincaid. "He's comin' for you. Sooner or later. He'll have his justice. If I was you, I'd find out who did kill the Calderons. That may be the only way you'll be able to get him to pull your horns in. That said, Kincaid, don't think he'll ever..."

Mannion let his voice trail off. He'd just seen a man standing at the bar scrutinizing him in the backbar mirror. When Joe's eyes had met his scrutinizer's, the man had jerked his gaze down and pulled his black hat down low on his forehead. Joe frowned, danger bells tolling in his ears.

Kincaid cast him an annoyed look. "Don't think he'll ever *what*?" he asked.

"See you as his father again. Your wife as his mother." Mannion narrowed an eye at the man. "You have no one to blame but yourself. You're the one who's been burning bridges. James is likely to finish the job and ride the hell out of here with the girl he loves, and you an' the devil can take the hindmost, Kincaid!"

"You go to hell, Man—"

"*Down!*" Mannion shouted, cutting the man off as Joe bounded up from his chair, shucking both his silver-chased Russians from their holsters.

During the tirade he'd lashed at Kincaid, he'd watched with one eye the suspicious-looking gent step too casually back from the bar, turn to his left, away from Joe, and then walk slowly and far too furtively, with obviously feigned nonchalance, toward the batwings.

Kincaid threw himself from his chair as Mannion leveled both Russians and bellowed, "Turn to stone, Harry Marcum, or you're wolf bait!"

The tall, pale, long-faced man wearing a black frock coat over a crisp white shirt and black vest, a ribbon tie knotted at his throat, swung around quickly, lithe as a panther. As he did, he filled his pale, long-fingered hands, a gold ring glittering on his left index finger, with his own two Colts. He was a blur of quick motion. Even though Joe had both of his Russians cocked and extended over his and Kincaid's table, Marcum almost got a shot off before both of Mannion's Russians leaped and roared in his hands, smoke puffing, orange flames stabbing from the maws.

Marcum screamed and fired his Colt into the ceiling as he went staggering backward, tripping over his own, black-booted feet. He got his feet set just in front of the batwings. Wailing, blood pumping from the twin holes in his chest, he brought both Colts down. His dark eyes narrowed along his long, hawk-like nose in his waxy-pale face, but just as he started to thumb back both hammers, Mannion's twin Russians roared once more, both bullets blowing the lunatic regulator and major thorn in

Mannion's ass, backward through the batwings and into the street.

A loud thud rose as he dropped. Through the gap beneath the louver doors and the floor, Mannion saw the man's boots shake as the regulator Harry Marcum shook hands with the devil in the smoking bowels of hell.

Mannion swung both smoking Russians toward the rest of the room and clicked the hammers back.

Several of the other wolves in the room had slapped leather, enervated gazes locking on Mannion.

Those hands froze. Those enervated eyes gradually turned away from Mannion, acquiring sheepish casts.

"Good god—what in holy hell was all that about?" This from Grant Kincaid, pushing himself up off the floor, creakily, brushing sawdust from his brown corduroy jacket and black trousers.

Mannion only half heard him. He'd just realized the room was considerably less crowded than it had been a few minutes ago. The table at which the six men whom Joe figured were the surviving members of Buzzard Lee's bunch had been vacated. Only empty beer bottles, shot glasses, whiskey bottles, and two overfilled ashtrays remained.

Joe slowly lowered his Russians, scowling curiously at the table.

The six toughnuts must have slipped out of the saloon when Mannion had been preoccupied with Kincaid.

Now, he remembered what Story had told him.

The circuit-riding judge was on his way to Battle Mountain town.

The six surviving members of Buzzard's bunch might have ridden out to welcome him with open arms. Or, more likely, hot lead.

Mannion pouched his pistols and ran across the room and through the batwings.

Behind him, Grant Kincaid shouted, "Get back here, Mannion. I'm not done with you!"

But Mannion was already in the saddle and galloping hard toward the east end of town and the open desert beyond.

CHAPTER 24

BEING JOSTLED AROUND IN THE FORMER STAGECOACH he'd had specially outfitted for his own specialized traveling needs, circuit-riding Judge Truman G. Newberry lowered his red silk neckerchief from his nose and mouth, slid the green, gilt-edged velveteen curtain away from the window on his left, and yelled up to the jehu in his froggy baritone, "Time for a nature break, Norbert. That carne asada I had in Cosmo has burned plum through my old entrails and is threatening to fill my drawers!"

"We're only a couple of miles outta Battle Mountain, Judge," came the driver's muffled response beneath the thunder of the stage's four-horse hitch as well as the clomping of the mounts on either side of the coach astride which the judge's two personal bodyguards rode—each a grim-faced, duster-clad, moon-and-star-wearing deputy U.S. marshal.

Clinging to one of the long leather loops hanging from the ceiling, the judge removed his stovepipe hat and poked his bony, nearly bald, bespectacled head out the window once more. He blinked against the infernal, billowing dust and roared, "That was a request, Norbert! Stop this contraption, or I'll have you bullwhipped!"

"Whatever you say, Judge! Whatever you say!" came the yelled response, followed by, "Whoa, ladies an' gentleman! Whoaaahhhhh!"

As the coach immediately started to slow, the judge pulled his head back into the coach, returned his hat to his head, removed his round, steel-framed spectacles, and smeared the dust around on them with his thumbs and index fingers. As he did, he cast his young, pale, bowler-hatted assistant, Manfred R. Blasingame, a devilish half grin and chuckled deviously.

"Judge, please," wheedled the prissy little man, a thin-blooded heir of English nobility in a clay-colored suit and dark-red foulard necktie pierced by a diamond stickpin. "You know what a difficult task it is to fill that seat." He nodded to indicate the driver's boot at the top of the rocking coach. "Pleeease, let's not lose another man! Mr. Thornburg came to us with good credentials—former packer and freight driver before driving coaches for some of the largest stage lines in the west...before the coming of the iron horse, of course."

"The iron horse is why he needs us as badly as well as we need him, Manfred, my good man. Please, don't take my fun away from me. When the day comes, I have to stop threatening those in my employ with the dreaded bullwhip; that's when I hang up my shingle and move into the Sherman Hotel in Denver and have my bunions rubbed by a flotilla of *doves du pave!*"

As the coach came to a stop, rocking on its leather thoroughbraces, Newberry threw his head back and roared with laughter before sobering abruptly; he frowned through the billowing dust at his overserious young assistant and said with a dry chuckle, "I'll be hanged if that doesn't sound rather attractive..."

He clapped his hands together once and roared once more, briefly.

Then the door to his left opened and, shrouded in clay-colored dust, stood the jehu himself, Norbert Thornburg, who pulled his green, polka-dotted bandanna down from his own, beak-like nose and mustached mouth, set a small wooden step down on the ground beneath the door, and said, "Nature stop, Judge. It's your timetable, not mine!"

He smiled unctuously and stepped back and to one side, throwing out his arm as though to indicate the rocky, bristling desert stretching away to the bastion of Battle Mountain hulking up against the brassy sky to the south.

The judge heaved himself out of his seat, grunting with the effort. "Ah, thank you, Norbert. Thank you. Doggone carne asada. I should know better than to—"

"Judge."

Newberry had just started to lower his left foot clad in a cowhide, side-buckle half boot. Now, he stopped and glanced over his shoulder at his prissy secretary. Blasingame held out a small stack of soft, white, cotton cloths, a deferential smile on his pink-lipped mouth atop which he was trying desperately but without success to grow a mustache.

"Ah," the judge said, chuckling. "Ah, yes—to help with the blasted cankers." He reached back for the cloths and stuffed them into a pocket of his broadcloth coat, and chuckling again, sheepishly, he let the driver help him down out of the stage.

Hooves thudded, and Newberry looked up to see his two bodyguards, each wearing the moon-and-star silver-

chased badges on the lapels of their own broadcloth jack-
ets, behind their long, cream dusters, ride up on their tall
steeds and look down at him from beneath the broad
brims of their dusty black Stetsons.

"Everything all right, Judge?" asked the dark-haired
Deputy Tom Sugar.

The dust his and Deputy Ranse Anderson's horses
had kicked up sifted in the still, hot, brassy air, settling
slowly down on the bunchgrass, creosote, and sage lining
the two-track trail climbing the steep incline toward
Battle Mountain town from the southeast.

"All's well," Newberry said, ambling off into the brush,
chuckling again—an elderly, stoop-shouldered man in his
late sixties, still tall and thin but arthritic and losing the
war against gravity.

"I don't know, Judge." The blond-headed, blond-
mustached Anderson sat his big buckskin, gazing off to
the northwest, in the direction of the town they were
headed for. "I spied something or someone—a couple of
riders, maybe—moving down in that ravine a few
minutes ago. Might be wise to keep moving."

He shared a dark, conspiratorial look with Tom Sugar.

"You two are worrywarts," the judge said, throwing up
a dismissive hand. "If anyone's on the lurk down there,
it's likely cowpunchers. Buzzard Lee's tribe is scattered to
the four winds. I looked into it myself. They're likely off
in Denver an' Las Cruces an' who knows where else,
drinking and dancing with the hurdy-gurdy girls."

The judge coughed, spitting phlegm as he turned
behind a large rock and settled into the shade behind it.
He laughed and added to himself, removing his coat and
draping it over a creosote shrub, "Which doesn't sound
half bad to this old bull. No sir, not half bad at all!"

He'd dropped his trousers and summer-weight

drawers and squatted down over a log, taking deep, even breaths and feeling the ooze that had become the carne asada when it had met his age-corrupted plumbing and dropped lower down inside him, burning and chirping like birds in the morning. To help himself relax further as his lunch came gushing out of him, wincing against the burn of the vile lunch he'd eaten, he hummed a little tune he'd learned as a boy: "The lilacs, the lilacs in the spring-tiime...oh, how they remind me of youuu. The lilacs, the lilacs in the spring-tiimmme...they will forever be yoouuu..."

He was about to start another verse, feeling better, lighter, and not as foul as he browned the sage brushing up against his old behind, but stopped when he heard men's voices. The sounds of tense conversation came from the direction of the stage parked on the trail a hundred feet away. A horse whinnied.

Then a man shouted loudly, shrilly.

The shout was followed by the crack of a revolver.

Another shout and then the shooting came fast and furious, drowning out the sounds—the grunts and screams of men dying hard and the fearful whickers and whinnies of the horses.

"Oh," the judge said, his heart racing, bucking up hard against his breastbone. "Oh...oh, my..."

Quickly, trembling, wincing with each loud blast ripping toward him from the trail, he wiped himself with the cloths. He tossed the cloths into the brush, and rising, pulled up his pants and summer-weight underwear. He pulled his Colt Lightning .44 from the shoulder holster under his left arm and moved out, heavy-footed, from behind the rock. As he did, the shooting dwindled... stopped.

A man screamed.

Running footsteps sounded and then Newberry saw one of the U.S. marshals—Anderson, he thought—run out from behind the parked coach. Hatless, a wing of blond hair bouncing over his eyes, the federal lawman ran down the trail in the direction from which Newberry's procession had come. It was a stumbling, shambling run. Blood shone in several places on the man's duster that winged out around him as he ran.

Behind him, standing around the coach, kicking over bodies, men laughed.

One man separated himself from the others and walked out away from the stage, raising a long-barreled, silver-chased Smith & Wesson. He was a large, shaggy-bearded, shaggy-haired man with a patch over one eye. He clicked the Smithy's hammer back.

Anderson screamed, "No! Let me live. Or sweet Jesus —save me from these devils!"

He'd just started to swerve toward the brush on the far side of the trail when the big, shaggy-headed man's Smith & Wesson roared, smoke puffing, a short bayonet of orange flames stabbing from the barrel.

Anderson screamed again, more shrilly than before, and went tumbling headlong into the brush.

Chuckling, the big man lowered the Smithy.

Smiling, he turned to gaze toward where the judge found himself frozen only a few steps away from the rock. His short-barreled Colt hung straight down against his leg. His knees felt like putty.

His heart hiccuped in his chest.

The big man glanced toward the parked coach that rocked as the frightened team shifted in their traces, wanting to bolt. The heavy brakes were locked. The big man canted his head to indicate the judge, and then five other men walked out from behind the coach to stand to each side of the shaggy-headed, one-eyed man, whose name, Judge Newberry just realized, was Buzzard Lee's second-in-command.

Luther "Lucifer" Cody.

Newberry had had the pleasure of hanging Cody's brother a few years back.

Now, however, he was rather wishing he hadn't done that.

The big man started walking slowly toward Newberry. The two men on his left and the three on his right—one was the albino, Victor Sanchez—fell into step beside him, matching his stride.

"Oh," the judge heard himself mutter. "Oh...oh...oh..."

He tried to lift the Colt. But his hand wouldn't move. It felt as heavy as an anvil, hanging there by his side.

Suddenly, cold sweat popped out on his forehead and dribbled down his cheeks.

His knees quivered.

Sharp swords of pain stabbed into his chest.

He groaned, grunted, dropped the Colt, and staggered backward. His throat was so tight he couldn't get air down it. He clawed with his left hand—the only one that worked—at the knot of his brown foulard tie. But then he lost the feeling in that hand, and it dropped down by his side.

He felt an iron claw grip his heart and squeeze.

Wheezing, trying desperately to draw a breath, he dropped to his knees, strangling.

Finally, he fell onto his side and then rolled onto his back, writhing like a turtle that had been turned onto its shell.

He lay like that for what seemed a long time, strangling, sweating, feeling that iron claw squeeze his weakly beating heart tighter and tighter.

The sky seemed to darken as he stared up at it.

A flock of crows swam in his eyes, cawing. Only, he knew they were not crows.

A head slid into view. The face of the shaggy-headed, shaggy-bearded man, a patch over his left eye, smiled down at him for a long time.

Then he lifted the long-barreled Smith & Wesson and aimed it down at an angle at the writhing, strangling, sweat-soaked judge's face.

As if from the bottom of a deep well, Newberry heard Luther "Lucifer" Cody say, "If you see Johnny, tell him hey from his big brother—will ya, Judge?"

He smiled.

The judge did not hear the Smith & Wesson's report.

Actual crows did. They lit, cawing raucously, from the branches of a dusty, lightning-split pine.

———

HEARING THE CRACKLE OF DISTANT GUNFIRE, Mannion swung Red off the switchbacking trail and down the steep decline to his left. Plunging, Mannion holding onto the horn with both hands, the big bay chose his route quickly but carefully.

The big horse dropped through a pine forest. At the far end of the forest, the land flattened out. The big bay dropped down another declivity, not as steep as the first, and then Mannion reined the horse to a halt.

Red stood blowing and switching his tail, wanting to keep moving.

The trail lay roughly two hundred feet below Mannion and the big bay.

The shooting had tapered off several minutes ago.

There'd been one last shot and then silence, save for the thudding and blowing sounds of the bay.

Mannion scanned the trail from his left to his right.

Then he saw it. The coach and six-horse hitch standing on the trail to the southeast, roughly a hundred yards away.

He booted the bay on ahead and down the declivity at an easy angle.

He and the stallion gained the trail and approached the obviously frightened horses and the stalled coach slowly. Mannion shucked his Yellowboy from its boot when he saw three bodies lying on the trail beside the coach. He inspected all three, checking for signs of life.

There were none.

He looked around for the judge, whom he knew to be an older man.

He didn't have to look long. A crow's fierce caw sounded from the brush on the east side of the trail. Yellowboy extended straight out from his right hip, and Mannion followed the cawing to its source. Three crows lit from the ground and, cawing even more raucously than before, royally piss-burned at having their meal interrupted, went flying up over a lightning-split pine to disappear quickly against the brassy sky.

Mannion stared down at the old man grimacing up at him, lips stretched back from chipped, crooked, ivory-colored teeth. Blood leaked from his eyes, still cast with the terror of his demise, where the crows had started their grisly work on the man Joe recognized as Judge Truman G. Newberry.

Only seconds later, Mannion was back in the saddle, galloping up the trail toward Battle Mountain town, knowing that if he didn't get there fast, a fate similar to the judge's awaited Sylvan Story.

CHAPTER 25

WHEN SYLVAN STORY LEFT MANNION AT THE BLUE Dog, he went back to his jailhouse to find that no one was guarding his prisoner. Willis Reed and Shoots-the-Coyote had disappeared, as Omar Sledge had earlier, leaving the two chairs on the humble building's front stoop vacant. The notoriously shy Earl was gone, too—likely off hunting rabbits or pocket mice in the desert.

Grumbling, knowing that the three troubleshooters always took the best offer, and that they had all doubtless gotten a better offer than Story's, the Battle Mountain lawman walked back into the small cellblock at the rear of the building to check on his prisoner. Buzzard was there, right where he belonged, behind lock and key. Lying on his bunk, looking at the pictures in the dime novel Story had given him to keep him busy and quiet—of course, Buzzard couldn't read—the big, ugly owlhoot curled his upper lip in a sneer at Story, and gave him the woolly eyeball.

No one could give the woolly eyeball the way Buzzard Lee could. He'd come by his nickname honestly. His gaze was truly that of a bald-headed, carrion-eating buzzard, sure enough.

Buzzard was Story's only prisoner. As was most often the case, Story's cellblock was otherwise empty, never mind that the town of Battle Mountain was teeming with owlhoots with none-too-shabby prices on their heads. Story was too old, stove-up, and just plain apathetic—not to mention smart—to brace any of the outlaw population. His only family was Earl, and he doubted Earl had it in him to put flowers on his master's grave. It was a lonely feeling, imagining your grave on a barren hill on a stark, brassy sky, with just a makeshift cross marking it, with never any decoration whatever, just the breeze blowing dust over it.

Story wanted to delay that bit of wretchedness for as long as he could.

When he and his former, dearly departed deputy had had a prisoner or two, it was usually some harmless drunk —one of the local shopkeepers or ranch hands—who was too drunk to put up much of a fight. Thus, Story occasionally justified his salary, little as it was.

At least, the job gave him and Earl a place to sleep at night and a few times during the day, for Story's only home was the jailhouse. He usually slept in the swivel chair behind his desk, boots hiked up and crossed on the desk's edge, hat pulled down over his eyes. Leastways, the employment gave him enough jingle for drinks at one of the town's two saloons, and a meal once or twice a day over at Ma Lonnigan's Continental Hotel. A man could do worse than filling his belly with Ma's rattlesnake stew or a big T-bone served with slow-cooked pinto beans.

Story returned to his office, locked the cellblock door, tossed the keys on his desk, and headed back out onto the stoop. He sagged down into his chair by the door, hiked his boots up onto the railing before him, crossing them, and set his double-bore twelve-gauge, across his thighs. Earl must have seen him return from the saloon, and that his three deputies were gone, because the short-haired, dun-colored cur lay at the bottom of the stoop steps, chowing down on a small jackrabbit he'd caught, growling pridefully and occasionally wagging his tail with satisfaction.

Story smiled and nodded as he watched the two carpenters putting the finishing touches on the gallows on the street's far side. One man was tripping the latch, using the carved wooden lever on the side of the grisly contraption's main, or "death," post from which the heavy hemp noose hung down over the trap door. The hemp was so new that Story could smell the creosote-like odor from where he sat. The other man was under the gallows, using a grease gun on the hinges.

A half hour or so later, the two men put their tools in their wooden toolboxes, set the toolboxes in the back of their wagon, climbed aboard, and nodded and winked at Story as they rocked and rattled up the side street toward the main drag and the lumberyard where they both worked.

"Gonna have us a fine hoedown as soon as the judge gets here!" one of them yelled, waving his gray cloth immigrant cap above his head, grinning back at Story.

"Should be rollin' into town any ol' minute," the marshal replied. "Likely have us a hangin' by noon tomorrow. Tune up your horns an' whistles, fellas!"

As the wagon and the two carpenters swung around the corner on the main street, Story fished his ancient, dented tin turnip out of his trousers, flipped the lid, and scowled down at the cracked glass face of the piece. He scowled, shook his head, and, returning the piece to his pocket, muttered, "Should be here. Should be here by *now...*"

He gave the back of his head a pensive scratch as he glanced toward the main drag where the dust from the carpenters' wagon was still sifting.

"He should be here by now," he said, pensively, hearing a vague apprehension in his voice. "Should be here by now," he repeated, glancing at the cur gnawing on what was left of the rabbit at the bottom of the porch steps. "What do you think, Earl? Shouldn't that old, whore-mongerin' reprobate be..."

He stopped as Earl stopped chewing on the rabbit, jerked his head up, and cast a wary look toward where the side street intersected with First Street. Earl pricked his ears and lifted his head, working his nose, sniffing the air.

"What is it, boy?" Story asked, feeling his own blood quicken. "What do you—"

He cut himself off suddenly when the dog gave a clipped mewl deep in his chest, lurched to his feet, and ran off into the brush on the other side of the street, tail between his legs and casting more quick, cautious glances toward the main drag.

Story turned his head to stare in the same direction, muttering, "Now, what in holy bla..."

Again, he stopped. The thuds of several horses reached his ears, growing steadily louder until six horse-back riders rode around the corner of First Street and started down the side street, heading toward the jail-house. Story almost squirted down his leg when he saw the big man riding in the center of the pack—a big, shaggy-headed, shaggy-bearded hombre with a patch over his left eye. He nearly squirted again when he saw the albino, Victor Sanchez, riding beside him.

Story drew a deep breath and let it out slowly as the big man's name drifted down out of his brain to deposit itself on his tongue, which was suddenly as dry as an old boot.

"Luther 'Lucifer' Cody," he wheezed, again tightening his sphincter muscles to keep from messing himself. He'd thought the judge had hanged Cody years ago.

Or...was that his brother, Johnny?

Story had a feeling he now knew why the judge hadn't arrived in Battle Mountain town.

He saw that one of the men was trailing a saddled horse on a lead line.

Story felt himself grow heavier and heavier as he sat frozen to the hide-bottom chair, watching Cody and the five other men grow larger and larger as they approached. As though all seven horses were tied to the same lead line, they all turned toward the jailhouse at the same time.

Where was Mannion? Story wondered. He'd left him in the Blue Dog around an hour ago.

The riders stopped their horses ten feet from the bottom of the porch steps, near where Earl had left the bloody rabbit around which flies were swirling, landing to finish off what the dog had left them. All six men held rifles, either on their shoulders or across their saddle pommels.

Story looked down at the Greener resting across his thighs.

It was a dead weight there. He couldn't have lifted the heavy piece if he'd tried. He had no compulsion to try. To do so, he knew, would be to die. What he should have done, he suddenly realized, silently castigating himself for another failure in a long life of them, was to have retreated to the jailhouse and locked the door behind him, warning Buzzard's bunch that any man trying to enter would get two loads of double-aught buckshot for his trouble.

Instead, he sat glued to his chair. His rifle was stuck to his thighs.

He looked at the six riders sitting their horses before him, the horses' snouts and withers streaked with sweat. He looked at one-eyed Lucifer Cody and then at the albino with strange, colorless hair curling onto the collar of Sanchez's duster. The strange, colorless eyes regarded Story flatly, the man's lips set in a straight line beneath a few colorless wisps of a mustache. The hot, dry breeze nipped at the broad brim of his weathered, salt-rimed, dark-green hat.

Cody looked at Sanchez. The two men shared a sneer.

Cody returned his demon's gaze to Story, canted his head a little to one side, and said, "Fetch Buzzard outta the lockup, Marshal, an' we *might* let you live." He cocked his Winchester one-handed and aimed it straight out from his right hip at Story. "No promises, though."

He curled one half of his upper lip in another bemused sneer.

The marshal's heart was racing. He glanced toward First Street.

The albino said tightly, "If you'r expectin' help from Mannion, forget it. His horse ain't at the Blue Dog. Musta done left town. Now, fetch Buzzard fer us."

Story moistened his lips with the tip of his tongue. "I can't do that," he said.

"You wanna die?" Cody asked him, closing his gloved hand more tightly around the neck of the Winchester he was aiming at the lawman.

Story shook his head slowly. "No. No, I don't. But I ain't gonna open that cellblock door."

The albino, Sanchez, said in his oddly high-pitched voice, "Is it worth dyin' for, old man? Pride?"

Story drew a breath. He tried to quell his racing heart without success. "All I know," he said, tightly, "is I gotta job to do. I ain't gonna get up outta this consarned chair and follow your orders. No, sir."

Again, Story wagged his head.

In the back of his mind, behind all his other concerns, he prayed for the Good Lord not to let him wet himself in front of these cutthroats. Oh, God, please don't let me do that. Dying was one thing, but he wanted to go out with at least a grain of self-respect intact.

Story heard the murmur of hushed voices. He slid his gaze to the north and saw loosely grouped men standing on the corner and on the other side of the street, most holding beer schooners in their hands. They were miners, woodcutters, mule skinners, and outlaws—jaspers, all. Mannion wasn't among them. They were staring with mild amusement toward the jailhouse, Buzzard's bunch, and Story.

Cody followed Story's gaze toward the two loose groups of men and then returned his own amused gaze to the town marshal of Battle Mountain. "Don't think you can expect any help from that quarter."

Keeping his colorless eyes on Story, Sanchez said to Cody, "What about Mannion? We shoulda killed him in the saloon."

Cody wrinkled his nose and gave his head a brief shake. "Mighta started a big lead swap in there. I wanted to make sure I was fit to kill the judge." Keeping his lone eye on Story, he smiled and blinked that one eye slowly. "Which I done did."

"Don't doubt it," the lawman said, fatefully, cold

sweat trickling down both sides of his face. "Don't doubt it a bit."

Cody glanced at the other three men gathered to each side of him and Sanchez. "Keep an eye out for Mannion, boys."

The other three glanced around, their faces as hard and savage as those of their two gang leaders.

"If he was in town, he'd be here by now," one of them said.

"My patience is wearing thin, Marshal," Lucifer Cody said. "You fetch Buzzard outta the lockup or one of my men will."

Story just stared at him and swallowed.

Fear was a wild stallion inside him.

Try as he might, he could not lift the shotgun from his thighs.

The albino gave a frustrated snort. "Oh, hell—I'll do it!"

Story's heart raced even faster, more and more sweat beads trickling down his cheeks, as he watched Victor Sanchez swing down from his saddle. The man tossed his reins over the hitchrack and glanced once more at Story.

The bald disdain in the albino's eyes, as though he were looking at something Earl had left on the jailhouse stoop, did what nothing else had been able to do.

Rage burned like a wildfire through Sylvan Story.

Bellowing, "I got a consarned job to do, an' by Jip, I'm gonna do it!" the town marshal of Battle Mountain rose out of his chair, raising the twelve-gauge double-bore in his hands, rocking both rabbit ear hammers back to full cock, and swinging the heavy piece toward Sanchez. He was just starting to draw back one of the steel eyelash triggers when the first bullet plowed into him—a heavy, hot fist smashing into his chest up high near his right shoulder. As he stumbled backward, the shotgun came up, and he triggered it into the porch roof, screaming, taking another two shambling steps backward, stumbling into the jailhouse door.

Wood slivers from the roof rained down around him.

More lead tore into him, several guns blasting, though he could barely hear the reports for the loud clanging of pain bells in his ears. He could feel the searing misery in his chest, gut, arms, and legs. Screaming, he dropped the Greener then sort of rolled away from the door, along the front of the jailhouse, and dropped heavily through his hide-bottom chair, busting it into sticks, before piling up on top of what was left of it, on the floor of the stoop.

He lay on his side and then rolled onto his back, staring up at the porch roof and his gourd olla in which the flat-handled gourd dipper resided. A bullet had smashed into it. Water poured out the .44-caliber-sized hole and onto his right leg, just above a bloody hole in his canvas trousers.

The shooting had stopped, though the blasting reports still echoed in his pain-fogged brain. He felt the resonation of footsteps through the wooden floorboards beneath him. A man stood over him. The bizarre, pink-rimmed, washed-out eyes of Victor Sanchez gazed down at him. The man shook his head and then turned away. His vision dimming, pain engulfing him, making him shake where he lay there on what remained of his chair on the floor of the porch, Story watched the man push through the jailhouse door and disappear into the office, leaving the door standing wide behind him.

He reappeared sometime later, though Story was so weak, his vision so dim, the lawman could barely make him out. Sanchez glanced down at Story and then moved off down the porch steps. Then it was big, beefy Buzzard

Lee—as hairy as Cody—staring down at Story. Buzzard had a Remington .44 wedged behind his wide, black belt. He pulled the hogleg out from behind his belt, grinned down at Story, and said something the lawman couldn't hear above the screeching of a hundred crows in his head.

He was able to read the big, ugly, bearded man's lips, however.

"Die slow and hard, you old fool."

Buzzard returned the popper to his pants. Story watched him turn and join the rest of his gang sitting their horses on the street, but he didn't see them ride away. Everything had gone dark by then.

CHAPTER 26

STANDING IN THE SLOWLY FLOWING BROWN STREAM glistening in the high-altitude sunlight, the cuffs of her denim trousers rolled above her knees, Giannina Calderon raised her hand high above her head and opened it palm up. She smiled her beatific smile, and for a moment, James, standing behind her, his own jeans rolled up, his shirt off, rifle resting across his shoulders behind his neck, his wrists hooked over it, thought she was awaiting manna from heaven.

Then a butterfly came down out of the hazy green pine shade, a monarch fluttering like a piece of delicate orange and black lace and lit in the palm of the girl's brown hand. She lowered her hand slowly, staring down at the creature in awe, eyes wide, lips parted. She turned slowly to James and held her hand out to show him the butterfly with its orange and black scallops, little splashes of yellow with many more, smaller, pinhead-sized dots of white in the black edges of the wings.

It just then occurred to him, as the girl looked up from the delicate creature in her hand, and smiled again, serenely, that he had never stopped and really looked at the simple yet complicated and otherworldly miracle a butterfly was. It warmed his heart. Then it occurred to him, also, that his heart never felt as warm as it did when he was in the company of this little, brown-eyed Spanish princess with small, fine teeth and full lips, adding a beguiling sensuality to her heart-shaped face.

The previous day, he'd taught her to shoot a pistol. She didn't take to the gun at all, but he'd convinced her she needed to shoot well enough to defend herself. The cabin was remote enough, the cabin deep enough, that he didn't think anyone would have heard the reports. He didn't have enough cartridges for much of a lesson, but at least he'd taught her how to shoot the pistol, though it would take her many more lessons to be able to hit anything from much of a distance.

But he felt better, knowing she could defend herself in close quarters if she had to. Today, he thought they'd spend time having fun together, because he doubted they'd have much of a chance at fun again anytime soon.

She turned away from him slowly and just as slowly raised her hand once more, high above her head. The butterfly lit from it, colorful wings flapping gracefully, as delicate as a wisp of orange and black smoke rising and falling on the sunlit breeze. Giannina watched the butterfly disappear back into the pine forest, climbing the ridge on the far side of the stream from the old trapper's cabin in which she and James had taken refuge.

Staring after it, suddenly her eyes grew large and round. Gasping, she closed her hands over her mouth, staring up the slope now as though she were seeing a grisly specter from a recent nightmare. Her long, dark-brown hair fluttered about her shoulders in the breeze.

"Giannina!" James said, frowning, walking around to stand in front of her. "What is it?" He glanced up the slope stippled with tall firs and pines. "What did you see?"

She looked up at him with her rich, deep-brown eyes, and lowered her hands from her mouth. Emotion glistened gold in those large, round orbs. "Mi mama...she was wearing her orange dress..."

"When?"

Giannina looked up the shaded slope beyond James, but he knew she was seeing something altogether different than the pine forest.

"When, Giannina?" James asked. "When did she wear her orange dress?"

Her deeply troubled eyes slid to his. "The night they came. The men in the night...to our estancia..."

Tears gathered in her eyes. A strangled sob escaped from between her lips, and looking down, she crossed her arms on her chest over the dark-blue wool shirt Ma Lonnigan had given her. She squeezed her eyes closed and bowed her head as though in prayer, tucking her lower lip under her upper front teeth. Her shoulders jerked as she sobbed.

"You remember it now—don't you?" James said. "More details about that night."

She'd remembered the attack, but only vague details. She'd remembered running in the night, in the rain, men galloping after her, and how frightened she'd been. She'd remembered falling into the canyon and being swept downstream and then Mannion finding her on the bank of the arroyo and taking her back to Battle Mountain town. Now, however, James could tell she was remembering more and more of it.

He lowered the rifle and looked around cautiously, making sure they were alone. Then, he leaned the rifle against a large rock on the bank. He was wearing his holstered six-gun, so he was entirely defenseless against a possible attack. He'd vowed he never would be again. He returned to Giannina and placed his hands on her shoulders.

"Oh, Giannina," he said, realizing now the horror she'd endured.

She looked up at him and gazed at him through the tears in her eyes. "They came in the night...before the rain. There were five of them. I was pumping water outside when they rode into the estancia. I saw they were trouble right away. I dropped my pail and ran to the house but already the men were shooting. Papa ran outside with his rifle, and they shot him down."

She was sobbing now, but speaking through the sobs, as though recounting what had happened would somehow purge the terrible memory from her mind. "They circled the cabin, shooting through the windows. Mama returned fire with a shotgun. I can see her wearing her orange dress." Giannina paused, shook her head, sniffing back tears, and continued. "She and my brother, Tio, held them off. Mama told me to run out the back. I did. I ran out the back and into the woods and then I heard Mama scream and call for Tio, and still the shooting continued. I ran so hard, my heart filled with fear, and then behind me, I saw the flames as they set fire to the cabin and continued shooting, killing the chickens, Tio's pig, and the mules. Then they came for me. By then it was raining. I hid in the hollow of a fallen tree, and when they rode around me, I ran again through the wind and the rain...such lashing rain, the thunder crashing all around me. I heard them coming again behind me and that's when the ground fell out from beneath me, and the muddy water carried me away!"

James drew the bawling girl tight against him and

rocked her as she bawled. When the cries let up, James held her back away from him and gazed down at her, rage searing him to his core. "Did you see them—these men? Did you get a good look at any of them?"

"Si," Giannina nodded. "One, maybe two."

"Tell me," James said, trying to rein in his own anger. "Tell me what they looked like."

"One was tall. He had long, yellow hair. Almost like a woman's hair."

James thought about it and nodded. "What else?"

"He wore a big, pale hat. A sombrero. Yes, a gray sombrero made of felt."

James nodded slowly, trying to keep from pressing his fingers too deeply into the girl's arms and hurting her. She'd just identified a local outlaw and troubleshooter, Omar Sledge. He thought he'd seen Sledge and two others around Ruth Kennecott's big stone house under Battle Mountain. Another white man and an Indian—a former scout, James thought he'd heard on one of his many supply runs to town, during which times, alone, he indulged in a single beer at one of Battle Mountain town's two saloons.

The supply runs had been his job and usually his job alone. That's all his father had ever thought he was any good for. Sometimes, he'd delivered supplies to Mrs. Kennecott and Athena, as well. That was when he spent some time with Athena, in the garden behind the odd, stone mansion. It was during those times that, despite the girl's obvious beauty, he realized he could never love her, though he'd resigned himself to the idea of his having to marry her, because it was what his father, mother, and Mrs. Kennecott had wanted him to do.

They probably thought that between the two families, they'd be able to make a man out of him. A man who deserved the precious Athena Kennecott.

"What else, Giannina?" he urged the girl before him now, the water flowing around their legs just below their knees. "What else can you remember...about the other riders?"

She looked up at him, squinting, tears bathing her face. She frowned as though another detail occurred to her. "When I was hiding," she said, "in the hollow of the tree. One of the riders rode past me, and I saw the brand on his horse." She paused and gazed up at James gravely. "It was in the shape of a horse's head."

James took in the information like a slap to the face.

But he'd already known his father had sent the riders, hadn't he? Not really all that surprising. Still, knowing now beyond the shadow of a doubt that his father had killed this poor girl's family—the family of the girl he truly loved—as easily as he hanged rustlers and nesters on land he considered his own even when it was really open range, was a sledgehammer blow to his consciousness.

"Oh, Giannina," James said now, wrapping his arms around her and again drawing her close against him. "My father...I'm...I'm so sorry, Giannina. Oh, God—how sorry I am!"

She lowered her head again and sobbed.

He closed his eyes, holding her close while the stream slid around them and the birds cheeped and the squirrels chittered just as though everything was calm and right with the world, as though nothing had so drastically changed in the past several minutes in which this girl had recounted his father's horrors.

As though James had not just now found himself on a course he could not turn back from. One that could very well kill him and deprive him of a life with the young woman he loved more than anything but a course he still could not veer away from.

When he opened his eyes again, his heart quickened. He squinted, trying for a clearer view of the two riders sitting two horses at the bald top of the forested ridge, high above the cabin. They were silhouetted against the western sky down which the sun was making its slow descent. They were mere shadows. Something in the delineation of each shadow, however, told him they were women. He thought he could see long hair gathered into mare's tails, hanging down from beneath their hats as they sat their horses half facing each other, curveted atop the ridge and gazing down at James and Giannina standing in the stream in the canyon below.

As James stared back at them, apprehension becoming a bug hopscotching along his spine, they turned their heads to gaze at each other. They neck-reined their horses around and booted them away from the crest of the ridge and out of sight.

James did not feel compelled to reach for his rifle.

No threat felt imminent.

No, not imminent.

But one was there, all right. Like a distant but dark and violent storm building to an intensity he had never seen before and would likely never live to see again.

CHAPTER 27

<small>MANNION RACED INTO TOWN FROM THE EAST.</small>

It had taken him longer to get back into town than leaving it, for Red had had to negotiate the steep incline up which the stage road switchbacked. He knew as soon as the first shops and stock pens and old, mostly abandoned log cabins rolled up on each side of Battle Mountain's main street that he was too late. It was too quiet. Just too damn quiet.

Mannion swung the big bay hard left down the side street on which Sylvan Story's jailhouse sat. The bay had taken only three long, hard strides before its rider checked him down. A cold stone dropped in Mannion's belly. Just as he'd thought, he was too late. A dozen townsmen stood around the jailhouse's front stoop, looking down. Story's dog, Earl, sat on the other side of the street from the office, whining softly, working his nose, shifting his sad weight from one front foot to the other.

Mannion cursed and put Red up to the bottom of the porch steps and sat the bay, gazing in dread at where Ma

Lonnigan knelt on one knee, shoving a red neckerchief against the big, old lawman's lumpy, bloody chest.

"Is he dead?"

Ma looked up at Mannion, eyes wide. She shook her head. "No! I don't know how he's not, but by god, he's still got a heartbeat." She rose quickly and swept her commanding gaze at the men standing around her, some on the stoop, some at the bottom of it. "Four of you men get him over to the Continental. Be quick, but don't jostle him too much." She hurried down off the porch and started striding toward the hotel. "I ain't much of a medico, but I reckon I'm all poor Sylvan's got! I'll get some water boilin' an' heat some knives. Snap to it, now! Snap to it!"

"Which way they'd head?" Joe asked a man he recognized as the grocer.

The man turned his head and nodded toward the big formation lumping up in the south. "Battle Mountain. Rode out fast. They'll likely lose themselves in those rocks up there before sundown."

"Not if I can help it!"

Mannion reined Red around and put him back on the main drag, heading for H.G. Finlay's Livery & Feed. Ten minutes later, Finlay emerged from the gloomy shadows of his barn, leading a stocky blue roan stallion that looked like a good cavalry mount—broad-barreled and built for speed in rough country.

"A good runner and climber?" Mannion asked the liveryman as he stripped Red's saddle off his back. He'd run the bay hard. He'd give him a rest and ride the roan. He didn't like tracking on an unfamiliar horse—he trusted Red like no other; they moved as one—but he had no choice.

"Best I have. I don't have much anymore, but this is

the fastest mount I have, and he's fast, too. He'd give your bay a run for its money."

"He's gonna have to."

When Mannion had saddled and bridled the roan, strapped his rifle scabbard, bedroll, and saddlebags into place, he patted Red and told Finlay, "Treat him right."

He swung up onto the roan's back and booted him into a hard run toward the cross street on which the jailhouse sat. Behind him, he heard the bay whinny in protest at being left behind. Mannion threw up and acknowledging arm, muttering, "I'm not gonna kill you, boy. Not a chance..." as he raced around the corner, heading south toward Battle Mountain and the dirty devils led by Buzzard Lee.

They'd left a clear trail along the two-track trace that led up an incline through cottonwoods and cedars, to the bottom of the high apron slope, a giant pedestal, on which the mountain was perched. Buzzard knew Mannion would be hot after him, so Joe held back a little, wary of an ambush. That's no doubt what Buzzard intended—to lead him into rough country and try to catch him in a whipsaw.

Mannion tried to hold back, to play it cautiously, but it was damned hard. He kept seeing Sylvan Story lying there on the stoop of his jailhouse, a bloody mess, likely having been shot five or six times. The age of the man, as well as his poor physical condition, made it unlikely he'd pull through. That fueled Joe's notorious rage to a blue flame. He also kept seeing the man's dog sitting across the street and heard Earl's grief-stricken whines.

Yeah, it was hard to hold back. But he had to. He owed Sylvan the bullets with which he'd cut down Buzzard Lee's gang.

He slowed his pace to a trot when he gained the high,

apron slope and the vast stone bastion that was Battle Mountain sweeping off to his left and his right. The formation was several hundred feet tall, with deep fissures running vertically as well as horizontally across its face. Gnarled cedars, pines, and aspens grew from these cracks, some of which looked hardly wide enough for a man to lie down in. The trail forked at the base of the mountain, one two-track tine branching off to the left, the other two to the right.

The intermittent tracks of six sets of horses followed the left tine. However, Mannion knew one or two of the riders might have somehow slipped around and headed west, the same direction as the right tine, intending to sneak up behind him and get him in that whipsaw he was leery of. Though it graveled him to do so, he kept his pace slow. It graveled the roan, as well. He likely hadn't been ridden in a while, and he was eager to blow off some of the stable green.

Horse and rider followed the base of the mountain for maybe a quarter mile. Then they came to a wide gap in the mountain wall on their right—a dry wash filled with willows and boulders that had been washed down from the higher reaches. Here, the trail forked again— one continuing across the arroyo, which was maybe fifty yards wide, the other one curving off to the south and following the west bank of the wash into the mountain.

Mannion checked the roan down to a stop.

He stared at the forking trail, smiled shrewdly and cursed.

Buzzard's bunch had split up.

The shrewd smile in place, Mannion nodded. Buzzard was smarter than he looked. They were going to try to get him in that whipsaw, all right. Now, he had a decision to make. Which tine to take?

Didn't much matter. He'd see all six riders again sooner or later, no matter which route he chose.

He chose the right tine, the trail following the arroyo into the mountain, for no other reason than he had to choose one. It was dusk inside the chasm, as it was late in the day, and the sun was falling behind the mountain on his right. He kept an especially sharp eye skinned on the way ahead as well as on his back trail. There were thousands of places for ambushers to hole up and either fire down on him from the rocks above, or from rocks on the trail ahead or behind.

He was foolish for riding in here alone, with three men likely ahead of him and another three men behind. But that was the man he was. If he'd tried to put together a posse back in Battle Mountain, it likely would have been made up of the same sort of jasper he was hunting. He'd have to have grown more eyes than he already had.

The trail followed the meandering course of the arroyo.

The farther he rode into the chasm, the harder his witch poked the back of his neck with that cold finger of hers. If he had ever imagined her before, he was not now. He could feel eyes on him from ahead and behind.

Suddenly, just as he was about to follow the mountain wall and the arroyo around another sharp bend, he quickly reined the roan off the trail and into the arroyo on his left. The stallion dropped fleetly to the arroyo floor seven feet below the bank. Buzzard might have been cagey, but Mannion had some wildcat sense of his own. Willows growing among the boulders, as well as large dead branches, screened him from the trail both ahead and behind. He swung down from the saddle and led the roan along a path through the boulders, generally heading toward a canyon mouth opening on the arroyo's far side—broad and deeply shadowed.

When he'd led the mount a hundred feet, he tied it to a willow and shucked the Yellowboy from its scabbard. Keeping low, he retraced his route back to the side of the arroyo he'd been traveling along. He climbed into some rocks, nestled into a niche that would shield him from view up the trail and that offered a view of about thirty feet of his back trail, between rocks and willows. He quietly jacked a live cartridge into the Yellowboy's action and set the hammer to half-cock.

He grinned at his cunning.

He couldn't wait to see the look on that slime-bogged lizard, Buzzard Lee's, face when he found it was his bunch who'd walked into it. Shouldn't be long now. Joe had a feeling ol' Buzzard wanted him off his trail by the end of the day, which it nearly now was. That was just fine with Joe. He'd like to send the son of Satan and his cohorts snuggling with the angleworms sooner rather than later.

He waited. The cold finger pressed against his neck relented a bit, and then he could hear the old broom straddler cackling in his ear. Presently came the sound of soft hoof thuds. As they grew louder, Joe could hear tack squawking slightly. A man said something too quietly for Mannion to hear clearly.

Then Joe could see them passing behind the screen of willows and stunt cedars.

As he'd suspected, there were three. He didn't recognize any of them, but the only one in Buzzard's bunch he knew on sight for sure was Buzzard himself. The others all just looked like your average, lowly, back-shooting lot of unwashed jaspers like every other outlaw in Battle

Mountain, pistols and knives bristling from varied and creative places.

When all three passed behind more willows roughly thirty feet from Mannion, Joe drew back the Yellowboy's hammer to full cock. When the trio rode into a gap in the shrubs once more, Mannion rose to his full height, rammed the Winchester's butt plate to his right shoulder, and commenced slinging lead. He grinned as he fired and cocked and fired and cocked and fired again until two men were down, their horses dancing and screaming. He'd blown the hat off the third and final killer of this bunch, who was trying to rein his black-and-white pinto back toward Mannion while also trying to bring his Henry repeater to bear.

Gritting his teeth, he shouted up the trail, "Bloody Joe pulled a fast one, fellas!"

Mannion howled and bellowed, "Die, you devil! This last one's for Sylvan!"

He blew the man—tall and lean and bald on top with dark, stringy hair hanging from a band around his head to his shoulders—out of his saddle. He struck the ground in a sitting position and inadvertently shot himself with the Henry through the underside of his chin. Brains and blood blew out the top of his head.

As his pinto went running back in the direction from which it had come, the man sank back in the trail and quivered wildly, spurs chinging raucously, as he died. Mannion sank back into his niche and, chuckling to himself with great self-satisfaction, began reloading the Yellowboy.

When Buzzard and the other two came—and they'd likely take their time—he'd be ready for them.

Mannion felt the rocks reverberate beneath his perch. He glanced down.

He heard a deep, guttural rumbling. It grew gradually louder until it sounded like the stirring of a long-slumbering god.

The roan whinnied fearfully in the willows behind him.

He looked up at the high stone wall vaulting over him just in time to see the cone at the top of a stone pinnacle break off and drop down against the side of the mountain, shattering. Another spire broke in half and came tumbling down the mountain, sending more and more tumbling in its wake, boulders breaking and rolling in jagged-edged hulks down the mountain to likely fill the canyon in which Joe sat, staring up, hang-jawed, knowing that he'd outsmarted himself once again.

Wasn't the first time he'd done it.

Wasn't the first time his shooting had nearly brought a mountain down on him and buried him in rock, either, in a giant stone sepulcher.

Almost.

Ha!

As the mountain continued disintegrating and tumbling toward him, the earth bucking beneath him, Mannion climbed up out of his niche and ran for all was worth, which wasn't much these days.

CHAPTER 28

Mannion grabbed the roan's reins, and he and the stallion ran down a narrow corridor between piles of rock. Meanwhile, the rocks tumbling down from the far side of the canyon struck the canyon floor with thunderous booms, making the ground beneath Joe's running feet reverberate.

Just before he ran out from a long finger of rock, heading for the side canyon, the roan screamed shrilly. Joe turned to see the bullet hole in the side of the poor beast's head. The crack of the rifle that had sent the bullet on its deadly course echoed.

"Ah, hell!"

The roan twisted around, eyes wide in agony, and just before it fell, Mannion grabbed his saddlebags and canteen off the horse's back. The horse fell in a heap, nearly taking Joe down with it. He managed to dodge the dead horse, and then, with the canteen and saddlebags hooked over one shoulder, he crouched behind a rock and pumped a round into the Yellowboy's action. He edged a look over the top of his cover to see none other than Buzzard Lee, the big bear of a bearded and duster-clad man standing in a long flue in the far side of the canyon, thirty feet up from the canyon floor.

The man grinned deviously as he racked a round into his own Winchester.

Mannion fired quickly, but the bullet only blew up rock dust as Lee stepped back deeper into the notch.

Mannion straightened and ran into the adjacent canyon, on the far side of the canyon from Lee. Buzzard fired at him twice quickly, the bullets blowing up gravel at Joe's boots. Joe climbed into the rocks, choking the canyon's far end. Buzzard leaped down off the canyon wall, dropped to a knee, and sent two more echoing rounds hurling at Joe. The bullets hammering the rocks to Joe's left.

Mannion went to ground in a small niche in the rocks, dropped his saddlebags and canteen, and stared down into the main canyon, ready to pump Buzzard so full of lead he'd rattle when he walked. Joe cursed as he spread his mustached upper lip back from his teeth.

The man was gone.

Probably heading off to join the other two.

Meanwhile, a great mushroom cloud of smoke-like dust rose from where Mannion had nearly sent that ridge wall crashing down on him.

He sighed, removed his hat, and ran a gloved hand through his sweat-damp, dusty hair. He'd lost a good horse, and he was on foot. Buzzard and the other two would likely come for him. Buzzard knew there was no quit in Mannion. He'd hunt him until he found him, and there would be little peace and beauty in the ugly outlaw's demise.

Joe looked around.

The canyon walls on both sides were craggy and tall. Mostly, the rock was sheer, but he saw the black mouth of a canyon up the wall at the top of a pile of boulders. He'd head there, secure the high ground, and wait for his stalkers to come.

With another ragged sigh—he was tired, weary, and too old for this anymore—he picked up his saddlebags and canteen and started up the canyon wall, climbing boulders, sometimes leaping from one to another, always keeping an eye on his back trail. He didn't need a bullet in his back for his trouble. He'd never be found in this dinosaur's mouth of rocks and boulders. Jane and Vangie would always wonder what had become of the man they loved.

Joe didn't like the thought, so he slid it to the back of his mind.

He gained the cave and stood breathing hard as he inspected it for signs of wildcats or wolves. None were there, though judging by the tracks, feces, and the partly furred bones of meal remains, they had been. It was "a little whiffy on the lee side," as the old saying went, too. It smelled as ripe as a lion's den.

Joe went on inside, having to remove his hat and crouch slightly.

He dropped to his knees and set his hat, saddlebags, canteen, and rifle down around him.

Then he dropped to his belly and gazed down toward the main canyon where the dust was still rising. He could see a few more rocks rolling down the canyon wall and heard them clatter to the floor. From here, he'd have a clear shot at Lee and his two cohorts. They'd probably already see that, and they'd likely wait to near dark or later.

Joe studied the sky. Dusk was a few hours away. He had a wait ahead of him. He unscrewed the canteen's cover and took a long drink, refreshing despite the brackish water. He returned the cap, set the canteen aside, and returned his gaze toward the main canyon, seeing nothing but a jumble of sun-blasted rocks, pines, and cedars.

He scratched the stubble on his jaw and waited.

Shadows moved around in the rocks below him and on the steep wall opposite him, the rocks changing colors. The only problem with his choice of location from which to do battle, he realized, was that he was trapped in here. He could see no way up the steep walls. Buzzard could wait him out, let him use all his ammo and water and the few bits of jerky in his saddlebags.

Then, he was doomed.

Oh, well. Not going back now. He was getting a might soft in his thinker box in his old age...

The shadows grew larger as they slid down the western ridge. Now, they would conceal three men moving through the rocks toward Joe's position. He crabbed a little farther back into the cave, holding his head down a little lower, and used his ears now as well as his eyes for movement, the slide of a shadow, the soft clack of a slealthy boot on rock. As he did, he reloaded the Yellowboy, plucking the bullets from his belt and sliding them through the Winchester's loading gate.

A few minutes later, a man shouted in Buzzard Lee's Southern drawl, "Hey, Mannion! You wanna die in there, old man?"

The voice echoed hoarsely.

Mannion scouted the canyon. He was sure the shout had come from straight across, but he wasn't sure until he saw the glint of a stray, remaining sunray off a rifle barrel.

Joe grinned, pressed his cheek up to his Yellowboy's rear stock, aimed, and fired.

Buzzard bellowed. Then: *"Ow—damn you! You grazed*

my cheek! You got eagle eyes for an old washed-up lawdog, Bloody Joe!"

"That's just the first blood I'll draw here this evening!"

A bullet rocketed in and slammed into the lip of the cave floor a foot in front of Joe. He was sure the following rifle roar came from beneath him and to his left, from a dark, rectangular niche between two boulders that still had a little salmon light on them. Mannion fired two quick rounds into the niche. No sound came from the niche, so he didn't know if he'd struck his target or not.

Buzzard bellowed again as he fired from across the canyon.

Joe pulled his head back and pressed his chin down against the cave floor.

Then, there were three rifles throwing lead at him.

When the shooting paused, Mannion looked down into the canyon where a man was climbing the rocks toward the cave, crouching low, holding his rifle across his chest—a stocky shadow in the gloaming, wearing a low-crowned cream hat. The man stopped suddenly, and Joe put two bullets into his belly. The man fell off the rock he was on and sat with his back to the cave, yelling. He'd lost his hat; Joe put a bullet through the back of his head.

Mannion pulled his own head back down as another fusillade was fired into the cave, most of the bullets peppering the wall behind him or the lip of the cave before him.

Then suddenly, the shooting stopped.

His stalkers knew they were only wasting lead. They probably didn't have any more than he did. They needed better positions. They'd have to wait for good dark.

Joe rolled back behind the cave wall on his left and edged a look down the rocky slope. Gradually, the darkness bled into the canyon, as black as ink in a bottle. The first stars shimmered to life. A coyote mourned from a distant ridge. Nightbirds made their piping cries. A gentle breeze moved down the ridges, cooling the air in the canyon, rustling tufts of wiry grass growing between the rocks.

Again, Mannion waited.

He heard an anxious breath down the slope on his left.

He edged a look around the cave wall. The man, whom Joe recognized was down on hands and knees, was crawling up the gravelly slope maybe twenty feet from Joe. Mannion grinned. He recognized the tall albino, Victor Sanchez, in the starlight and shot him. Sanchez grunted, fired his own rifle wild and then rolled down the slope, arms and legs pinwheeling.

A rifle stabbed flames from down the slope on Joe's right, fifty feet away. Three quick, wild shots, Buzzard Lee bellowing, "Why the hell can't anyone kill you, Joe?"

Pressing his back against the cave wall, Joe grinned and shouted, "I'm too mean to die, Buzzard—don't you know that?"

He stepped out from behind the wall and fired three quick shots of his own from the hip. Buzzard twisted around, yelling, and dropped his rifle. He ran, staggering down the slope, falling on the rocks, getting up and running again. He seemed to be holding his right arm across his chest.

"Leave me be, Bloody Joe. I'm hit. You've caused me enough grief!"

"I'm just getting started, Buzzard."

Mannion followed the big man's silhouette across the

rocks and down the slope. Buzzard fell on the last rock, heaved himself to his feet and ran in a shambling fashion toward the main canyon. Mannion leaped down off the last boulder.

"Turn around or take it in the back, Buzzard. Not that you deserve anything better after killing Sylvan Story. I should have just killed you rather than going to the trouble of hauling your mangy carcass here to kill both the judge and his contingent and Sylvan himself. I'll likely pay for that once I'm planted, and I deserve to!"

Buzzard stopped stumbling over his boot toes.

He stood staring straight ahead. Then he suddenly swung around. Starlight glinted off the barrel of the hogleg in his hand.

Mannion shot him from the hip. Buzzard screamed and stumbled backward, triggering his own gun into the ground at his boots. He stretched his bearded lips back from his craggy teeth and dropped to his knees. He looked up at Mannion.

"You gotta take me in, Joe. That's the law!"

Mannion gave a cold grin. "I follow only Bloody Joe's law. You should know that by now, you dumb, murdering fool!"

He followed it.

Then he went back to the cave and spent the night.

The next morning, he retrieved his saddle from the roan, threw it onto one of the dead outlaws' mounts, and headed back toward Battle Mountain town. He'd ridden in from the south when it was plain that while he'd been gone, all hell had broken loose.

CHAPTER 29

THAT SAME MORNING, JAMES OPENED HIS EYES ON THE musty cot in the old trapper's cabin.

He lifted his head, listening.

Giannina lifted her head from his chest. "What is it?" she whispered in the dawn's early light.

"Heard somethin'," James said, tonelessly. "He's coming. Likely to finish the job he started."

"Your father?"

"Yep."

James rose and moved to the window right of the door.

His father, Kincaid's new foreman Pat Winslow, C.J. Harriman, and Tyrell Brand were just then riding across the creek, Kincaid in the lead, his craggy features set grimly. He rode his big, black stallion as though he were the major in charge of a cavalry contingent. He wore his gray wool coat, the sheepskin collar pulled against the morning mountain cold.

Anger rose in James.

He moved from the window, stepped into his boots, grabbed his Winchester from where he'd hung it above the door, and told Giannina to stay down.

"James, I'm scared."

"Don't be. It's time to end this right here and now."

He moved to the door.

————

OUTSIDE, KINCAID REINED UP IN FRONT OF THE CABIN. Winslow, Harriman, and Tyrell Brand flanked him. He turned to Winslow, and said, "Go in and pull them both out of there. James is coming back to the ranch to eat his just desserts. I'll deal with the girl in town, send her off to Denver on a stagecoach, get her out of my hair once and for all."

"You got it, Mr. Kincaid," said the foreman, and swung down from his horse.

He dropped his reins and walked up to the front door, knocking with the end of his fist. "James, come on out of there. Your father wants you back at Horsehead."

"This is downright embarrassing!" Kincaid put in.

"Come on, James," Winslow called again. Again, he knocked on the door.

It came open suddenly, and James stood in the doorway, holding his rifle out from his right hip, aimed at Winslow's belly. He cocked it loudly and bunched his lips in anger as he said, "Tell my father he can go to hell."

"How dare you talk to me like that," Kincaid said. "Have you gone mad?"

"No, I've come to my senses. I know you had Giannina's family murdered and their farm burned. I'll be the one taking Giannina off to Denver by stage. And I'll stay there with her." He raised his chin as well as his voice, adding. "I'm going to marry her."

"You will not!" Kincaid pounded his saddle horn.

"You'll come back to Horsehead with me if I have to drag you kicking and screaming! Pat, pull him out of there!"

Winslow looked down at the rifle in James's hand. He glanced over his shoulder, and said tensely, "I don't think he's comin', boss."

"He is, by god!" Kincaid booted his horse forward.

James swung the Winchester at him. "One more stride, Pa, and I'll give you one in the belly."

Kincaid stopped, his face swollen and fierce, blue eyes bulging in exasperation.

James reached into the cabin. "Come on, Giannina."

The girl came to him and took his hand. She was still dressed in Ma Lonnigan's wool shirt and denims, a felt hat on her head. Her hair was pulled back in a queue.

"My horse is saddled and waiting out back. We're going to ride him to town. You try to stop me, I'll shoot you. Keep all the men here. If they try to stop us, I'll shoot the first one in the belly. If that's you, Pa, then so be it."

The men sat their horses in mute astonishment, Winslow remaining on the porch as James led Giannina around behind the cabin. Two minutes later, they galloped out of the yard and across the stream, James keeping a close eye on the men behind them.

None made a play.

A little over an hour later, James and Giannina rode into town. They passed the Blue Dog out front of which Omar Sledge, Eddie Shoots-the-Coyote, and Willis Reed stood watching him and the girl with soapy beer mugs in their fists.

They leered.

Rage burned in James.

He didn't know how he was going to do it, but they had to die.

They'd been at the Calderon estancia that night with both Hattersby and Plum.

————

MA LONNIGAN SETTLED JAMES AND GIANNINA INTO A room at the top of the stairs once again.

She'd seen them ride into town from where she sat, smoking her corncob pipe in her famous chair on the porch of her humble hotel. She'd also seen the three toughnuts giving them the leering eye, daring James to challenge them, and anger smoldered in her own.

Now, James washed at the stand in the room while Giannina had laid down to rest. It had been a trying several days for the poor girl.

James dried himself, put his shirt and hat back on, and told the girl he'd journey over to the Western Union office and find out when the next stage was due. But as he headed for the door, he saw out the room's only window his father and his three hands ride into town. They were just then passing the three hardtail killers still standing outside the Blue Dog. Neither party acknowledged the other. James didn't blame them. They were accomplices in cold-blooded murder.

As Kincaid and his men lined their horses up outside the hotel, James opened the window to glare down into the street. "I told you not to follow us, Pa. You're not stopping us!"

"If you won't listen to me, maybe you'll listen to Mrs. Kennecott. I stopped by her place on the way into town. She is riding down in her carriage." Kincaid shook his head with dire warning. "You and that girl, as pretty as she is, don't belong together. You're a Kincaid, by god, boy!"

Behind the man, James saw the fancy, black, leather, red-wheeled carriage roll down the steep hill from the Kennecott house. It entered town, and there were two other riders coming up behind it. After a minute, James saw they were both young women attired in riding gear— a blonde and a brunette.

His sister Sydney and Athena Kennecott.

James's heart burned with even more anger. They were ganging up on him? Then he knew for sure that it had been Sydney and Athena staring down at him and Giannina from the ridge the night before, and they'd told his father where they were holed up.

Meanwhile, Omar Sledge, Eddie Shoots-the-Coyote, and Willis Reed watched the procession with drunken delight, nudging each other and sipping their beers.

My god, what a mess, James thought. What a holy damn mess!

The gall of his father to confront James in the company of three of the five men—he...and possibly Mrs. Kennecott, as well, she had a heart of stone—who were standing on the same street. And here comes Sydney and Athena to watch it all with delight, as well!

They wanted to humiliate him for not taking part in the arranged marriage.

They wanted to see him dragged back to Horsehead and be returned to the whipped dog Grant Kincaid had raised him to be. They wanted to see Giannina dragged off to some brothel in Denver.

James picked up his rifle, cocked it, and shouted down through the window, "Get out of here! All of you! You're as bad as those three standing over there with the beers in their hands!"

Giannina came to stand behind him, her hand on his shoulder. When she saw the people in the street, she gasped—all of the people involved in the killings of her family gathered in one place.

Athena Kennecott glared up at him from where she sat her horse behind her mother's carriage, beside Sydney. "You think I wanted to marry you anymore than you wanted to marry me?" she cried. "You were your father's whipped cur, but that you turned me down in favor of a cheap little Mexican whore was too much for me to take!" Her eyes turned to her mother. "Yes, I stole the money. I learned the combination by looking over your shoulder. I stole the money and hired those vermin who worked for you, Mother, and two more to burn that scuzzy Mexican family to the ground!"

She threw out a gloved hand to indicate Sledge, Shoots-the-Coyote, and Willis Reed.

Again, Giannina gasped and covered her mouth with her hands.

"Hey, now, wait a minute," Sledge said, raising his free hand, palm out. "We didn't have nothin' to do with murderin' that family!"

"Yes, you did!" Athena stubbornly countered. "I paid you the five thousand, and you killed them and burned their farm!"

Sledge dropped his beer mug and drew the six-shooter hanging low on his right hip. "Shut up, you damn uppity bitch!" He raised the weapon, aimed, and shot Athena through her forehead. The bullet punched her out of her saddle.

"*Athena!*" Mrs. Kennecott screamed.

Sydney also screamed and stared down in horror at her dead friend.

Sledge stepped into the street and turned to face Mrs. Kennecott and Kincaid. "Go to hell, the lot o' you, or we'll gun you all right here an' now!"

"I don't think so!" James thrust the Winchester out the second-floor window of the Continental, and fired.

A puckered blue hole appeared in Sledge's forehead, just above his nose.

The gunman staggered backward, eyes rolling up in his head.

His two cohorts slapped leather, but before they could draw their weapons, another rifle barked twice. Both men were punched back to land with hard thuds on the boardwalk behind them. James turned to see Joe Mannion sitting a dun horse on the street twenty feet from the others, his rifle still aimed out from his shoulder, smoke licking from the barrel.

As the others, including the sobbing Mrs. Kennecott, hurried over to gather around Athena, James and Mannion locked gazes. "I heard it all," Joe said. He looked at Giannina standing beside James, sobbing. "You two going to be all right?"

James put his arm around his future wife and nodded.

"Sylvan?"

"He's still alive if you can believe it. Ma did a good job on him. She thinks he might even make a full recovery."

"Whang tough."

James smiled.

"Tell him I'll be back to harass him again one of these days."

"I'll do that."

Joe pinched his hat brim to both him and Giannina and gigged the outlaw horse over to the livery barn.

An hour later, he was astride his prized stallion and on the trail back to his wife and daughter in Del Norte.

Damn this crazy world, anyway.

In the action-packed conclusion to Peter Brandvold's bestselling Western series, rough 'n' tough "Bloody" Joe Mannion is pushed to the deadly brink.

In the heart of Colorado Territory, Mannion faces a whirlwind of troubles—a foreboding dream that hints at his demise and a vengeful man seeking justice for his family's slaughter.

With a mysterious assailant determined to see him and his deputies dead also on the horizon, Mannion races against time to unmask the perpetrator and understand their motives. But when his family is kidnapped, everything becomes clear—a band of outlaws aims to eliminate Mannion and his team in order to execute a daring train heist, leaving the town reeling from their blood-thirsty robbery.

As tensions mount and time runs out, Mannion must confront his own mortality. Will he and Deputy Henry McCallister catch the train robbers...or will fate deal Bloody Joe his last dance?

In a tale of bravery, betrayal, and the unyielding spirit of the Wild West,* Bloody Joe's Last Stand *delivers an explosive conclusion readers won't see coming.

AVAILABLE NOW

Peter Brandvold grew up in the great state of North Dakota in the 1960's and '70s, when television westerns were as popular as shows about hoarders and shark tanks are now, and western paperbacks were as popular as *Game of Thrones*.

Brandvold watched every western series on television at the time. He grew up riding horses and herding cows on the farms of his grandfather and many friends who owned livestock.

Brandvold's imagination has always lived and will always live in the West. He is the author of over a hundred lightning-fast action westerns under his own name and his pen name, Frank Leslie.

Made in the USA
Monee, IL
14 March 2025

14001522R00163